Be Mine Forever

A St. Helena Vineyard Novel

Also in Marina Adair's St. Helena Vineyard Series

Kissing Under the Mistletoe
Summer in Napa
Autumn in the Vineyard

Be Mine Forever

A St. Helena Vineyard Novel

MARINA ADAIR

 Montlake
Romance

The characters and events portrayed in this book are fictitious. Any similarity to real persons, living or dead, is coincidental and not intended by the author.

Published by Montlake Romance, Seattle

www.apub.com

ISBN-13: 9781612184739
ISBN-10: 1612184731

Cover design by Kerrie Robertson

Library of Congress Control Number: 2013915254

Printed in the United States of America

To my amazing critique partner, Brittney,

for the friendship, never-ending belief, and
around-the-clock tech support.

This journey wouldn't be the same without you.

CHAPTER 1

Trey DeLuca hated hospitals. Almost as much as he hated himself right now.

Four calls. He'd received four calls over the past two days from his family, which he'd selfishly chosen to ignore. Another three came in while he'd been in transit from Paris to San Francisco. All from his oldest brother, Gabe. And all with the same message: *Call me.*

So he had. And was sent straight to voice mail.

Trey reached the emergency room entrance and was hit by the smell of ammonia and a sterile vibe that gave him the willies. It was a pretty quiet night. Most of the seats in the waiting room were empty. Then again, St. Helena, California, with its not-quite-six-thousand residents, wasn't exactly a hive of activity.

Stopping at the information desk, he tugged his coat tighter around him, sending rain drops scattering to the floor. "Excuse me, can you tell me what room ChiChi Ryo is in?"

"Sure, Mr. um . . ." the woman standing behind the nurses' station looked up from the computer screen and trailed off with a smile.

"DeLuca. I'm her grandson."

"Hey, Trey. It's been a while." Her smile grew . . . flirtier. She came out from behind the desk and gave him a hug—the kind of hug that people who had history shared, the sweaty and gasping-for-air kind of history. She pulled back, a little frown creasing her forehead. "Kayla, remember?"

Blonde with a tight body and nice rack. She was hot too. Even in those scrubs. But familiar? Trey couldn't say. Had he not been jet-lagged and crazy with worry, he might have been able to place her face, or that cute little ass, but right now all he could focus on was his nonna's message. The one begging him to come home, telling him that she needed him by her side.

At first he'd just thought it was one of ChiChi's "stop breaking your grandmother's heart and come home" calls—something he avoided as much as possible since it meant caving in to the guilt and agreeing to an elongated happy-family stay—so he'd ignored it. Then he'd received a call from each one of his three brothers, in succession, telling him to zip up his pants and get home, ASAP. Which would have been funny, except that Trey's pants had been firmly fastened since last fall when his only remaining single brother, Nate, finally succumbed to domestication.

Christ, even Marc, the known playboy of the family, was leashed, trading in his man-card for a minivan, and leaving Trey the odd man out.

Yeah, nothing about this situation was funny.

"Right, Kayla. Good to see you again," he lied.

"How long are you in town for?" she asked, her tone a flat-out offer.

"I'm not sure, but—"

The two swinging metal doors crashed open and a gust of moist, cold wind blasted through the emergency ward. Orders and commands were shouted, and the room erupted into chaos while three paramedics pushed a bruised and bloodied woman on a gurney right past them into one of the surgical bays.

Just watching the fluid bags swinging made Trey think of needles—and that made him queasy.

Eyes back on the pretty nurse and off the team of green scrubs now rushing down the corridor talking in elevated voices, Trey said, "I really need to see my nonna. My brother texted me that they were here but didn't tell me what room."

That was when Trey had lost it. Four little words on a screen had him struggling for breath, struggling to keep it together.

At St. Helena Memorial.

"I can help with that. She's on the third floor. West side of the hospital. Last door on your right," she said without even consulting the screen, which did not make him feel any better. "Do you know where that is or do you want me to walk you there? Better yet, if you want to wait, I get off in ten minutes."

She could not have been more obvious if she'd written her number on his forehead.

"Thanks, but I've got it," Trey said, already heading toward the elevator.

He knew every inch of this hospital. His parents had died here over a decade ago, after he'd lied about being sick so that they'd come home early. Only their sedan had driven over the embankment, head-on into a concrete pylon.

Trey exited the elevator on the third floor and made his way past another nurses' station decorated with cut-out hearts, down the corridor, stopping at the last door. He took a deep breath and tried to get his hands to stop shaking. Latex, iodine, and that cooked cabbage smell notorious with hospital cafeterias only made the shaking worse.

God, he just needed her to be okay.

Trey pushed opened the door, took one step inside, and froze.

Holy Christ, if the smell of Bengay didn't make him want to run for it, the sight of saggy breasts slung up in sequins did.

He'd been played. They'd dangled his grandmother's health in front of him and he'd come running. Instead of lying on her death-bed with his family standing in silent vigil, his nonna was at the back of a small cafeteria, where the tables and chairs had been shoved up against the wall to create a makeshift dance floor, draped over some silver fox's arm as though he'd caught her mid-faint.

Dressed in a flowy red dress and matching orthopedic shoes, and wearing enough hair spray to ignite with a single spark, ChiChi sashayed around the floor, twirling through a good portion of the town's retired sector, and going for the dramatic dip under a giant poster that read: ST. HELENA'S SALSA SOCIETY: WE PUT THE HEAT BACK IN WINTER.

"Trey?" ChiChi said mid-toe flick, looking about as startled to see Trey as Trey was when she adjusted her goods and—ah, *Christ*, he had to look away. "You came?"

"You say that as though you didn't leave a half-dozen cryptic messages on my cell implying that I needed to come home before it was too late."

"And here you are, such a good boy," ChiChi praised, smooth-ing a hand over her gray updo and coming over to give him two kisses to the cheeks. "Just in time for—"

"You'd better say 'my resuscitation.'" He ran a hand down his face. "I thought you were . . ."

Dead. He'd thought she was dead. He'd spent the past eighteen hours on an airplane, praying he'd make it in time to tell his grand-mother he loved her, and berating himself for being a selfish prick for staying as far away as possible from his family. He wasn't even sure what time zone he was in anymore. "You said it was a matter of life or death. Christ, Nonna."

"Watch your language," she chided. "And this is life or death. The Winter Garden Gala is less than a month away."

Trey exhaled a weary breath. "I walked out of a meeting with our biggest French buyer, went straight to the airport, flew here, then went to the hotel where I borrowed Marc's minivan." He threw up his arms. "A minivan, for God's sake, so I could come straight here. In the same suit I've been wearing since yesterday. All so that we could talk about the Gala?"

"Why, yes," ChiChi said as though he were the dramatic one. "Because you, my favorite grandson, get to be my dance partner and I wanted to tell you in person. Isn't that wonderful?"

Yeah, wonderful.

Trey let his head fall back and stared at the disco ball spinning overhead, as he worked overtime not to lose it. St. Helena might not be *Dancing with the Stars,* but people here took their swing time seriously. And the Winter Garden Gala, the Valentine's Day celebration put on by the St. Helena Garden Society, was pretty much the hottest ticket in town.

"Gabe is your favorite." *And better with this kind of stuff,* he thought, remembering the last time he'd gone to the Gala.

Trey had been fifteen and his mom was a nominee for Winter Garden of the Year. With his dad stuck in a snowstorm in Chicago, his brothers claiming two left feet, and Trey having had seven years of parental-enforced dance lessons, he was the only possible candidate to partner with his mom in the celebratory waltz that was held every year during the Gala.

Only Mollie Miner, with her blonde hair and way-too-full Cs for a sophomore, had asked him to meet her in the garden. Even at fifteen, Trey knew that she wasn't looking to waltz. And since dancing with his mom in front of the entire town sounded like social suicide, he'd snuck out to meet More Than a Handful Mollie.

They'd rounded second that night, Mollie had turned out to be a bra stuffer, Trey missed the waltz, and four months later his mom died.

"Yes, well, Gabe is busy being a husband and proud papa." ChiChi patted his cheek. "And you drew the short straw."

"I wasn't here to draw."

Every year the brothers drew straws to see who "got" to escort ChiChi and partner with her in the waltz. And every year Trey somehow managed to weasel out of it. Apparently this Valentine's Day, his brothers and Cupid had their pointy little arrows aimed at Trey. Too bad for them, tomorrow morning he was going to be on the next flight back to Anywhere But Here.

Being home was hard enough. Being home around Valentine's Day was not going to happen.

"No, you weren't. You were off to God knows where, with Lord knows who," ChiChi said. Trey had been at a wine conference. In Paris. Alone. Selling the family's wine. "So, I drew for you."

"And just how many straws were there to draw from?"

"One. Congratulations, dear." ChiChi clapped as though he were the luckiest man in the world. And maybe he was. His grandma was alive. Which was the only thing keeping him from wringing her neck, because underneath the anger at being misled, a deep relief poured through him. But there was no way he was going to that dance. One of his brothers would have to man up.

The door to the cafeteria opened, causing everyone in the room to turn, and every man in the room to smile. Trey glanced over his shoulder as a tiny woman entered, burrowed under a bright-yellow rain slicker and a sorry looking blue-and-white knit cap. She was carrying a broken umbrella, which explained the drowned kitten look, and a duffle bag big enough to hide in.

"Sorry I'm late," a sweet but slightly harassed voice came from beneath the slicker as she struggled to pull it over her head—only the wet vinyl got stuck. "Some jackass in a minivan parked diagonally taking up three spaces so I had to circle the lot a few times."

"Maybe they were in a rush because of a family emergency," Trey said, sending ChiChi a stern glare.

"Yeah, well." The woman, who he assumed was the dance instructor, dropped the broken umbrella to the floor to work harder on that raincoat. "There were no more spots, I looked. So after five laps I decided to squeeze in beside him. I mean, I figured my car is pretty compact. It should fit, right?"

Trey hoped to hell it had. Otherwise he was going to have to explain to Marc how he'd "borrowed" and dented his new minivan. Which kind of served him right for trading in his truck for one.

"Wrong." Giving up on the buttons, she reached down for the hem and tugged up. "I heard the scraping of metal and instead of stopping, I panicked and gunned it."

Trey's stomach bottomed out. *Scraping?* Minivan or not, Marc was going to kill him.

"Oh dear, are you okay, Sara?" ChiChi said, concern lacing her voice as she took a step forward. Several other worried hums erupted from the senior gallery.

"Outside of eating my front bumper, the minivan looks fine." Which explained her shaking hands. And the way she was frantically fumbling to get out of her coat. "I left a note, but the wind blew it away. I stood out there for a few minutes waiting for the owner to come out."

Her movements were jerky with what Trey thought was frustration and a good dose of adrenaline. In fact, if she wasn't careful in her disrobing, someone was going to get hurt. One of the senior males with bad hips and dentures was already closing in to help.

With a frustrated huff, she dropped the duffle bag, bent at the waist, and started shimmying out of the slicker and—*holy shit*—a shapely, sequin-clad, nowhere-near-qualified-for-a-senior-discount ass emerged from beneath the raincoat.

Trey had always considered himself a leg man, loved them long and wrapped around his middle. But after seeing that exquisite heart-shaped handful, he was a changed man. Not that her legs weren't toned and silky. But that backside? Perfection.

"You need help?" Harvey Peterson, the town's podiatrist asked, his hands already reaching for her waist.

"No, I'm fine. Really, Harvey." If anything, Mr. Peterson's offer got her moving even faster.

Harvey, however, looked disappointed. Trey felt for the guy.

He stepped around the forming crowd, so as not to lose the view, while Sara wrenched and yanked the wet material until she made some progress and—*thank you, Jesus*—it got stuck on an even more incredible set of breasts—on the smaller side, maybe a full B, but incredible all the same. And they were just as slick as the rest of her.

Always the gentleman, Trey stepped forward to do his part, lending his hands to the cause. "Here, let me help."

"I'm fine, really," she said, her hands batting at his, which rested on her hips to steady her. And yeah, she was tiny but packing a ton of delicious curves.

"Sorry, can't hear you through the material," he lied, grabbing her wrists and guiding them to the bottom hem of her thin tank top. "But if you don't stop flopping around you're going to take someone out. Or," he leaned in and quietly added, "give Harvey over there the chance to goose you and call it an accident."

She froze.

"So, work with me here. Hold your top down so I can pull the slicker up and . . ."

"Okay," Sara whispered. "Better?"

Abso-fucking-lutely. First, the woman did just as he asked—that in itself was a miracle. Second, she pulled a tad too hard, causing the scoop of her neckline to ride blessedly low, giving him an inspiring view of teal lace and tan cleavage. The best part was when he gave the final tug and the slicker and knit cap came up and off, leaving behind the most beautiful woman he'd ever seen.

Which didn't make sense. Trey had been around a lot of beautiful women. Spent the past few years traveling the world and getting up close and personal with a good number of them. Women who were stilettoed, stacked, smoking hot, and satisfied with one night. This woman was maybe five-two with bouncy brown hair, girl-next-door freckles, and a pair of no-nonsense shoes that were definitely more Mary Ann than Ginger. And he was a Ginger kind of guy. Always had been.

Nothing about her said simple, short term, or easily impressed, so why then was he having a hard time breathing?

Dry spell. That was it. The main reason he was staring at Pollyanna had nothing to do with the way those big brown eyes seemed to look right through all of his bullshit, or the way her sweet kiss-me mouth curved up into a smile that made his pulse pound. Nope, the simple truth was, it had been way too long since he'd gotten laid.

"Isn't this interesting?" ChiChi murmured, patting Trey on the back, no doubt already picking out great-grandbaby names. "Sara, this gentleman here is my grandson. My *favorite* grandson."

"Thank you, *favorite grandson*." Sara smiled, two little dimples winking his way. He'd never been into dimples, but on her they worked.

"My pleasure," Trey said, wondering what kind of dance she taught and if she would be open to a private lesson—of the tangled-sheets variety.

He flashed her that smile he knew women loved, because why the hell not? Flirting with a pretty woman seemed like a much better way to spend his evening than arguing with his brothers or making funeral arrangements.

She tried not to smile, but one slipped out and—*hello sunshine*—it even lit up her eyes, which had little flecks of gold and green in them, making them distinctly hazel.

"Shouldn't you two exchange information?" ChiChi nudged.

Right. The minivan. "It seems silly since I've already helped you undress, but I guess we've reached the information portion of the evening where I ask for your name, number, and if there is anyone at home you can call?"

"Information? Okay, um, no there is no one at home." A hint of pink tinted her ears, which he found oddly endearing, and she wiggled a naked ring finger. Before Trey could clarify the reason behind his questions, she pulled out a business card and handed it to him. "My number is on there and . . ." Trey shot her an amused look, "what?"

"Bolder Holder?" He read the frequent buyer card she'd handed him. He was right—a 32B. "Your local lingerie pusher-upper."

"Oh, God." She snatched it back and produced another card. Still not the insurance card he expected, but before he could explain, she looked around at the room of students who were all smiling back, then to him, and damn if her entire face wasn't glowing with embarrassment. "I'm Sara Reed and as you can tell I'm not really good at this."

Even her name was sweet. And flirting disaster would be putting it mildly. Not that he minded. There was something about her shy interest that got to him.

"Trey DeLuca," he said. She placed her hand in his extended one. Her skin was soft and a bit chilled—and packed one hell of a punch. "I'm the asshole who ate your bumper."

And wasn't that just her luck. For the first time in twenty-two months and eleven days, Sara Reed had felt a small flicker of interest. Nothing big or life altering, just that tiny zing of attraction reminding her that she was, indeed, still a woman. So what did she do?

Hit his car.

Then hit on him.

"Oh, my God, I'm so sorry. About the car and the really embarrassing . . . moment we just shared that everyone here witnessed."

In her defense, she hadn't been on a date or so much as flirted with a man since her husband died. Something she absolutely did not want to think about while staring up at an extremely sexy—and if she wasn't mistaken—interested man who was standing less than a foot away, smiling down at her with the most perfect set of teeth on the most perfect face she'd ever seen.

"I did try to leave a note," she explained. "But the wind—"

"You said. And that was very *sweet* of you."

Ouch. Last she'd heard, "sweet" wasn't on the list of requirements for hot and sweaty hookups. Not that she was looking for a hot and sweaty hookup. Between renovating her new house, getting her dance school in the black, and raising her son, there wasn't room for another man in her life. Although a coffee or maybe a casual lunch sounded nice.

Then again, maybe this moment was the universe's way of telling her that it was still too soon. But throwing a charming, underwear-model look-alike in her way as a reminder that she wasn't ready to start dating again was a little cruel.

"Do you want me to call Stan so he can tow your car to his shop?"

Realizing she was staring at his mouth, she looked up. "No, really, it's only the front bumper and your car is fine."

"Why don't we go check it out and see?"

"It's pouring and you already look . . ." *edible* she almost said as she took in his dark hair, moist and slightly disheveled, his black peacoat that did little to conceal the broad chest beneath, and a pair of slacks that looked spectacular on him.

He cleared his throat.

"Wet," she said.

"Wet?"

"Yes, wet." She nodded confidently as though she hadn't been caught checking out his goods. "And if you have someplace to be, I don't want to keep you any longer. Plus the bumper is gone, poof, just fell off, so it's not like I'd be dragging it around town."

He raised a brow. "Is there a reason you are so determined to not let me see the damage?"

"No!" she shot out and, *wow*, that sounded guilty. Trey must have thought the same thing because he just waited, watching her, his lips curled in amusement.

"Good, because I want to make sure you won't be stranded here. And," he leaned in and whispered, the twinkle in his eyes turned to full, "the thought of wrestling you back into that raincoat sounds almost as fun as it was wrestling you out."

She laughed and felt an absurd rush of heat—to her face and other more southerly places. Maybe her guy-dar wasn't as off as she'd originally thought. She knew that smile, had seen it before, and when combined with the wink he was currently sending her, it wasn't just a playful grin. It was an invitation.

"He's right, child," ChiChi said, collecting Sara's things and shoving them into her hands and *them* toward the door. "We can't have you driving around in a car that might not be safe. Not in this storm. Why don't you head home?"

"But what about class? The Gala is only a month away."

"Missing one lesson won't kill us," ChiChi said, then stiffened, going dead serious. "As long as you aren't giving that Deidra Potter extra lessons on the side."

"I'm not giving her extra lessons, ChiChi." Sara tried not to roll her eyes, but it was nearly impossible. She had no idea what went down between the two older ladies, but bad blood would be an understatement.

"Enough, Nonna." Trey's stern tone was in direct contrast with the gentle kiss he pressed to his grandmother's cheek. "And we'll talk about *this* later."

"Looking forward to it, dear." Now it was Trey's turn to roll his eyes. "And Sara, don't you worry about a thing. Pricilla and I can handle class tonight while Trey takes a look at things and you two work out . . ." ChiChi waved a regal hand between the two of them, "whatever it is you need to work out."

"It's probably best to get out of here so we can get this *thing* worked out," he joked quietly, placing his hand at the small of her back and making her breath catch. It felt possessive and warm and in no way like a joke. In fact, it felt exciting.

Safe.

Tingly.

Things she hadn't allowed herself to feel since her husband's commanding officer had shown up on her doorstep holding a Silver Star for gallantry in action, and a Just in Case letter her husband had written—because the worst "just in case" imaginable had happened.

In the letter, Garrett reminded her that life was a series of adventures. Since theirs had come to an end, it was her job to live twice as hard, take twice as many risks, and love their son enough for the both of them.

Sara promised herself that she would live her life balls out—as Garrett used to say—and be open to life's adventures. Easier said than done for a single mom with control issues, but she was trying.

She had already shared the greatest love two people could share, knew how hard it was to find, and didn't expect to get that lucky again. But she was open to finding a love built on friendship and respect.

Not now. Maybe someday. And she wasn't saying that this was love. But there were enough warm fuzzies from the simple contact of his hand on her back to let her know that she was ready. Ready to put herself out there again and slowly recapture the part of her that she'd buried. Ready to ask a charming man out for coffee, because that was what her sister-in-law said single people did these days.

"You ready?" Trey asked when they stepped out of the room.

They took the elevator to the bottom floor, and she couldn't help snatch a few peeks at him—only every time she looked over, she found him already looking back. Only he didn't go red and quickly turn away.

The doors opened and he led them through the main lobby toward the emergency room, stopping at the double doors.

Taking the jacket from her hands, he unbuttoned it and held it open.

"I'll pass," she said.

He dropped his gaze to her legs and raised a brow. She knew what he saw. She hadn't dressed for the weather. Her dance pants and tank, which now seemed way too skimpy and clingy, would be as effective as tissue paper in the rain.

"I don't want to get stuck again," she admitted.

Trey raised his right hand. "I solemnly swear to help you get out of your clothes. Anytime. Anywhere. All you have to do is ask."

She shouldn't have laughed. It was obviously some lame pick-up line. And if his delivery had felt even the least bit threatening, she wouldn't have. But his eyes were crinkled with humor and he made the offer seem so charming, she couldn't help herself. Flirting with him was easy, and kind of fun. Two things she needed more of in her life.

"Fine," she agreed and let him help her into her coat. She watched as he buttoned it with ease, his fingers getting higher and higher until he reached the one between her breasts and she heard a small groan. And damn if it wasn't her. This was what two years without a battery-assisted orgasm got her.

Trey stilled, then delivered a smile that registered a solid *oh my* on the panty-melting scale. "Should I stop?"

Sara shook her head and, channeling some balls-out confidence, said, "Only if you promise to let me buy you a hot cup of coffee afterward."

His fingers were hovering over that button and a cute little frown split his forehead. "So I have the choice between coffee or disrobing you?"

That wasn't what she meant. And she couldn't tell if Trey was joking or serious. Even worse, she didn't know what to say, because neither was slow or safe or easing her way into anything—other than his bed. Which meant that she must have hit his car harder than she thought because coffee was no longer what she wanted, and option B didn't seem as scary as it had a minute ago. In fact, her lady parts were already sighing at the mere idea.

"I'm kind of new to this whole dating thing, but if you want—"

"Trey?" a woman said coming out from the employees' room. "Perfect timing. I just clocked out and was waiting for you."

Her voice was low, in that gravelly, nine-hundred-number-operator kind of way that was part purr, part proposition, and— *holy God*—the woman had legs to her neck. And that wasn't even the sexiest thing about her. She oozed attitude, which worked well in the painted-on jeans and body-hugging sweater she was sporting. She had blonde hair and big blue eyes, which were almost as big as her boobs. In a nutshell, she was Florence Nightingale gone Playboy Playmate.

"Hey, Kayla," Trey said, his eyes on Sexy Nurse as she swished her womanly curves over and wrapped herself around him in a hug.

To his credit, Trey looked more uncomfortable than anything. Then again, Sara had just asked him to coffee. Safe, boring coffee.

"Do you know Sara?"

"You own the Tap and Barre School of Dance, right?" Kayla asked and then before Sara could even answer she went on, "My niece takes ballet from you."

Translation: I am at least five years, one kid, and a major broken heart younger than you.

"I was just heading out to check on Sara's car. It was great seeing you again, Kayla," Trey said.

"Oh, but I was hoping we could go grab a drink." Her perfectly manicured hands wrapped around Trey's arm and that's when Sara saw it. Trey and Kayla *knew* each other—in the biblical sense. "And catch up."

"Actually—" Trey began and Sara cut him off.

"That's okay, really, I'm fine," she lied. She wasn't fine. She felt like a grade-A ass. "Like I said, the damage is only cosmetic, plus I really need to be getting home. But thanks for . . ." *For what? Not laughing at me when I obviously made a big something out of an embarrassing nothing.* "Helping me with my jacket. But I'm kind of tired and need a shower." She exhaled hard, took a step back, and clarified, "A hot shower. To warm up." She wanted to slap her palm on her forehead because, damn it, that didn't sound any better.

"Hang on, let's just make sure that everything is all right." Trey stepped closer, so much concern on his face she felt hers flush with embarrassment. She stuffed her cap low on her head and took two huge steps—backward. In every way possible.

"I'll call my insurance adjuster when I get home and have him contact you in the morning. In case you find a scratch or paint on your bumper or something. Which you won't, but, okay, yeah, nice meeting you. Both. Nice meeting you both. Bye."

Sara turned and rushed out the door, shuffling her sequin-clad butt toward her car. And if that wasn't a big enough clue to take dating off of her newly formed bucket list, then the really big, hard balls of ice falling from the sky and pelting her head sealed the deal.

Sara Reed. Dance instructor. Widow. Single mom.

Period.

CHAPTER 2

C UPID WANTS YOU.
    Trey stopped in his tracks when he saw the giant banner with glittery silver and pink letters, which hung between a plasma screen showing ESPN highlights and a NINERS' TERRITORY sign. It was a poster of his niece, Baby Sofie, dressed in nothing but a gummy smile, a diaper, a heart-tipped arrow, and a sash reading WINTER GARDEN GALA.

He'd seen the posters plastered around town. He understood Valentine's Day was fast approaching. He even understood why all of the local stores had rolled out their rose-petal welcoming mats, and why people were farting hearts and talking about love that lasts forever. But to invade his favorite sports bar was wrong. On so many levels.

The Spigot was the only place left in Trey's world that wasn't dripping with domestication or girly shit. They didn't serve skinny drinks or run their hours around nap time or offer a gluten-free menu. It was about beer, bros, business, and ball. Which was why

Trey felt himself relax when he saw his three brothers lined up at the bar, shoving each other and arguing about, Trey assumed, who was going to win the Super Bowl.

"You made it," said Nate, the second oldest and most tightly-wound of the brothers, from the far end of the bar. "Good."

It was good. Trey had been home for three days, due to a disappearing passport that "somehow" wound up in ChiChi's purse, and this was the first time that everyone's schedule had allowed for any kind of brother bonding.

Trey slid up to the bar and pulled out a stool. "I was just on a call with our buyer in Paris and he wants to reschedule—" He froze. *What the hell was going on?* "Is that an umbrella in your drink?"

Nate slid a pink, foamy concoction, complete with pineapple slice and cherry skewer, down the bar. That was when Trey noticed that each one of his brothers was double-fisting not beer, not Jack, not even a glass of wine, but the most un-manly drinks ever ordered at this bar—and they were smiling about it.

"Frankie wants to finalize the Frankie-Nate signature drink for the wedding. She's calling it Pink Paradise and asked me to help narrow down the choices," Nate said as though *that* wasn't the pussiest sentence in the history of mankind.

Signature drink? This had to be a joke. There was no way ball-buster Frankie with her steel-toed boots and wicked right hook would go for this. "Pink? Really? Are you shitting me?"

"Hey, real men drink pink," Marc said and Trey choked.

Only two years apart in age and sharing common interests, mainly their love of women and freedom, Marc and Trey had always been close. Until Marc hooked up with his high-school crush, Lexi. Now his big brother was married, expecting, and so damn happy you could smell the marital bliss wafting off on him.

In fact, all of his brothers stank of happiness, something Trey hadn't smelled on a DeLuca since his parents were alive. Proving that, once again, right when Trey thought he'd finally caught up to his older brothers—in his newly appointed position as VP of Sales for DeLuca Wines, no less—he came home to realize he was still several steps behind, and now even playing in the wrong game. A place he'd spent his entire life trying to outgrow. Without much luck.

"Yeah, well, do real men walk around with babies attached like accessories?" Trey asked, flagging down the bartender to order a real drink.

"Says the man who uses the word 'accessories,'" Gabe, the oldest brother, laughed. "Besides my girls are the cutest damn accessories I've ever had."

"Real babe magnets too," Marc laughed. "Lexi sees me cuddling Baby Sofie and she is yanking me out the door back to our place."

"Holding Baby Sofie and Holly's hand at the same time, potent stuff." Nate and Marc high-fived and Trey wanted to punch someone.

"*This* is my problem." He dropped his head to the counter, everything making sense. His dry spell, why he was so drawn to Little Miss Manners the other night, why he couldn't even look at a baby without breaking out in a sweat. "This is why I haven't gotten laid in three months."

"You haven't gotten any in three months?" Marc asked, sounding pretty damn shocked. That was all right, Trey was shocked himself. He hadn't gone this long without a woman since high school.

"How can I, when every time I meet someone, we start talking, vibes start flying, she gives me *the* look, and before I know it, my sexy one-nighter suddenly morphs into a pregnant woman in a wedding dress?"

Although Sara hadn't morphed and she had given him *the* look. Then again, she was too sweet to morph and too nervous to follow up on *the* look. Hell, she couldn't even follow up with returning his call.

Still, as far as Trey was concerned, there was nothing settling about the idea of settling down. In fact, he was pretty sure he'd developed a severe allergic reaction to commitment, compromise, and kids the day his parents died.

The bartender set down his beer and Trey took a large swig. "I don't want to talk about this. I came here tonight to let you all know that I can't escort Nonna to the Gala."

"Sorry, bro," Marc shrugged. "Rules are rules, you drew the short straw."

"Rules my ass," he mumbled. "We all know there was only one straw. And I'm turning it over to Nate."

Nate was the peacemaker of the family, the problem-solver go-to guy. There was no way he would say—

"Nope. Sorry."

Trey choked on his beer. "What?"

"Frankie's my date. I'm still making it up to her for taking Sasha Dupree to the prom. And since Frankie already has a dress for the waltz, and I like my nuts right where they are, I'm taking my fiancée. Sorry, bro," Nate said, not sorry at all.

"Marc?" Trey asked, his voice sounding a little desperate.

"I filled in for you last year and, I believe, three years ago as well. Plus, Lexi is really looking forward to this, and I am looking forward to her in red."

"Nonna expects me to brush up on my ballroom. By taking dance lessons," he explained.

Marc flashed a smug-ass grin and added, "Time to man-up, Trey."

"Don't look at me," Gabe said before Trey even had the chance to look his way. "Regan is convinced that this is her last time to dance before she looks like a beached whale, her words not mine, because if you ask me, when she's pregnant—"

"I'm not asking you, nor have I *ever* asked you, so can you—not." Trey held up a hand. He couldn't do it. He just couldn't listen to one more detail about married, pregnant sisters-in-law who rocked his brothers' worlds. Tonight was supposed to be bro-time. And bro-time didn't include talking about feelings, swollen feet, or color palettes—ever. "Bottom line is, I can't stay."

"It's three weeks, Trey," Nate said as though Trey could just clear his schedule at will.

"I don't even have three days. I walked out of a meeting with one of our biggest French buyers, and if I don't get back to Paris ASAP, they might decide to go with someone else."

Gabe shrugged. "Do it by phone."

Was he even serious? "And get the kind of numbers you guys are expecting? No way. Not to mention, I'm meeting with a company in Long Beach to take over all of our domestic shipping and tracking. I need to get down there and see their setup before we can finalize the contract."

Last summer his brothers had signed a deal with one of the nation's largest retailer food and beverage distributors, and as a result, DeLuca wine was available in supermarkets around the globe. Making sure the wine got to its destination on time was becoming a hundred-hour workweek on its own, meaning Trey was falling behind on their other customers. Which was why he was meeting with a logistics company, hoping to outsource some of the work—and outsource some of the burden.

"I can do it," Marc offered, sucking his drink through a dainty little straw. "I'll be in Santa Barbara the week after Valentine's Day. I'm taking Lexi on a little babymoon."

"Nice, man," Gabe said, as if Marc were making complete sense.

"This isn't just something you can tack on to a few days away," Trey said. "I've been researching this for months, know the process, know what to ask, what to negotiate."

"It isn't rocket science," said the guy who was just getting all girly over a freaking babymoon—whatever the hell that was.

"Maybe not, but it's my job and I can't drop everything to hang out here and take dance lessons. I have plans."

"Yeah, well, change them," said Abigail, his sister, sliding up to the bar next to him. She was so tiny that even with him sitting and her standing, she barely reached his chest. "I need you to help finalize the sale for the Fairmont Hotel and make sure everything runs smoothly for a big delivery in Santa Barbara."

"As I was just explaining, I am kind of strapped for time right now. At the rate DeLuca Wines is growing, there's no way I can take on Ryo."

Four years ago, Nonna ChiChi and Abby opened Ryo Wines, a boutique winery in the valley. Female-owned, female-run, and female-branded Ryo Wines was estrogen in a bottle. Every time Trey set foot in that office, he felt his nuts shrivel.

"Sorry, sis. Your sale, your mess," Trey said. "And last I checked, I have too much penis to be a part of your woman-run company."

"Could have fooled me," Marc choked out and Trey slid him a wanna-go-there? look.

"Come on, when have I ever asked you for a favor?"

She had a point. Abby hated when her brothers interfered with her life. So of course, the DeLuca brothers had mastered interference. But this time, she was here on her own.

"I have some deals already on the table that need finalizing. In Europe," he explained.

"Please?" Abby begged, batting those big lashes his way.

Oh, hell no. This was a no-lash-batting-allowed, Y-chromosome-required event.

"No. And since when do you join in on guys' night?"

He'd already lost his brothers the other six nights of the week, but Thursdays were their nights. If they broke man-night code for Abby, it wouldn't be long before the wives started coming. Immature or not, he didn't want to share.

"Since a Mr. Rossi e-mailed me about a perfect piece of property in Italy." Abby pulled up a stool and slid a packet, complete with photos, across the bar. "It's fifty hectares."

"About one hundred and twenty acres," Nate said picking up the photo and studying it. "And it looks to be nearly all planted."

"It is," she went on, her face one big smile. "Half Sangiovese and half Barbera grapes. It's located right on the coast, making it a perfect destination-villa. Think about it: I could design it, Marc could oversee the facilities end, and you three could add the vineyard to the DeLuca umbrella."

Great, more wine to sell.

Trey spread the aerial photo of the property out on the bar top. It was an incredible piece of land. And Abby was an incredible designer, specializing in wineries, but lately the only jobs she'd been getting were small remodels. This was the kind of project that would put her on the map. It would also mean some serious family time with everyone working together.

Another reason to say no.

"Abby," Gabe said quietly. "This is amazing, it really is, but there is no way we are in the position to expand right now. Not into Italy."

"I know that this isn't the best time with all of the new contracts and Nate's new property." Abby shrugged. "I figured, what's the harm in checking it out? The owner promised he would give us first option, but that generosity expires at the end of February."

"No way." Trey could barely manage his schedule now. Fitting in a trip to Italy, on top of the meetings he already had to reschedule because of his unscheduled trip home, was out of the question. At the rate he was already pushing himself, he'd need a permanent vacation from his life. "I can't fit in another trip."

"No one is asking you to," Abby said.

"Not that he'd have time, what with Nonna looking at dance shoes online. Men's dance shoes," Marc said, and Italy suddenly seemed doable. "Wing-tipped ones. Black and white. Very Fred Astaire."

The corner of Gabe's mouth tilted up. "She was bragging to all her friends about how she is going to out-waltz Deidra Potter. With you on her arm."

"Will you two stop?" Abby said, reaching around and smacking Marc on the shoulder. Eyes back on Trey, she said, "I am just asking you to cover a few of my meetings this week so I have time to do more research and check out the land. And if I think it is a good move for the family, that you all back me."

Gabe opened his mouth, no doubt to say *hell no*, when Marc sat up straighter, his eyes going wide. "This is the same town that Great-Grandpa DeLuca grew up in."

"It's the same property. The house where Great Grandpa was born is still there. It needs some love, but it's still standing."

Her statement was like a fist to the gut. There had been a time when Trey would have loved the idea of creating something with his family. Even as a kid he'd had a clear vision of how the family business would grow, and where he'd fit into it. Things were different now that his parents were gone, and being around his family, especially while reconnecting with their roots, would be a constant reminder of what he'd cost everyone.

"That house," Marc said, pointing to the map, "right there?"

"Yup," Abby said, a little hope back in her voice because, just like that, Marc was in. She knew it. Trey knew it. Hell, the whole damn bar knew it. "When his parents moved to the United States, they sold the family's vineyard to Mr. Rossi, who owned a neighboring vineyard, and it has been in the Rossi family ever since. Only now, they are looking to sell."

"That's a lot of grapes," Nate pointed out and Trey allowed himself to sit back and relax. There was no way Nate would sign off on this. Not after he'd recently sunk over seven million dollars into a piece of land that was only worth five.

"They're DeLuca grapes," Abby explained. "Half of the plants are from the original DeLuca vines. The others are the Rossis'."

"No kidding." Nate smiled and, Jesus, the guy looked like he'd just gotten a pony for Christmas.

Two down and Gabe to go. And in Gabe's hormonal, my wife-is-pregnant-so-I-have-to-be-a-sensitive-prick state, it probably wouldn't take much. Meaning, Trey would have to be the bad guy.

"I was thinking that we could build the vacation destination here, and a smaller house, just for the family back here so it would be private." Abby leaned across the table and pointed to an empty patch right by the cliff's edge—overlooking the Mediterranean Sea. "You know, a place where we could all visit. Vacation together as a family."

"How did you find out about this?" Gabe asked. And yup, he was on board. Any hesitation about being stretched too thin, international headaches, and cash flow were replaced with Holly and Sofie running down to the beach with their cousins, pails in hand, the Italian coastline at their backs.

"I've always dreamed of designing a place in Italy and thought it would be special if it was in the village where Great Grandpa was born," she explained, really piling on the family-history and roots BS. "A few years ago, I found out where he grew up and contacted the owners. At the time, the Rossis weren't interested in selling, so I made them promise to call me if they ever changed their mind."

"And they changed it?" Marc asked.

Trey sat back and shook his head. Couldn't they see that Abby was using the same magic she wove when they were kids?

"What about the new vineyard Nate just bought, or the distribution deal we signed last year? I think we have enough going on," Trey pointed out, trying to be the voice of reason. But when his brothers just glared, he knew he was the odd man out.

"One week, Trey. That's all I need." Then Abby went and said something that nearly broke his heart. "It's what Mom and Dad would have wanted us to do."

And damn if Trey didn't have an answer to that.

"Twenty-five hundred dollars?" Sara asked over the sound of the air compressor. She stared down at her engine, wondering how there was so much damage. "It's a bumper."

"The bumper isn't the problem," Stan O'Malley, the local mechanic and owner of Stan's Soup and Service Station, called out from under the car. "It's the blown head gasket."

She had no idea what a head gasket did, but for that much money, it had better make her coffee in the morning. What she did have though, was a better idea of why her insurance company was being so difficult. A lost bumper claim was not two-and-a-half grand.

"How long did you say you were driving around with that log sticking out of your grill?"

"It was more of a twig," she clarified, and Stan rolled the dolly out far enough so that only his forehead and eyes could be seen— eyes that were calling her a big fat fibber. Sara took a sip of latte and admitted, "Okay, maybe it's a branch and since Monday night."

She hadn't lied when she said the minivan was fine. She'd just left out that, in order to avoid hitting it completely, she must have jerked the wheel, because when she got out to inspect the damage, her car was partially up on the curb, its front end making nice with a giant shrub.

"Well, that *branch* went through the grill and pierced your radiator." Stan rolled the dolly all the way out and slowly stood. The man was agile for being somewhere between seventy and one of the original settlers.

Grabbing a work rag he wiped off his bald head then dragged it down his face and shaggy beard, making more of a mess than anything. "Which means you've been driving around town with a cracked radiator for the past four days. Surprised it didn't blow sooner."

He tapped what she assumed was the radiator.

"I should have just called you." *Or let Trey take a look at it*, she silently admitted. But she'd had a sleepy son to get home to and an embarrassing situation to run away from, which included the sexy do-gooder whose sense of chivalry she'd mistaken for interest. "How long will I be out a car?"

"Let me go see how soon I can get the parts, but best guess is a week."

"A week?" How was she supposed to get Cooper to school, buy groceries, do all of the things that single moms did, without a car? Not to mention, a week's worth of damage sounded like a whole lot more than she could afford.

Stan must have seen the panic in her eyes because he gently patted her on the arm and said, "Don't worry, Sara, we'll get you fixed up. But while I'm checking on the parts, could I interest you in a bowl of my famous chili? On the house."

"No, I'm fine," she said, holding up her coffee.

"Suit yourself." Stan stopped at the door to his office. "But if you change your mind, I've got a box of sweets on the tool bench."

With a heavy sigh, she walked to the pink box—just for a peek. And—well, look at that—it was a mouthwatering selection of pastries from the Sweet and Savory across the street. Thankful she had on her dance pants with the elastic waist, she settled on her favorite, a lemon drop cupcake, and walked back over to her car. Licking off the icing, she peered into the hood, trying to locate the head gasket without much luck.

She didn't know a lot about cars. Didn't have to. Garrett could fix anything with wires or wheels. For all she knew, a head gasket cost eleven dollars and Stan was short two grand to his bookie. Although, with his bushy eyebrows and stark white beard, he looked too much like Father Time to take advantage of her. At least that was her hope.

"Well, now I know the secret to getting a peek under your hood," a low, mellow voice said from beside her.

Sara looked up from the radiator, past the broad chest beneath a dark-blue button-up, past the faint stubble that shadowed his face, and into a set of deep-brown eyes that had her heart crashing to the garage floor.

Taking in her cupcake, he leaned a casual elbow against her fender and Sara forced herself to swallow a huge bite of frosting because it wasn't just any man. It was the hot man whose car she'd "gently tapped," then asked out to coffee, only to flee the scene after he helped her out of her clothes.

The same man who had called three times over the past four days, and she still hadn't found the courage to pick up the phone. Was that the equivalent of a dating hit-and-run?

"Stan is a licensed professional," Sara said, dragging her gaze to his face. "He also bought me coffee."

Trey leaned in and the movement caused the collar of his shirt, which was unbuttoned at the top, to open and his slacks to pull taut in the back.

Don't look, don't look, don't look.

So of course she let her eyes wander down to take a peek and, *whoa,* he sure could fill out a pair of pants.

"Pumpkin-spice latte?" He sniffed. "Good choice."

"My favorite." Sara forced her gaze to his mouth, which was turned up in an amused smile.

"And if it was credentials you wanted to see, you should have said so. Under-the-hood assessments are my specialty. I'm also good with wet rain slickers."

Sara found herself smiling, just like the other night. Trey had an easy way about him that was infectious. And after a long chat with her insurance company, and then hearing Stan's preliminary estimate on her car, she needed a reason to smile.

"How did you know I was here?" she asked.

"The sign on your studio said, 'Gone to Stan's, be back in ten minutes.' That was an hour ago." Which explained the wet hair and shoes. "And since you don't seem to be returning calls, or at least my calls, I figured this was the best way to see you."

"I am so sorry, I'm not avoiding you."

He raised a disbelieving brow.

"Okay, I am avoiding you, but not because I don't intend to pay you for any damages. I do. And I know how this must look, but to my credit I was waiting to get Stan's assessment before I called, because my insurance company is being impossible." She took a breath and went for honesty. "And because I was too embarrassed to ask you if we could avoid the insurance company all together and make some kind of deal, you know," she lowered her voice and peeked to make sure Stan wasn't around, "just between us."

"Between us," he rolled the words around and leaned even closer, enough that she could smell the rain on his skin. "I like the sound of that."

"Me too," she admitted, her heart in her throat, because, she was flirting. And she was pretty sure that he'd started it.

"But if we're going for honest, I came here to cash in my rain check for coffee." His eyes dropped to the cup in her hand. "But it looks like I missed out, once again."

"What about your car?" Every message he left specifically referenced the minivan.

"Not a scratch. I was using it as an excuse to see you." His eyes sparkled with a boyish gleam and something crackled between them. It was definitely chemistry—and completely mutual.

Before Sara could process what *that* meant, or the way it made her thighs tingle, Stan came out of his office with a printout in hand. "All right, the parts are on order. I put a rush on 'em so they should be in by Monday. And your car will be my top priority."

"Thanks, Stan," Sara said, taking the bill and choking. Apparently the twenty-five hundred had been for parts only.

"I'll give you a call when it's ready." Stan disappeared toward the front of the shop to help another customer.

"Can I give you a ride home?" Trey asked.

Yes. That was all she wanted to do. Go home, take a hot bath, and go to sleep—for a year. But she pictured the stack of billing statements sitting on her desk that needed to be stuffed and sent out first, and the downstairs toilet, which, due to an unfortunate Play-Doh accident, was in desperate need of a plunging. And when that was all done, and she finally had a chance to sit down, it would be in a big house. All by herself.

The mere thought had her chest tightening and her palms sweating.

"Have you ever just not wanted to go home?" The minute the words left her mouth, she felt like a terrible person. She loved her home. She just preferred to be in it when her son was there. Which, according to her watch, was a good two hours away.

The charm-your-pants-off smile that she'd come to connect with Trey DeLuca faded into something softer, something almost sad. "Story of my life."

Not hers. Sara had spent so much time at her mother's dance studio growing up that home had always felt like a sanctuary. Then when she'd married and had Cooper, home was where she felt the most alive. Lately, though, when it was quiet and empty, it felt more like a coffin, slowly sucking the life out of her.

"What do you do instead?" she asked.

"I get lost." No hesitation, no apologies. Nope, Trey DeLuca spoke those words like he was an expert on the subject.

"Get lost," she repeated, trying it out. Even the way the words fell from her lips felt irresponsible and reckless and so incredibly luxurious that she laughed. And that felt exhilarating.

"In your case though," he said, looking down at the bill in her hand and giving a low whistle, "I'd say get lost somewhere where I can buy you a drink."

God, a drink sounded good. A drink that didn't come with a built-in straw or dancing fruit on the carton sounded even better. Getting lost with a sexy man who made her laugh sounded exciting and terrifying all at the same time. Exciting because it would be another small step toward moving on with her life, and terrifying because for the first time since Garrett's death, the thought of moving on without him didn't rouse the hollow ache that always sat right above her breastbone.

"What if I told you that I have ninety minutes before I have to be found?" she said.

He grinned and it was so ridiculously sexy that a jolt of heat went right through her, causing her entire body to tremble. Had she not been so nervous about what that smile meant, or wondering just how lost in him she was willing to get, she may have found the courage to smile back.

"Sweetheart, I can do a lot with ninety minutes."

CHAPTER 3

"First rule in getting lost," Trey said, unlocking the door to one of his family's oldest tasting rooms and flicking on the lights. "No contact with the outside world. If they don't know where you are, they can't find you."

"Just a sec," Sara mumbled, her fingers flying over the keypad on her cell. "I just need to remind the other dance teacher about the stack of billing statements that—"

He slipped the phone out of Pollyanna's little hands, pocketing it when she reached out to grab it back, loving how her lips went plump as she frowned.

Sweet and stubborn. The perfect pairing.

"I can see I'm working with a first timer here." She sent him an amused look. "That's okay," he said. "I'm an excellent teacher."

Placing his hand a little lower on her back than was polite, to test the waters, he nudged her through the doorway. Trey took in a deep breath, inhaling the familiar scents of aged oak and cherry tobacco mixing with the rawhide of the barstools. One sniff and all

of the tension he'd been carrying since last night's sorriest-excuse-
for-a-guy's-night-ever evaporated.

For Trey, this place felt more like home than anywhere he'd ever
been.

"Then teach away," she said, sending him a sidelong glance.

"Rule number two, no talk of business or family. What's the point
of playing hooky if all you talk about is what you're trying to escape?"

Their footsteps echoed across the expanse of the room that lay
in front of them as he led her toward the tasting bar. He patted the
stool on the far end and, when she hopped up, he slipped behind
the bar.

"Right," she nodded seriously, and he had to fight back a smile.
"No contact. No talk of family, work, or problems." She paused,
then looked across the bar at him, those big hazel eyes so confused
he wanted to kiss her. "Then what do we talk about?"

"How about we start with preferences. Red or white?" he said,
pulling out two bottles of their special reserve from behind the
counter. "And I promise not to embarrass you by sharing that I've
had a thing for ballerinas ever since Judith Carr danced the Sugar
Plum Fairy at our fifth-grade talent show." She laughed and he felt
it in his chest. "I swear, it's something about the short skirts and
tight buns."

"I'm wearing my hair down," she explained.

He smiled. "I wasn't talking about your hair."

Sara flushed an adorable pink, but tried to hide it by studiously
examining the wine bottles he'd selected. With her distracted, Trey
took his time to studiously examine her every curve.

He hadn't been kidding with the ballerina thing that she was
rocking. If the ass-hugging leggings didn't do it for him, then that
sheer, white skirt she had on did. And yeah, he was a guy, so ignoring the creamy swells that peeked over the lacy edge of her little top,

or the way her body reacted to the chill in the room was impossible. So he didn't even bother to try.

"Today is about adventure, right?" She sat up straight, all proper and prim, and folded her hands on the bar top. "So surprise me."

Only fair, since she kept surprising him. The other night when she'd crashed into his life, she'd come off as sweet and sunny and, if he were being honest, a little frazzled. Today though, in Stan's shop, he'd really looked at her. Looked past the smile, past the wide eyes and smattering of freckles, and past the good face that she was putting on for the world, and damn if that didn't do something to his chest.

"I say it is a day to go bold, live loud, and since we are limited on fun time . . ." he said and went to work. Reaching for five globed glasses from behind the bar, he lined them up in front of her. "Let's start with our house Zinfandel, move our way through the medium-bodied wines, and end with a glass of our reserve Cabernet. How does that sound?"

He poured a generous tasting of the Zin into the first glass and slid it her way. "Since this is my first time playing hooky *and* wine tasting I will leave the choices to you." She wrapped her elegant fingers around the stem, took a dainty sniff that made her nose crinkle, before pressing the rim of the glass to her mouth and taking a sip. "This is good. I don't know what I'm supposed to taste, but—"

Instead of launching into his practiced spiel about the luscious deep flavors of cherry with a hint of spice, one that he'd given a hundred times, to a hundred different women, he said, "Are you serious? You've never been wine tasting?" How the hell did she live in the wine country and never go tasting? "Ever?"

"I know. It's awful. I keep telling myself that I have to get out of the house more, actually experience where I live, but between getting my studio up and running and making sure that my so—"

He placed a finger over her lips, and God, she had great lips. They were full and soft and damp with wine.

"Rule number two. Remember?" She nodded and he could feel her breath against his fingers come out in shallow bursts. "And since this is your first tasting *and* first time playing hooky . . ." he paused to look at her. "Really, not even senior ditch day?"

"Nope, I made it through four years of high school with perfect attendance."

His day kept getting more interesting by the second. Trey didn't know what he expected to happen when he followed her into Stan's. But suddenly, his usual go-to game plan didn't feel right.

"I assume that since you're behind the bar acting like you own the place, you do." She slid the empty glass forward, already eyeballing the next bottle.

"My family does." He wanted to make that clear. And when she didn't seem disappointed by the news, her eyes widening with genuine interest instead, he added, "This was my Grandpa Geno's favorite tasting room. His father built it back in the twenties. There is even a secret room in the cellar where men would come to buy wine during Prohibition." Trey felt himself smile. "My grandpa used to take me down there when I was a kid and sneak me a glass or two. Point out the different flavors, what made one unique over another."

Those were some of his favorite memories as a child. With his grandfather, he never felt as though he had to prove himself. He could just be in the moment.

Kind of like he was now.

"It sounds like you two had a special connection," she said quietly. "I had the same kind of relationship with my grandmother. My mom taught me everything she knew about dance, but it was my grandmother who shared her love for it with me." She gave a shy shrug, almost embarrassed, but unlike him, she went on. "After she died, I realized that I wanted to teach dance, help little girls experience the same magic that she shared with me."

That was exactly what his grandfather had said to him about wine and why he loved what he did. Grandpa Geno believed wine brought people together, cemented relationships, and allowed special moments to happen.

"I'm not around enough to share," he admitted and had to glance away. The way she was looking at him, as though he'd passed on his grandfather's legacy the way she had her grandmother's, made him feel like a fraud.

"Well, you're sharing it with me."

He stared at her, surprised that she openly held his gaze when most people would look away. She might think that she was playing hooky, but the woman was so amazingly open and grounded there was no way she could ever be truly lost. Something that Trey admired.

"Thank you," he said and, before he could grab the next bottle, she reached out and touched a finger to his, letting it rest there. The simple connection reminded Trey of just how long it had been since he'd talked to someone like this.

"Now, share with me your favorite wine," she said. "Not the ones you give customers or people you're trying impress, but the one you'd pick for yourself if you were here alone."

At that, he smiled. She was beyond good at reading him and calling him out. "Deal. Give me a minute."

He walked to the end of the bar and selected a bottle of Chianti from his secret hiding place. Then he palmed two of the un-sexiest tumblers in wine country, smiling because they were what his grandpa had used when he'd come here to drink with his cronies. It wasn't about the packaging, it was about the experience.

Opening it, he placed the cork beneath Sara's nose, the side of his finger lightly brushing her lips and igniting one hell of a spark. "Close your eyes and tell me what you smell."

With an amused smile, her lashes fluttered closed and she inhaled, her chest slowly rising and then holding. After a long moment, her warm breath washed over his skin and she opened her eyes.

"It smells charming." He watched as her cheeks slightly flushed and her smile became coy as she looked him dead in the eye. "Will it taste the same?"

Something inside of Trey shifted. Unable to stop himself, he leaned in until their mouths were a breath apart and whispered, "You tell me."

Then he kissed her. And charming was the last thing he felt. Not while her mouth gently worked his as though she'd also been fantasizing about this all week.

He teased the seam of her lips and she gave a breathy little moan that shot straight to his core. The taste of her sent blood pumping through his body at an accelerated pace. She teased back, creating enough of a spark to get his chest vibrating, his ears ringing.

Twice.

"Trey," she breathed, his name whispered against his mouth. "It's my phone."

"First rule, no contact with the outside world." He nipped her lower lip, moaning a little when she nipped back. "We haven't finished the tasting."

"I know, and I'm sorry, but I have to go." She pulled back just enough so that he could see her eyes were wide and dazed with heat, and a little humor. Her hands were cupping his face and she was leaning so far forward across the bar she was plastered to his chest. "My world needs me again."

"How's the car?" Heather Reed asked and Sara froze. Hand on the doorknob, mid-sneak, she turned and offered up an innocent smile.

Heather was Sara's dance-assistant-slash-nanny-slash-best friend. Who also happened to be her sister-in-law. And right now she was aiming an accusatory glare in Sara's direction.

"Not good," she admitted, feeling as guilty as a teenager who'd been caught sneaking off with her boyfriend. Not that Trey was her boyfriend, or that she even knew what that kind of guilt felt like, since Sara had never sneaked in her life. Until today. "You were right, more than a damaged bumper."

"Yeah, well the log sticking out of the front and the steaming engine kind of tipped me off," Heather said, pulling her long leg underneath her, freeing up a spot on the couch. A spot that Sara was not going to take. She sucked at secrets. Keeping one from Heather was impossible, which was why she walked into the family room and casually plopped down in the armchair—on the opposite side of the coffee table.

That's when she noticed how incredibly clean the house was. The floor had been vacuumed, toys put away, not a single LEGO left out to step on. There was even a bouquet of fresh flowers on the mantle.

It was Sara who pinned Heather with a look this time. She wasn't the only one being sneaky. "What's going on?"

Heather smiled. Way too big. "Remember the audition I went on last month?"

"You mean the musical I said you were perfect for and forced you to go on even though you said you were too tall to blend in with the other dancers?"

"Yeah, the director called today and they passed. I was too tall to blend in with the supporting dancers."

"Oh, Heather, I am so sorry."

"I'm not. He also said that the lead tore her ACL and he wants to talk to me about filling in while she recovers. The lead!" Heather's face lit with a joy that Sara hadn't seen since before Garrett died. "It's just for a few months, and I don't even know how many other girls they are considering, but I figure it's worth a meeting."

"Heather, that's incredible. Well, not for the lead who tore her ACL, but you know what I mean," she said, crossing the room to pull her sister-in-law in for a hug.

Heather was *beyond* talented, a dancer with megastar factor. Her potential had outgrown St. Helena the day they moved here.

"I know, right?" She hugged Sara back, tightly, and Sara felt her eyes start to burn. "He's going to be in San Francisco for the week and wants me to meet the choreographer. Tuesday."

Sara froze. "Tuesday?"

"I know, I'm sorry," Heather said, and she was. She also wasn't finished with her favor. "If things go well, then I might have to stay through to Wednesday."

Tuesdays were the studio's busiest days. If Heather was gone, Sara would have to cover her classes and Cooper wouldn't get to bed until nine. She'd start bright and early at seven sharp and go straight through to their evening senior lineup, which included— *oh God*—Heather's brainchild.

"Senior Pole Dancing," she groaned.

"I'll make it up to you." Heather tugged Sara's hand and she was already beginning to cave. Two months as the lead in a Broadway musical could be the career changer Heather needed.

"Fine, I'll do it," Sara said. Heather launched herself into Sara's arms with a resounding *oomph.* "As long as you admit that I was right. You are not too tall."

"Only if you admit that the whole 'Sorry I'm late, I hit some guy's car' story the other night was really code for doing the backseat tango."

"It was not."

"Then explain why the driver looks just like Sexy Italian Guy who came into the studio last night looking for you."

That was news to her. News that made her shiver with delight. "He was just checking to make sure I was okay and to tell me that his car had no damages."

Heather snorted. "That must have been some checkup, since you stopped answering your phone like an hour and a half ago." Heather shot Sara a knowing look. "Especially since Sexy Italian Guy happens to go by the name Trey DeLuca."

Oh my God. "You know Trey?" The idea made Sara's stomach sour because her sister-in-law was tall, willowy, and endowed. One glance at her centerfold body sent most men to their knees in awe.

"Sara, every available woman in town knows Trey. Or at least knows of him. He is like the Jedi master of panty whisperers."

Sara rolled her eyes. "You make him sound like some kind of urban myth."

"According to the ladies in my yoga class, the word you are looking for is 'legend,' not 'myth.' Apparently, he can talk his way into a pair of panties in under two minutes, and his way out of a commitment before breakfast." Heather waggled a brow. "So . . . your panties—"

"Are still intact, thank you very much." *Although he could work a button like nobody's business,* she thought, remembering her raincoat.

"Mommy!" Cooper squealed from the top of the stairs.

"Hey, honey." She stood, thankful for the interruption.

Trey was sexy and gorgeous and so far out of her comfort zone that just thinking about seeing him again made her nervous. It shouldn't matter that he was a shagging legend. But for a moment there, Sara had felt like they'd shared something—something real and special. A connection.

Or maybe they just shared a kiss and some wine and she wasn't experienced enough to know the difference.

Refusing to overthink the afternoon, she put out her arms just as Cooper came tearing across the rug, not bothering to slow down as he launched himself at Sara. Arms wrapped around her waist, legs locked around her ankles, and his head firmly butted into her stomach, she managed to hold back a grunt. The kid might be small, but he packed some serious velocity.

Hugging him as tightly as she could without crushing him, she placed a kiss on his head. He smelled like Jell-O and bath time.

"I missed you so much," he whispered.

And that, right there, was all she needed.

"Missed you too, kiddo."

He nodded and then let go. Sara dropped to one knee and gave her full attention to her entire world, who was dressed in a San Diego Chargers ball hat, a matching jersey that hung to his knees, and nothing on the bottom except, she'd bet a million dollars, Batman undies. "What happened to your pants?"

"Don't need them," Cooper explained.

"He said pants slowed him down too much," Heather clarified, with a look that said she'd drop the subject of Sexy Italian Guy. For now. "And we also learned today that warm glue and excited hands are a bad combo so I got him in a bath. When it came to getting him dressed for bed, well, the pants weren't happening."

Sara was surprised Heather managed to get him in the jersey. Cooper was going through his tough-guy phase, which translated into walking around the house in his underpants and not much else.

"Pants are for babies," Cooper said. Lately anything he didn't want to do was because it was for babies.

A knock sounded at the door and Cooper's face went flush with excitement as he yelled, "I'll get it," and took off.

"Don't open the door until I get there," Sara reminded him but he was already swinging it wide open.

"Roman!" Cooper squealed and started jumping up and down. "Mom, look. It's Roman. At our house!"

"I see," Sara said, coming up behind her son and resting a hand against the door. "Hey, Roman."

"Hey, Sara," he said and flashed a flirty smile.

Roman Brady was good-looking, everybody's friend, and a single dad who had an honest way about him and a killer body that made women melt.

"Is Matt here?" Cooper poked his head around Roman's legs and scanned the front porch for his best friend.

"Sorry, buddy. Matt's at his mom's tonight," Roman said, extending a paper bag with Cooper's name scrawled in crayon across the front. "But I found this by the garbage can after pickup and I knew that you spent a lot of time picking it out, so I wanted to drop it by."

"Thanks," Cooper mumbled. "Hunter took it and wouldn't give it back."

Sara shot Roman a worried look. Hunter Lock was a bully of the worst kind—mainly because his parents refused to see him for what he was. For whatever reason, he'd selected Cooper as Target of the Year.

Sara was about to ask him what transpired today, when Cooper opened the bag and, with an enthusiastic *yes*, pulled something out and waved it in front of Sara's face. "Look, Mom! It's not broken."

"What do you have there?" she asked, moving her head and narrowly escaping a collision. "Is that a block of wood?"

He frowned as if truly surprised no one else saw the true awesomeness of the block.

"It's a car." He ran the block of wood down Sara's knee. "Well, it will be. It's for the Mighty Mites Pinewood Derby."

"Pinewood Derby?" This was the first time she'd heard of it.

Mighty Mites was an after-school program and Cooper's time to hang with his buddies, learn how to tie knots, identify bugs, and make farting sounds with his armpit. It was also how Sara was able to manage her studio without sending him to day care. Something she refused to do.

"I sent a flier home last week," Roman explained. Not only was he the St. Helena fire chief, he was also Cooper's Mite Hive Commander. And as of recently, Sara's friend. "The qualifier race is next Saturday."

"We have to turn that hunk of tree into an actual car that rolls? By next Saturday?" Sara asked, wondering how she was supposed to accomplish that task.

"Yup." Cooper gave a decisive nod. "I'm going to win."

"There are directions in the bag," Roman said softly, leaning in close. "They're pretty detailed. I also put in an extra flier about the big swarm race that is held at the end of the month. The top five winners from the qualifier square off against the best Lady Bug racers. It's a pretty big deal for the kids."

"Cuz everyone who goes gets a trophy." Cooper's little arms stretched as wide as they could, the block of wood dangling from his fingers. "A big one."

"Garrett did it when we were kids," Heather said, coming to the door. "I used to watch him and my dad slave for weeks over it. We're talking top-of-the-line pine-car engineering and aerodynamics. A real testosterone, mine-is-bigger-than-yours competition."

"It's a wood car with detailed instructions. How hard can it be?"

Heather snorted. "Although it was made really clear at pickup today that this is supposed to be a 'parental supervision project'"— she made exaggerated air quotes and shot Roman a pointed look— "the dads were already grunting their engineering superiority."

"Great," Sara said, watching the excitement in her son's eyes as he raced his hunk of wood across the carpet.

"We got to pick out our own wood and I picked this one cuz it has a dark line right here. Built-in racing stripe, see." Cooper held it up and, sure enough, it had a dark grain cutting right through the middle. Getting that stripe to go up the middle of a car was a whole other problem. "Like Daddy's car."

Heather shot Sara a sympathetic look and, just like that, she felt her heart drop right to her toes. She saw how excited her son was, knew how important getting the car perfect was going to be, and yet she couldn't even park a car correctly, let alone whittle one.

"And we got our own piece of sandpaper. But I'm not allowed to use a saw unless an adult supervises, right, Commander Roman?"

"Right, kiddo," Roman said, but she could hear the apology in his voice.

Did they even own a saw? And wasn't five too young to race wood cars chiseled from semiautomatic tools?

Born the only child to a single mother who ran a ballet company, Sara's experience with men was limited. Which was why she'd fallen so hard and fast for Garrett. Her husband had been smart, funny, and 100 percent military-grown male. Everything that her world as a dancer was not.

When Garrett was alive, Sara never had to worry about Cooper getting in his "guy-time." Now that her son had turned five and was better at identifying sickled feet during a pirouette than a good football pass, she was getting worried. Which was one of the reasons she'd put him in the Mighty Mites to begin with. The other was that Garrett had been a Mighty Mite.

"It's a nice piece of wood," Heather said, tapping the bill of Cooper's cap. "Now, say thank-you to Roman and then you and I will go brush your teeth and pick out a bedtime story."

Cooper's face fell. Fun over. With a mumbled thank-you, he picked up his block of wood and slowly made his way to the bathroom. Apparently bedtime was for babies too.

When the sound of water hitting the sink sounded, Roman tucked a piece of hair behind Sara's ear. "I didn't mean to make tonight hard on you."

"No, it's not that," she admitted, taking a sudden interest in her shoes when Roman's gaze strayed to her lips. "Just sometimes being a single mom sucks."

"Yeah," he smiled down at her, which made Sara smile because he got it. His ex-wife might have Matt tonight, but Roman had primary custody and was the main parental influence in his son's life. He was in this all alone—just like Sara. "If you need help with the car or the saw or whatever . . ." Roman's eyes darted to her lips and hung there, letting her know that *whatever* was still on the table, she only had to give him the go-ahead.

Sometimes Roman popped in for one of her ballroom dancing classes at the studio. And sometimes they'd talk afterward, about their kids, school, parenthood, the Mighty Mites. They'd flirted once or twice, but whenever he'd pressed for more Sara had backed away.

She hadn't been ready.

Understanding as ever, Roman had shrugged and said maybe another time. Apparently another time was now, and Sara was ready—only not with him, because all she could think about was a sexy Italian with way too much swagger and experience.

"Thanks for dropping this by," Sara said abruptly.

Roman just smiled warmly. The man was stable and thoughtful and loved her kid. That should count for something. Yet she just stood there, awkwardly grinning and having no idea what direction to go in.

"No problem. Tell Cooper I'll see him tomorrow." He gave a small wave and walked backward down the porch steps, never taking his eyes off her. "And I'll see you at class this week."

Sara felt herself blush as he winked while climbing into his minivan. After he pulled out of her driveway, she closed the door and turned around—to find Heather standing at the top of the stairs grinning.

"So, are you going to see him again?" Heather asked, making her way down the stairs, and Sara had a bad feeling she'd just been set up.

"My guess is Tuesday night. At Swinging Singles."

"Not Roman." Sara followed Heather into the living room where Heather took a seat and waved her hand dismissively. "Trey."

"Oh," Sara said and felt her face heat—but for a whole different reason this time. "I don't know. I think it was just a one-day thing."

Although today was exactly what Sara had needed—her lips still tingled from that kiss—Trey was apparently some kind of smooth-talking panty whisperer. And even if Sara's panties were whisper worthy, which they were not, she wasn't sure if getting horizontal with a guy who had more nurses on call than the local ER was the kind of adventure she was looking for.

"That. Right there," Heather waved her palm to encompass Sara's entire being, "is terrifying proof that you have been sniffing the Play-Doh too long. I mean, have you not seen his ass? It's incredible. A solid ten on the squeeze-scale. And don't even get me started on those eyes. He could wink and my clothes would melt off."

Trey was a ten bazillion on the squeeze-scale. He scored even higher on the best-first-kiss-ever scale. And she hadn't stepped back.

Instead, she'd dug her nails into his hair and pressed her body against his.

Heather crossed her arms in challenge. "We made a deal that if I started following my dream of dancing on Broadway again, you'd start dating."

"We were drunk, and I said I'd be more *open* to dating, which I have been." Sara sighed. "It's just hard."

"I know it's hard," Heather said softly. "And I know my brother broke your heart when he reenlisted, and then shattered it when he never came home, but it's been two years. Two years of spending your Saturday nights watching Cooper snore. You moved to St. Helena to start a new life. When are you going to start living it?"

She wanted to argue that she was. Nine months ago, she'd taken the first huge step toward living. She packed up eight years of memories and her five-year-old, and moved her family to St. Helena for a fresh start. Admitting that Garrett was really gone had been difficult. Agreeing to get back out there in the dating pool was terrifying. Taking off her wedding ring had nearly killed her. But she'd done it. For Cooper and for herself.

And she was ready—she just wasn't sure if she was ready to take on a guy like Trey. "I'm taking things slow, to make sure that I'm ready."

"That lie stopped working when you kissed Sexy Italian Guy."

"Who said I kissed Trey?" Her cheeks went even hotter.

"You have lipstick smeared all over your face."

Sara touched her lips, feeling her face burn up, as she realized that was what Roman must have been staring at.

"And I know it wasn't Roman since I was standing right here. My money is on the panty whisperer."

CHAPTER 4

Exhausted and covered in pink and red glitter, Sara sat down and dropped her head on the bistro's table. It was only ten forty-five on Tuesday and already she needed a nap. Or a pick-me-up. She'd sucked down a large pumpkin-spice latte. It hadn't helped.

"I need a Cupid's Arrow, double shot. Pronto," Sara said.

"I've been telling you that since you moved to town," Regan DeLuca said.

Sara lifted her head long enough to glare. Regan was drawing little pink hearts on a piece of vinyl that stretched across six tables. Strings of hot glue draped from her hair and pink Sharpie stained her fingers.

"The drink," Sara clarified, although the idea of a little romance in her life didn't sound as terrifying as it had last week. She remembered the smoking-hot kiss she'd shared with Trey, felt her palms start to sweat, and reminded herself that she had to tread especially carefully around Trey's sisters-in-law. "Make that light on the Cupid and heavy on the arrow."

"Don't you have a Tiny-Tappers class in fifteen minutes?" Alexis DeLuca asked, screwing the cap on the cotton candy–colored glitter.

Dressed in custard-speckled jeans, an apron that read GONE ITALIAN, and an enormous baby-bump, Lexi co-owned the Sweet and Savory with her grandmother Pricilla. The locals-favorite bistro was famous for rustic French fare, to-die-for pastries, and Cupid's Arrow, a drink with one shot espresso and two shots homemade chocolate liqueur and strong enough to knock you on your butt.

"No, I'm covering a private lesson for Heather," Sara said. "Then I'm meeting a woman at town hall to ask about getting on this summer's recreation calendar to hopefully drum up new students, *then* I have my Tiny-Tappers class," Sara mumbled into the vinyl cloth, a piece of arrow-shaped confetti sticking to her lip.

"I forgot that Heather had that audition today," Lexi said with sympathy lacing her voice. "You're stuck covering all of her classes?"

Sara nodded against the table. "And if she doesn't make it home tonight, I have to cover her Waltz and Rumba class with Handsy Harvey." Sara looked up. "Which is why I need something to get me through until bedtime."

Sara's day had started at the crack of dawn, which wasn't unusual since Cooper liked to rise with the sun. Unfortunately, she had passed out on the couch last night before she'd managed to finish stuffing and sealing all of next month's billing reminders, and was dreaming about death by paper cuts, when Cooper woke her up by spilling a carton of OJ on the floor while trying to make Mommy a special breakfast in bed.

They cleaned up the mess, the kitchen floor good as new, just in time for Cooper to accidently flip his syrup-coated pancake off the plate and, two-second rule in full effect, shove it in his mouth.

She dropped Cooper off at school, ten minutes after the bell and, since she was still short a car, walked back to the studio where she went straight into her Mommy and Me Scoot and Shake, followed by her Pre-School Promenade class. Then she locked up her studio and headed over to the Sweet and Savory for a pick-me-up.

"If you get one, I get one. And since that isn't going to happen . . ." Regan's voice trailed off as she smoothed her hands over her swollen belly. "I know things can get crazy when Heather's gone, so thanks for helping with the banner for the Gala."

"No problem." Sara stood and, reaching for the finger paint, poured a thin layer of pink onto one paper plate and a pile of matching glitter on another. Fisting her hand, she sank the side of it into the paint. "Where do you want Cupid's little footprints?"

"I was thinking along the bottom of the banner, right under the word 'Gala.'"

"Speaking of the Gala," Lexi said. "I heard that the sexy fire chief is looking to pin himself a dance teacher this year."

"Pin?" Sara asked.

"At the Winter Garden Gala. It's tradition," Regan explained. "Everyone shows up with a flower to pin on their sweetheart. Kind of like staking their claim."

"Only with class," Lexi pointed out. "And Roman was asking what kind of flowers you liked."

"That's thoughtful of him," she said, plunging her hand back in the paint and focusing on making more baby Cupid feet.

"Maybe she's just holding out for someone else," Lexi mused.

"I wasn't planning on going with anyone," Sara said truthfully. Going on a date was one thing. Going on a date to a Valentine's celebration was a whole other ball game.

"Really," Lexi said with a casualness to her voice that sent Sara's pulse skyrocketing. "I thought you were holding out for the youngest DeLuca, who I heard you ran into the other night and swapped all kinds of personal info—"

"It was more of a sideswipe," Sara said.

"—then he helped you out of your clothes and offered to look under your hood."

Regan froze, her eyes going wide. "Why is this the first time I am hearing about this?"

"There is no *this*. I hit the man's car, he helped me out of my raincoat, and I gave him my card in case there was any damage. No big deal."

Both women raised disbelieving brows that, combined with the crossed arms and pointed looks, had Sara squirming in her dance pants.

"Then why are you blushing?" Lexi asked.

"I am not blush—"

Sara touched her face and felt cold paint drip down her heated skin. *Great.* Releasing a big breath, she rubbed her cheek off on her shoulder. The cotton sleeve came away with pink, glittery smudges.

"Fine. He came to see me Friday to make sure my car was okay. I happened to be having a bad day. So he took me wine tasting." Where Sara had the pleasure of tasting a very special vintage of DeLuca. "He was sweet and . . . what? Can you two stop doing that sister-in-law silent conversation thing?"

"You're just the first woman who has had a *run-in* with my brother-in-law and described him as sweet," Lexi said.

"Well, maybe you're just talking to the wrong women."

"Apparently," Regan said and they both laughed.

Sara ignored them and dusted glitter over the wet footprints. "He was sweet and charming. And just being nice." But she was talking to herself because the pointer sisters were back to their non-verbal discussion. "And, okay, he kissed me."

Everyone at the table froze, even Sara, who was wishing she could take back her last admission because just thinking about that

kiss had her face flushing and her lips tingling and—*oh my God*—
would they stop staring at her like she'd lost her mind?

"End of story," Sara said firmly. "Now, if you two are done talking about me in front of my face, Cupid's feet are finished and I have
to get ready for my eleven o'clock."

Sara spun around and walked right into a solid wall of muscle
that smelled like warm, yummy man. Her hand rested on his pecs.
His were on her hips, steadying her and—*whoa*—pulling her closer.

Reminding herself to breathe, Sara slowly looked up at Trey,
and *whoa* was an accurate statement—there was nothing sweet
about the way he was looking back.

"For the record," Trey whispered, the gravel in his voice sending
zings of anticipation racing through her body, and something much
more primal south, "I think you kissed me."

"Really? I wasn't sure. It happened so fast," she said, remembering just how *fast* it had happened and how thrilling it had felt.

"Yeah," he smiled, "me neither."

Dressed in a crumpled suit, yesterday's stubble, and an epic case
of bedhead, Trey looked like he'd just rolled out of bed. The ridiculous part of Sara hoped it was his own bed. A warmer part, the part
she'd shut off when Garrett died, noticed that he looked tired—and
a little lost. Almost like he needed a hug. So she gave him one.

Sara knew that she was in trouble, because he hugged her back.

Christ, what was he doing?

Trey wasn't a hugger, but he couldn't make himself let go. The
way she smelled, like paint, a hint of something spicy, and all
woman was almost as good as the way she felt pressed against him.
So he pulled her closer, all the tension of the past few days fading.

One touch and, for the first time since he'd walked into that hospital, he wasn't itching to leave.

"What was that for?" he asked.

He felt her shrug and out of the corner of his eye watched the wide scoop neck of her shirt slide down her shoulder, exposing a lot of silky skin and a single black, lacy strap. Even with pink paint smeared across her cheek, he found her ridiculously hot.

He was about to bury his face in her neck and maybe take a little bite, when she cleared her throat and pulled back. "You looked like you needed a hug."

What he needed was a hell of a lot more than a hug. Like her, beneath him, panting his name for the next few days.

He took in her lithe body, the way her black leggings hugged her hips and how nicely, he imagined, they stretched across her exceptionally toned butt, and changed his mind. Top, bottom, standing up, he didn't care as long as they were both naked and moaning.

"Trey," she whispered, her mouth moving sensually as she formed his name. She had a great mouth.

"Yeah."

Then she hit him with those warm hazel eyes. "I am so—"

Into you . . . Horny . . . Turned on . . .

"—sorry."

Not the word he was hoping to hear.

She took a small step back and, sadly, her hands were no longer on him. In fact, they were palms up and—*what the hell?*

He looked from her hands to his shirt where two very pink, very dainty handprints stained his coat, one on each pec. When he turned, the light hit it, and . . . *oh hell no.* He sparkled. His six-hundred dollar, tailor-made, Italian tweed overcoat looked like one of Holly's art projects.

But instead of being mad, he found himself grinning—like an idiot. Because she was staring at his mouth, and he knew she was thinking about their kiss.

"It's still wet. Here, let me see if I can—" She reached out to help him then looked at her paint-coated palms and stopped. "Give me two seconds to wash my hands and let's see if I can get that paint off."

Having had a particularly crappy weekend, one that he was certain Sara could've helped alleviate, he leaned in to her and lowered his voice. "I have a better idea. I'm staying at the Napa Grand. Right next door. It has a shower, a really big one with fluffy robes. We can get cleaned up, have one of the hotel's famous oyster platters brought up with a bottle of wine, and finish," he let his eyes drop to her mouth, "that tasting."

Her mouth quirked up at the corners as though she thought he was an idiot and he wondered what the hell went wrong.

Most people thought he was charming. Especially women. One of his basic go-to lines delivered with his DeLuca smile was enough to make them hot and bothered. Not Sara. Nope, he just made her laugh—and not in the hot-and-bothered way. And he couldn't figure out why.

"Actually, I have to go, but you can send me a bill for the coat."

"Another bill?" His grin became a full on smile. He couldn't help it. "You've got to be kidding me."

"I wish I were," she laughed. "I don't know what's gotten into me lately. Your property clearly isn't safe around me."

They stood smiling at each other, before Sara broke the contact and looked at her watch. "I do have to go, though. I have a private lesson starting in a few minutes and I don't want to keep my client waiting."

"Lucky client," Trey said.

"He's a special client," she clarified, her eyes going soft and dreamy, and Trey found himself wondering how to qualify for the special-person's package. "It's someone looking for a second chance at love."

"So you're a romantic?" Of course she was. Girls like her with those big trusting eyes had white picket fences and grand gestures built into their DNA. Yet here he was, trying to figure out how to get more time with her.

"It used to be easier for me." Her smile turned unsure. "But I'm working on it."

There was a vulnerability in her eyes that he felt all the way to his chest and the only honest thing he could say in that moment was, "Me too."

She stopped smiling and that tug he felt every time he was with her tightened, because he could tell by the openness in her expression that he hadn't totally blown it. Not completely. And more than anything, he wanted her to keep looking at him like she was right now. "Forget the room, how about a cup of coffee?"

She looked at his sisters-in-law—who were practically teetering over to listen in, something they picked up the moment their last name officially became DeLuca—then back to him and silently nodded. "That sounds nice. Why don't you call the studio later and we can set up a time?"

He started to say that he'd already tried that when a leggy blonde entered the bistro and talking became dangerous. In fact, Trey stood perfectly still and tried to become one with the crowd. Too bad Tammy of Tammy's Wine Country Tours had the same uncanny ability of picking out a former fling as she did a good Syrah, because her eyes locked on Trey's and he knew that any hope he had for coffee with Sara—or anything more—was over.

He watched Tammy go all bubbly with recognition as she sauntered over to give him a proper Tammy Welcome Back, and after their run in with Kayla, he could only imagine what Sara was going to think.

"Well, well, well, Trey DeLuca's back." Arms flung wide, completely oblivious to Sara, she plastered her generous breasts against him in the most uncomfortable hug of his life.

"Hey, Tammy." Two cordial pats between the shoulder blades and Trey stepped back, untangling himself. Even though Trey and Tammy hadn't hooked up since college and were nothing more than friends now, suddenly seeing his life through Sara's eyes made him uncomfortable—and a little embarrassed.

"Talk about weird timing," she went on, wiggling her fingers at his sisters-in-law who wiggled back—fully amused at his situation. "Last night I dropped off one of my regulars and his current arm candy at the Napa Grand. Told them to be sure and order that famous oyster platter. Always a winner, right?"

She winked and he was screwed.

"I hear they have fluffy robes too," Sara said with a laugh, confirming that he was a total and complete idiot. With an amused look of her own she glanced down at his coat. "Send me the bill."

"How about you give me a private dance lesson and we call it even?" he offered but she was already hugging his sisters-in-law good-bye.

"Even better," she said. At her comment, he felt his shoulder relax a little. He still had a shot to make this right. Then she added, "Call the studio and ask for Heather. She handles all privates."

He started to argue that Heather couldn't handle *all* privates, since Sara was headed toward a "special" one right now, but she had her umbrella in hand and was through the door before he could even open his mouth.

He watched her cross the street and wanted to throttle himself because, yup, those leggings looked as good going as they did coming. And he was never going to get that dance.

Ten minutes and a stern lecture from his sisters-in-law later, Trey ducked through the revolving glass doors of the Napa Grand Hotel. One of the more well-preserved beaux-arts masterpieces on the West Coast, the Napa Grand was the oldest hotel in town. It was also the only hotel in town. This week, Trey happened to call it home.

Marc's hotel was the only place left in St. Helena that was connected to his family and didn't reek of domestication. Or painful memories.

Shaking a few globs of glitter off of his coat, he rode the elevator to the top floor and strode down the hallway, loosening the top button of his shirt. It had already been one hell of a week and it was only Tuesday. Thanks in part to Abby's "few" meetings, which had turned into a catastrophic calamity of errors. Starting with a shipping error of the worst kind and ending with Trey stuck in the minivan for a grand total of twenty-two hours—since its retractable seats made it the *only* available car in the family that could handle the fifteen cases that needed to be rush-delivered to Santa Barbara. Something his brothers found freaking hilarious.

He didn't know how it happened, but it seemed as though every time he came home, he was thrust into a shitstorm of problems he was expected to fix. None of them his.

Blaming his mood on exhaustion, Trey fished out his key and opened the door. All he wanted was to eat lunch, take a hot shower, and go to bed.

Strike that.

All he wanted was to eat lunch, take a hot shower, and go to bed—with Sara. But since Sara wasn't interested in playing hooky today—or ever again, thanks to Tammy—and his suite was filled with DeLucas, Trey didn't think he'd even get to eat his lunch.

"Nice coat," Marc said, taking in the pink handprints. "Do you have a matching clutch?"

"I was going to ask to borrow yours." Trey dropped his to-go bag on the entry table and shut the door with his foot. "Glad to see that this hotel respects their guests' privacy and security."

"You should complain," Marc said, resting his feet casually on the coffee table.

"Yeah, but I hear that the owner is a total prick."

Trey purposefully remained standing, hoping that they'd all take the hint and get out. Not that there was any place to sit. Even if he wanted to pull up a cushion and share some small talk—which he most definitely did not—Marc, and all six foot three of him, pretty much consumed the entire couch, and Nate made himself at home in the overstuffed chair.

Gabe stood silently at the window, practicing his disappointed glare at the approaching storm outside. The air was so thick with tension, and the space so overflowing with DeLuca attitude, the room felt more like a casket than a luxury three-bedroom suite.

"Abby wants to make an offer on the land," Gabe said. "I'm still looking into things on this end, but I came across a snafu that it seems only you can fix."

He wasn't sure exactly what the problem was or how he could fix it, but since Gabe's tone gave him the feeling that this wouldn't be a kid-brother-saves-the-day kind of talk, Trey decided to take that seat.

With a sigh, Gabe turned around and—*Jesus*—Baby Sofie was strapped to his front in some kind of parachute harness for babies.

Face red, lips pursed, she took one look at Trey and started flailing all four limbs. "Da-da-da-da-DA!"

"With how fast the owners want to sell, and how difficult it is for a US company to acquire Italian land, I wanted to make sure we were all buttoned up on this end, just in case," Gabe said over Baby Sofie's jabbering. "So I called Drew. He suggested that *you* buy the land. Imagine that?"

Trey felt his stomach bottom out. Followed by his chest, then his heart. "I was going to tell you."

Two years ago, Trey started looking into gaining Italian residency through their grandfather's lineage. He'd called Drew, their lawyer and expert in all things corporate and foreign policy, to help him with the process. What started out as a temporary answer to an insane travel schedule quickly became a solution that would save his sanity.

"Really? When?" Gabe's tone all business. "Would that have been before or after you shipped your stuff overseas and sent out housewarming invitations?"

Trey was delirious. He had to be. Because it took everything he had not to laugh. Or point out that gently bouncing up and down in tandem with a diaper monster while snarling words like housewarming and invitations was *not* intimidating. Then again, Trey had big, sparkly, pink hands on his chest.

"I don't get to hang out at home and watch the business grow," Trey pointed out. "Last year I spent more time in an airplane than I did in a bed. I hit a hundred thousand miles before summer even ended. I thought that buying a place I could use as a home base was a good idea."

"I agree. Buy one here," Gabe countered.

"We're two hours from an airport." And right in the middle of a tsunami of memories and regrets. "Between managing Marc's hospitality friends, Nate's new high-end collectors, and you dominating the domestic wine industry with your one-grocery-store-at-a-time campaign, I don't even have time to sleep, let alone focus on new markets."

Silent dialogue shot around the room from brother to brother as though he wasn't sitting right there.

When their dad died, Trey went from having one father to three, making it three times harder to live up to expectations. The constant feeling that he somehow managed to always come up short was becoming suffocating as hell.

"I'm tired of dealing with corporate suits," he explained. "There is no connection, no history there."

"All right," Nate said, surprising Trey. "What do *you* want to focus on?"

He thought about his day with Sara, how great it felt to talk over a glass of wine. How intimate the situation had been compared to the sale he'd just handled for Abby. It wasn't that he wanted to quit his job, he realized. He just wanted to redefine it.

"I want to focus on the individual customer again, the ones who buy and sell over a good meal and a better bottle of wine. And I'd like to do it in a place that values the things that Nonno Geno built this company on. With people who don't do business over the phone." He shot a look at Gabe.

"Then moving to Italy has nothing to do with the fact that ever since Mom and Dad died, you can't seem to keep your feet planted around home?" Gabe asked quietly and Trey felt that familiar knot, the one that took up residence in his chest a little over a decade ago, tighten to the point of pain. "Especially this time of year."

"No." Moving to Italy would allow him to feel connected to his family, without having to be reminded that he didn't deserve them.

"Why didn't you come to me before?" Gabe asked.

How to answer that?

"Between weddings and babies and everything else, there just wasn't a good time." And Trey had wanted to prove that he could handle it. As ridiculous as it was, he always felt like he was the tag-along. As though no matter how old he got, or how many deals he closed, he still had to prove that he was tough enough, man enough, worthy enough, to hang out at the big kids' table.

Gabe gave a weary nod. "Then let's talk about hiring a sales team to handle the domestic end."

Trey blinked. "Are you serious?"

"It's smart," Gabe said, but Trey couldn't help noticing that he sounded disappointed. "We've grown too fast for one person to handle. I'm just sorry that I've been too busy to notice. So if this is what you need, then I've got your back. Which means that you have until the end of the month to put a domestic team together. I want them local."

"The end of the month? As in four *more* weeks?" Trey choked. "Here?"

"Yup." Gabe grinned. "It will take you that long to put a stellar team together. Plus a few weeks with your family before you move to another continent won't kill you."

Maybe not, but the way his chest kept ratcheting tighter and tighter, it sure felt like it. But since Gabe was pretty much giving him everything he'd asked for, and more, including the belief that Trey would make the right decisions and, more important, the freedom to leave when it was over, Trey acquiesced. "Fair enough."

Then he stood to politely ask his brothers to get out, when the door burst open and there stood ChiChi, dressed in a fur-collared, fuchsia rain slicker, matching galoshes, and a strand of pearls. Her hair was stuck to her head, her hand clutching a rolled-up newspaper, and her temper was dialed to seek-and-destroy.

Trey glared at Marc. "What? Is there a vending machine in the lobby with everyone's room key in it?"

"Nope, just yours."

ChiChi slammed the door and narrowed her eyes. Right. In. On. Trey. "I just got off the phone with Sara from Tap and Barre School of Dance."

Well, at least Trey knew that Sara had the ability to use the phone. Now he had to figure out a way to get her to use it with him.

"She said that you haven't signed up for lessons yet," ChiChi chided, hand over her heaving chest. "Deidra Potter's got forty years of dance on you, young man, and she is out to take what's mine."

Trey stood, walked over, and kissed ChiChi on the cheek. "Nonna, Mrs. Potter is not—"

ChiChi smacked the day's issue of the *St. Helena Sentinel* right between the two handprints on his chest. "First she sells me tainted soil, killing my best pansies to up her chances of winning, and now she's out to ruin my Valentine's Day." She smacked him again. "Read."

Trey took the paper, unfolded it, and looked down at the headline and the six photos that followed, then read aloud, "Finalists for Winter Garden: Best in Show were announced Sunday by the St. Helena Garden Society. First finalist, Peg Stark, owner of Stark Corking, the largest plastic cork company in the valley—"

ChiChi flapped her regal hand impatiently. "Peggy got the green vote. Her granddaughter stuck her in a retirement home last Christmas. Her patio's only six-by-eight. She recycled all those malformed corks from that discounted cork-making machine her son bought off eBay, and fashioned them into planter boxes. Keep reading."

"Second finalist, Charlene Love—"

"Pity vote. For God's sake, get to the important part. Here."

ChiChi pointed her pudgy finger at the bottom of the page with so much force she nearly punched a hole right through it.

"Holding the county record as an eighteen-time finalist, and nine-time winner, Chiara Amalia Giovanna Ryo, co-owner of DeLuca Wines and Ryo Wines . . . Congratulations, Nonna." Trey looked up and went in for the hug but ChiChi fended him off with one arched brow and a pair of very pursed lips.

Trey sighed. ChiChi was nominated every year and every year she acted surprised, which meant that every year, Trey and his brothers were expected to act surprised. Only this year she looked pissed. Which could only mean one thing.

Skipping to the photo of Deidra Potter in feathers and some kind of weird flamingo, showgirl costume, Trey read the last line, ". . . will face off against the nineteen-time finalist, and eight-time winner, Deidra Potter, owner of Petal Pusher: Buds and Vines."

"If she wins, she'll tie me for the county record and her picture will go up next to mine in the Hall of Fame." Trey refrained from pointing out that the "Hall of Fame" was a stretch of wall between the men's room and a janitor's closet in town hall. "She'll put up that picture of her in those stripper clothes and shame us all. Make a mockery of the most treasured event in St. Helena history."

"I thought the unveiling of Randolph the Reindeer was the town's most treasured event," Gabe said, referring to St. Helena's version of lighting a Christmas tree in town square.

ChiChi ignored him and started fanning herself. "And she's not against playing dirty, even if she resorts to sabotage. By poison."

"You told me that the gophers ate your prized pansies," Nate reminded her as he stood and pulled her in for a hug. "Which is why I spent six weeks in the rain placing no-kill cages around the property and the next two finding a safe sanctuary for them to roam."

"That was before I remembered that Deidra sold me all that fertilizer. Plus, she's an agricultural professional. Professionals can't compete in an amateur contest! It's against the rules!"

"I've never seen that rule," Gabe said, bending down and kissing ChiChi on the head. ChiChi plucked Baby Sofie from her slingshot and sat down next to Marc, who leaned over and kissed both grannie and baby.

"Well, we're going to march right in to that Garden Society meeting and petition that it be added to the bylaws, aren't we, *amore*?" ChiChi cooed and Baby Sofie squealed. Babies were like little, drooling mood enhancers—only with legs.

"Not a smart move, Nonna," Marc said, taking Baby Sofie and standing her on his thighs. He steadied her while her pudgy little legs pushed up and down, like she was revving up to take off. "Since you'd only end up disqualifying yourself."

"Why?"

"You own a vineyard." When she feigned innocence, Marc added, "Several in fact. All around the world, which would make you an international agricultural professional."

ChiChi harrumphed. Then she reached for the newspaper and spread it open on her lap. Silently, she traced a shaky finger over the photo which accompanied her nomination and bio. Trey sat down next to her and—*holy hell*—his lungs stopped working.

The photo was of Nonno Geno gracefully dipping ChiChi under the twinkling arbor at the last Winter Garden Gala they attended together. ChiChi wore a sash declaring her Best in Show, and Geno was smiling down at her like she was his entire world. And in the background—Trey had to squint because the page went a little blurry—were his parents.

Happy.

In love.

And so alive.

ChiChi took his hand and when she spoke, her voice was so fragile it nearly broke his heart. "With your brothers getting married and giving me all these beautiful grandbabies, this is my last year to be the woman of the house, the only woman in all of your lives. Next year, Regan or Lexi or," she looked at Nate and grimaced. "Well, Regan and Lexi will have gardens of their own to enter in the contest, prized pansies that *their* husbands gave *them*. And I can't square off against my granddaughters and steal their chances of winning. It wouldn't be right."

ChiChi took out a cloth napkin and dabbed her eyes. Trey was already mentally picking out dance shoes. "Thanks to Deidra, I can't get those flowers back. I don't even know if I can win. But I'd like to dance, like in this picture, just once more. And you look and move so much like your grandfather, it melts my heart. Please give this old lady one last spin around the dance floor."

Trey pulled her close and breathed her in. She felt so small in his arms and smelled like his childhood. Even though coming home was painful, there was nothing in the world more important to him than his family.

He'd missed this same dance with his mother. If he stood up ChiChi, he didn't think he could forgive himself a second time, not that he'd ever forgiven himself the first time. And if this was to be her last Winter Garden Gala as a nominee, then he was going to give her the best damn waltz of her life.

CHAPTER 5

Wednesday night, Sara was still trying to wring the rain out of her hair when the bell on the studio's front door jingled. She looked into the dance mirrors and watched three of her favorite senior dancers enter. Decked out in their best USO costumes for the Tuesday night Swinging Singles Social, the self-titled Foxy Ladies—ChiChi, Lucinda, and Pricilla—made their way across the dance floor.

"Thanks for introducing me to Brooke," Sara said, kicking off her rain boots and grabbing her dance shoes before coming out from behind the counter. "When Heather called to say she'd miss class tonight, I didn't know what to do with Cooper."

Heather's audition had gone so well that the choreographer and director wanted her to meet the male lead, which meant one more night in San Francisco.

"My pleasure," Pricilla Moreau said as all three ladies sat down on the bench to swap out their shoes. "Brooke's a sweet girl. Reliable too. Works Saturdays at the bakery helping run the cash register and doing odd jobs."

"She's babysat Holly a time or two," ChiChi added.

"Stan said your car was still out of commission, so if you need anything," Lucinda Baudouin said, placing a pudgy white ball of fluff with whiskers and a black necktie on the bench next to her. The woman was all bony limbs and sharp edges. Mr. Puffins, the cat, was all fur and attitude. "A ride to work, groceries, dinner, doesn't matter the time, just call."

Her offer reminded Sara of a similar visit, last summer, when the same three ladies showed up on her doorstep, burnt almond cake and a bottle of homemade angelica in hand, for a welcome-to-the-neighborhood visit. Three hours later, a blubbering Sara was inducted into St. Helena's Widowed Warriors, Cooper had gained three surrogate grannies, and she'd somehow been swindled into adding Swinging Singles Socials to her schedule.

Part dance class, part speed dating, and open to everyone who was old enough to buy a glass of wine, it was the studio's most popular class, besides Pole Dancing.

"And I will have Trey stop by for a neighborly visit of his own to fix you right up," ChiChi added with a wink.

"He's quite handy," Pricilla said.

Sara could just imagine how handy Trey could be, especially with the female sector of town. One shake of that underwear-model posterior and anyone with a set of boobs would be lining up to test the equipment. The new adventurous side of her wanted to make that call. Then the intelligent, more realistic side piped up, reminding her that sexy stud muffins and widowed single mothers played in vastly different leagues.

"That's nice of you, but I don't need any fixing up." Three sets of silvered brows rose above the rims of their glasses. "Tonight, I am the instructor and you are the single ladies. Now, would someone like to explain why you're here," she glanced at her watch, "twenty minutes before class starts?"

"We're here on official business," Pricilla said, her round face flush with excitement. "And to solve your problem."

"Could you narrow down which problem you are referring to?"

"You need more students," Pricilla said. "Students who don't require a doctor's clearance before they can join your classes."

Did she ever.

Sara had walked away from a prestigious yet demanding position as a professor of dance and creative movement at the University of San Diego with dreams of opening a children's dance academy here, in a town that embodied the close-knit community she craved for her son. Teaching at a less-competitive level would give her more time with Cooper, and her son the kind of life he needed. One that didn't include day care and nannies. In theory, it had seemed like the smart choice.

Too bad theory didn't always translate well into reality. As it was now, Sara spent more evenings at the studio teaching senior classes and doing paperwork than at home reading bedtime stories.

"You have any ideas?" She had exhausted all of hers.

She knew growing her school would be a slow process, so she gave herself a year to make it happen. But when summer had turned to fall and fall to winter, and Tap and Barre School of Dance was still in serious lack of tot-size students, Sara had become nervous. If she didn't get some students who didn't require girdles and evening classes soon, she was looking at financial trouble on top of everything else.

"The Winter Garden Gala is in desperate need of spicing up," Pricilla said, leaning closer. Sara got a heavenly whiff of vanilla and tannins. The woman always smelled like cookies—and wine. "We want you to provide the opening entertainment."

"Are you serious?" Sara said. Butt firmly on the bench.

Providing the opening entertainment for the biggest social dance of the year was exactly the kind of exposure her studio needed. It would give her visibility, community approval, and something tangible for her to point to when mothers came in asking if she was qualified to prepare their toddlers for Julliard.

That it was hosted by the Garden Society, which was constructed of the PTA mafia and other ladder-climbing mommies of wine country, only made the opportunity that much more amazing. Once they learned that there was to be a performance at the most exclusive ball of the year, every aspiring ballerina and tot-size tapper within a three town radius would be twirling through her door, their mothers begging for classes.

"Before you go dreaming of sugar plum fairies, you need to sign here. Make it official." ChiChi handed over a thick contract and Sara felt her heart drop.

"What's this?"

"Finalizing your appointment as the official Gala Entertainment Chair," Pricilla said with a smile. "You should be proud. You beat out three other applicants."

Sara flipped through the very long, very binding contract. "I don't remember applying."

"Oh, we did that for you," Lucinda explained. "When Peggy threw out her hip and the committee found themselves short one coordinator, we immediately thought of you."

Peggy was the owner of the Paws and Claws Day Spa and therefore knew every old biddy and business owner in town. She was outgoing, a gossip, and perfect to plan such an event. Sara, on the other hand, was fairly new to St. Helena, kept to herself, and had never mastered the art of gossip.

"You run the event and your studio gets hired to provide the opening entertainment." Pricilla patted Sara's knee. "Just think about all of the exposure your studio will get."

All Sara could think about, as she read through the list of itemized responsibilities of things still left to be done, was all of the time it would take to coordinate an event like this. Opening ceremonies, hiring a band, finding an MC, mandatory Garden Society meetings—the list went on. Even with Heather helping out at home and in the studio, between her classes and Cooper's schedule, it would be exhausting—if not impossible.

"Is *anything* on this list checked off?" she asked.

All three ladies shook their heads.

"Peggy's a procrastinator, but she always comes through," Chi-Chi defended. "Always."

Apparently not this year, Sara thought.

"I can help with the opening entertainment, but run the whole night?" Sara shook her head. "I have no idea where to find an MC or a band and even if I did, there is no way I can do this without giving up more time with Cooper."

"I've been spending time with Archie," Lucinda explained. "He plays Old Blue Eyes for Rat Pack Redux, a cover band from the local Masonic Lodge. Let me tell you, that man sure knows how to fly me to the moon." The older woman sighed and when Sara choked, she added, "Don't give me that look. Just because you aren't getting any doesn't mean the rest of us aren't."

Now wasn't that wonderful? Even the senior section of town had a better love life than Sara.

"We'll act as your liaisons at the Garden Society meetings,"

Pricilla offered diplomatically. "Representing your ideas and helping execute the Gala's agenda in any way that you see fit."

"Uh-huh." Right now, they were being diplomatic, but the first time Sara's ideas clashed with theirs, she knew that there would be a battle. In the end, the only agenda that they would push would be the one that benefited their own ideas.

"Now hurry up and sign before Deidra shows up for class," ChiChi snapped.

"Mrs. Potter from Petal Pusher: Buds and Vines?" Sara asked. Deidra's flower shop was right next door to the studio, and even though it was obvious that ChiChi wasn't Deidra's favorite person, Sara couldn't imagine why they wouldn't want her to head up the entertainment. She'd be perfect.

"One in the same," Lucinda said. "Deidra didn't even wait for the plaster to dry on Peggy's cast before she was propositioning the Garden Society with a *new* idea for the entertainment."

"Entertainment?" ChiChi spat, as though anyone who believed that was dimwitted. "She's flying in her old stripper friends from Vegas."

"Deidra was a showgirl," Sara corrected, in a neutral tone. The last place she wanted to be was between a feud involving two of her students.

"They danced in unmentionables and feathers for money, sounds like a stripper to me," ChiChi argued, her hands shaking. "And if she gets elected, she won't just stop at the entertainment. She'll make the whole night about her."

"This event means a lot to a lot of people," Pricilla explained. "Especially ChiChi here. We want to make sure it stays true to the season. The Gala is a sweethearts' ball, designed to celebrate family and forever, and the amazing power of love and eternal commitment."

"That's why it's held on Valentine's Day," Lucinda added. "The sweetheart pinning is our town's oldest Valentine's Day tradition."

Just like that, Sara's heart started to ache.

For Sara, Valentine's Day wasn't only her anniversary, it was a painful reminder of how much she had lost when Garrett passed. Though she had worked hard over the past two years dealing with her grief—learning how to forgive Garrett for leaving her behind and trying to move on like he would have wanted her to—she wasn't exactly up for being forced to spend her wedding anniversary with half the town's sweethearts.

Then again, maybe being around people who were in love would remind her how wonderful it feels.

"If you decline the position, the Garden Society will have no choice but to appoint Deidra, and she'll make it so that she's the only one who gets to shine," Pricilla finished.

"There is someone special who is going to be there and I've been waiting a long time to catch his interest. I think he's finally pulled his head out of his backside, so I'm ready to make my move. This year I want to wear his flower," ChiChi whispered, and that's when Sara saw it. The older woman wasn't looking to snag herself a man, she was hoping to find love.

"Plus, there is a five thousand dollar stipend that comes with it." Lucinda always cut right to the important parts.

"Five thousand dollars?" Sara sat up straight, neutrality going out the window. With five grand she could afford to hire another dance teacher to take over some of the evening classes. It would give Sara more time with Cooper at home. Something they both desperately needed. "Who am I to get in the way of Cupid?"

"Wonderful," ChiChi said with a clap of her hands as Sara grabbed the application and signed her name to the bottom. The older woman folded the paper and slid it into her purse. "Now that that's taken care of, my grandson has agreed to escort me to the Gala. He needs to brush up on his dancing and I need to glide across that floor, so I told him to ask you about booking some private lessons."

Sara swallowed. She knew exactly which grandson ChiChi was referring to. "I told him that Heather can help him with that."

"The one who dresses like she puts out?" Lucinda asked stroking her cat.

"She does not dress like she puts out," Sara defended. Heather couldn't help it that she had a knock-out figure and oozed sex appeal, two of the main reasons her studio had such a large senior male clientele.

"Tell that to the men who come to tango with her. She takes all the good ones. Or at least the ones with working limbs and real teeth."

"I'm sure that's not true," Sara chided.

"She's right, dear," Pricilla said apologetically. "When you're here, we only get half the turnout for Swinger's Night. The female half."

Lucinda leaned in and whispered, "Maybe if *you* started dressing like you put out, you'd have higher numbers." Then she stood and walked toward the mirror to practice her swivel hips. Mr. Puffins sat regally on the bench and watched.

Sara wanted to laugh at Lucinda. Taking fashion advice from a woman who wore a pinstriped zoot suit with red wing tips was ridiculous. But as she looked at herself in the mirror, all her humor faded.

She was wearing strappy dance shoes, a yellow-and-white polka-dotted knee-length skirt, which had the perfect flare radius when she spun, and a fitted, cream long-sleeved top. Her hair was secured back in a ponytail with a yellow flower and she looked polished, professional, and perfectly boring.

Then again, she was the instructor and speed-dating mediator, not one of the singles who'd come to mingle and dance with the hopes of finding Mr. Right—or even a Mr. Tonight.

With a sigh, Sara grabbed a glass fishbowl and a stack of dance cards off the counter and walked over to place them on the table by the dance floor. She folded the cards in half and, dropping them in the bowl, mumbled, "What's wrong with the way I dress?"

"From where I'm standing, not a damn thing," Trey said striding in the front door.

His eyes locked on her and even from across the room, she could feel the heat arch between them. The way he took his time, sizing her up as though liking what he saw had something deep within her belly tightening. What really got to her was the easy smile he sent her way as he walked toward her. That tired and scruffy guy from yesterday had vanished, and in his place was the relaxed and charming Trey she'd spent a wonderful afternoon—tasting.

Oh my God, did her face just flush?

"Although I'm partial to the ballerina look, this fifties housewife thing you've got going on is sexy." He brushed the flower in her hair with his knuckles and they came away damp with rain. "To think, just a minute earlier, and I might have gotten to help you out of your slicker."

"ChiChi said that you wanted to talk to me about privates, but—"

He held up a hand. "I know, you only do privates for special customers. So how about you and me go play hooky again so I can work my way up to the special package?"

She looked around the studio, and thought of a night spent playing geriatric matchmaker to the senior sector, referee to Deidra and ChiChi, and making sure Harvey's hand stayed north of the equator. She looked back to Trey and what he was offering. An escape.

Then again, he was the number-one escape plan for women everywhere. She was a single mom who married her college sweetheart and lacked the necessary experience to tango with a guy like Trey. It was obvious he liked them tall, curvy, and blonde—everything she was not.

"I can't," she said, proud of how confident she came off. She didn't falter, didn't elaborate, didn't explain. Cut and dry. Then to her horror she added, "But maybe Tammy or Kayla is free."

Trey shot her an amused smile, one that showed all of his teeth and released a lethal dimple. "I don't want Tammy or Kayla. I want to get lost with you."

His tone was light and easy, his swagger dialed to smooth, and even though it was obviously a line, it didn't feel like one. Not this time. Which was ridiculous since the man was so practiced and polished he had no doubt broken many a girl's heart. More proof in the ever growing pile of evidence supporting why "he" was a bad idea.

So she channeled her best teacher tone and said, "I have a class to teach."

He shrugged, as though he could work with that. "All right, when is it?"

"You want to take a class. With me? Tonight? "

"Sweetheart, if you're teaching, I'm interested." There went the other dimple. "Plus, ChiChi's been after me to get some lessons from you."

"Lesson one." She held out the fishbowl trying to bite back a smile, and failed miserably. "Pick a blue card and when a lady calls your number, you're up."

Trey knew once he saw the fishbowl that tonight was not going to go as he'd imagined—which started with Sara dancing in his arms and ended with her naked in his bed. Nope, not only was the naked bed-hustle not looking good, but the class, which focused on swing—the only style he'd never taken—was almost over, and he hadn't managed to snag even a single dance with Sara.

Instead she was dancing with Roman "local hero and all around badass" Brady, whose body was swaying a little too close for a simple student-teacher relationship, and the smug-ass grin on his face said he knew it. Just like Trey knew by the way Roman moved, that this was not his first time swinging with Sara.

To make matters worse, Trey was stuck holding Mrs. Potter, the woman who, prior to killing his nonna's prized flowers, used to dress up as Mother Goose and lead story time at the elementary school. Tonight she was dressed in a sailor's hat and some weird Navy-inspired dress that displayed enough folds of cleavage that he was afraid with one misstep, he'd fall in.

The only thing that remained of the grandmotherly lady he remembered as a kid was the goose part, which happened every time he wasn't looking—meaning every nine seconds since he was trying to listen in on Brady sweet-talking Sara.

"And I don't like long walks or the beach, not anymore." Mrs. Potter stopped to lift up her skirt—exposing fishnets and a garter that should be illegal on women past menopause—and tapped her knee. "Titanium."

Trey didn't hear anything else because Sara was twirling closer. And laughing at something Roman said. Roman leaned in and so did Trey, but Mrs. Potter was going on about her stamina and all Trey could catch was, "Just the night and a million stars."

"That sounds amazing," Sara responded with a laugh—which, if you asked Trey, sounded forced. When he made her laugh, it was rich and husky.

Then she said something that sounded an awful lot like,

"Would hate to miss it," followed by, "I have to check my schedule," when Trey twirled Mrs. Potter—right into Roman.

"Sorry, man," Trey murmured and Sara looked up at him. He took the moment of direct eye contact to silently plead with her to change the song and call time—so they could have their dance.

She sent him a sweet smile and pointed to his feet in return.

"Triple step, triple step, *rock* step, Trey," she clarified. And yeah, yeah, he got it. Only every time he rock stepped, Mrs. Potter came in faster than expected and pressed herself against him.

"Mrs. Potter was just showing me her new knee," Trey deadpanned.

"The titanium one?" Sara asked, fixing Roman's hand grip as though this was a normal conversation. "How's it working out?"

"Much lighter than the steel one." Mrs. Potter leaned in, as close as she could get, and whispered, "And we're both adults now, Trey. You can call me Deidra." There went her hand. One more pinch and Trey wouldn't be able to sit for a week.

Mercifully, the song switched and Sara clapped her hands.

"All right, time to switch partners. Since this is the last dance of the night, it's open call and ladies' choice." She pulled out a flashcard, her eyes darting over the page before she looked up. "Pick your partner and share your favorite color, favorite hobby, and what your dream date would be."

"Thanks for the dance," Trey said, taking a step back, desperate to get some air that didn't smell like a perfume bottle, when Deidra pulled a card from the little purse that hung across her body and slipped it in the waistline of his pants—right next to the five dollar bill Mrs. Moberly had stuck there earlier.

"It's a coupon for a free floral consultation. But for you, I'll just say a free consultation of your choosing."

Lovely. "I think Roman is waiting for you."

Deidra wiggled her fingers and with a wink sashayed away, her hips working that knee overtime. A group of ladies stood in the wings ready to grab him, so when Sara went to walk off, he snagged her by the hand and drew her in close.

"I've been waiting all night to dance with you," he said, loving how she smelled. Fresh and bright, and like—he dropped his hands to her hips and pulled her in a little closer—the beach?

"You're just scared of Mrs. Moberly."

"She's the librarian. Has been since before I was born. She used to check Disney books out to me, now she's checking out my butt." Something that he wouldn't mind doing to his new dance partner, so he gripped her hips lower.

"This is the swing, which means that we hold both hands when we dance," she corrected, but he noticed that she didn't pull back.

Taking that as a green light, he slid his fingers around her back, stepped into her and, damn, she felt good. Warm and soft beneath his fingers. She must have liked it too, because after a moment, she rested her palms on his chest and leaned into him. She hadn't done that with Mr. I Carry a Hose.

"After that last dance, I think my swinging days are over. No more wild fishbowl parties for this guy."

"I would have thought that this was right up your alley," she said innocently. The effect was ruined by the humor sparkling up at him in her eyes.

He gave her a wry expression that made her laugh, but she didn't look away.

He liked that about her, the way she always held his gaze. He also liked the way her mouth turned up at the corners and parted slightly when he brushed up against her. So he did it again and, *oh yeah*, that got to her.

A flush tinted her cheeks, working its way down her elegant neck and right under the deep V of her shirt, which of course drew his full attention because . . . how could it not? The woman was beautiful.

"Groping aside, I think it was wonderful the way you charmed them. You made their night, Trey." Her fingers absently played with the fabric of his shirt. "Did you at least have fun?"

"Yeah," he admitted. The strange thing was, he had.

He'd come here tonight because it sounded a whole hell of a lot better than ordering room service and working in his suite until sunrise. Yet being here with Sara, even when he'd been propositioned by his grandmother's friends, had somehow been the most fun he'd had since—he looked at her lush mouth—their wine tasting excursion last week. Even though he would have liked more time with her in his arms and to throw Roman out on his ass for touching her. But just seeing her had made the stress from the day disappear.

"I'm glad." She pressed her lips together as though to stop herself from grinning. "A few of the ladies wanted to know if you're coming to the ballroom medley class on Saturday."

He should say, *nope, sorry, won't be around.* He never hung around longer than one night. Ever. And Sara was clearly not a one-night-stand kind of girl. A spontaneous kiss and some harmless flirting, sure. But a casual fling?—not the type. Not to mention, his sisters-in-law would kill him if he hooked up with Sara with less-than-honorable intentions.

Then why did he find himself asking, "Are you teaching it?" and when confirmed that, yes indeed, she would be here Saturday night in some other fantasy-inducing outfit, adding, "Then count me in."

Which was stupid enough in itself. Especially since they weren't dancing or even swaying. They were just staring at each other in the middle of a crowded dance floor. Only, he couldn't stop there. No, he had to persist. "Okay, no more stalling, favorite color, favorite hobby, dream date."

He made sure to put extra emphasis on the last one, hoping to hell she didn't say anything about a night under the stars.

"Color, red. Hobby, hmm. Let me think." She paused and bit her lush lower lip, as though thinking long and hard about the next question. Of whose answer he didn't hear, because he was too busy staring at her work that mouth of hers with her teeth, which only made him want to work that mouth of hers with his tongue.

"And for the date, I don't know." Her shoulders rose on a deep breath, but when she exhaled it sounded more like a huff than a sigh. "I never really thought about the questions when I wrote them, but they're hard to answer."

"Yellow-and-white polka dots, playing hooky, and anywhere with you," he rattled off then smiled. "Nope. Easy. Your turn. Dream date. And be specific."

"I haven't had a lot of time to date, let alone think about what a dream one would be. But an empty tasting room with a charming," she looked up at him, "wine sounds pretty dream-worthy."

Before he could have her elaborate, or ask if she was interested in a replay—like now—the music stopped. She stepped back, signaling that the dance was up and so was his time.

"How about that private?" he asked. "Tomorrow night?"

"I'll think about it," she said and, *oh yeah*, he was in. The smile on her pretty face told him as much.

CHAPTER 6

With Italian families, there's a fine line between being brotherly and being blackmailed. Trey was being blackmailed. Plain and simple. The embarrassing part was that his blackmailer was a five-foot-nothing of a sister-in-law and her baby bump.

"Those are your choices, Trey," Regan said for the third time, as though *he* were the one not listening. "Either take me to Lamaze orientation or pick up Holly and drive her to dance."

Pregnancy made women crazy. Period. That was the only explanation he could come up with. Three minutes ago, Regan had plopped down next to him at the pub in Marc's hotel, a carton of rocky road in hand, Baby Sofie strapped to her front, *asking* him for a favor. Only when he'd regretfully passed, she got hostile. Then she ate all of his fries.

"Shouldn't Gabe be going with you to um . . . Lamaze?"

"He's in Italy with Abby," Regan said, placing the palm of her free hand on her lower back and exhaling.

Abby had negotiated the terms of the deal, everyone was in agreement, then they'd hit a snafu. So she called in the big gun— aka Gabe.

"Maybe Lexi could take you," Trey said in a soothing voice he'd heard Gabe use. He even set his burger down to show Regan she had his full attention.

"Lexi offered to watch Sofie while I'm at Lamaze. With you. Unless . . ." Regan looked down at the drool monster, who was babbling at a level that would scare off rabid dogs, "you want to switch and be on diaper duty and handle breast milk?"

Trey pushed back his plate. He was done. Lunch ruined. Day ruined. His innocence ruined. "What about Frankie?"

"In a class with babies? Are you kidding me? They'd kick me out and never invite me back."

Trey saw her point. Frankie was worse with kids than he was. Last time she was left alone with his niece, Holly ended up with a new haircut. "I've been on the waitlist for this class since we discovered I was pregnant. With Sofie."

"Plus, Frankie can't," Lexi said, flopping down next to Regan, her eyes narrowing in on Trey's plate. Whereas Regan looked like she was carrying half-a-basketball under her billowy blouse, Lexi appeared to be concealing an entire NBA team in her belly—a team that obviously needed feeding because she wouldn't take her eyes off his burger. Or her feet off the chair next to him. "She's taking everyone to the airport."

"Everyone?" Trey shoved his plate toward his sister-in-law. "What the hell do you mean 'everyone'?"

"She and Nate picked up Marc about an hour ago." Lexi snatched his burger, poked it, sniffed it, and then put it back. Her face went a little green and she started wafting her hands. "Oh, God, can you move . . . that?"

Why not? It wasn't like he was going to eat it now.

"Dooz-dooz-doozzzzzzz," Baby Sofie sputtered, her legs flapping and a whole lot of pissed-off female in her voice. Regan handed the ice-cream carton to Lexi, shoved her way to standing, and started pacing.

"Marc went too?" Trey asked, that familiar pang of disappointment pushing at his chest.

He wasn't surprised that Gabe had left him behind. Could even understand the need for it since he controlled the family purse strings. Nate, the family grape god also made sense. But Marc?

"Why the fu—" Regan covered Baby Sofie's ears and raised a condemning brow that damn near singed his soul, "—udge did Marc get to go?"

And why the—again with the fudge—hadn't anyone bothered to invite him? Or even asked him if he minded being left out and, subsequently, left behind?

"There is already another interested party, and if we want the land, we have to move quick," Lexi said and Trey wondered when the *fuck!* "we" started including everyone but him. "And since Marc is heading up the facilities part of the deal, him going made complete sense."

As opposed to Trey going, because why the hell would they need to consult the sales end of the business before engaging in a new venture whose success depended on *sales*? The other day he felt as though he'd made ground with his brothers. That they were all on the same page. That he was finally back in the loop. Apparently not.

Different project, different day—same old bullshit.

"I was given strict instructions that until they return, you were the DeLuca to go to if I needed anything," Regan said, her pacing having no impact on the kid's vocal exercises.

"Let me guess, Lamaze falls under the umbrella of anything."

"So does diaper changing and midnight feedings," Regan clarified, while gently swaying Baby Sofie, whose eyes started to flutter closed—thank God. "So I suggest you keep your phone on."

He thought staring down his oldest brother with that mean-ass scowl was bad, but his pint-size wife with her little belly was by far the scariest DeLuca he'd ever faced.

Trey looked at the overflowing inbox on his laptop, the seven conference calls and two interviews he had scheduled, and not a single e-mail from his family telling him they were headed to Italy. He felt like he was being strangled—slowly. "And Lamaze class is . . . ?"

"A bunch of hormonal women looking at birthing videos, breathing heavily, and complaining about swollen feet and lady parts. It's very inspiring," Regan deadpanned and Trey actually felt the walls closing in. "I mainly threw that one out there to make Holly's audition sound like an easy break."

"Right." He found himself breathing deep. "And Holly's class is where?"

"It's from three to four at the Tap and Barre School of Dance. At the end of Main Street, right next to Petal Pushers." And suddenly being the go-to guy didn't sound so bad.

Holly's class would give him a reason to see Sara again, to move that "I'll think about it" to a solid "Name the time and place." Playing the doting uncle in the process couldn't hurt. Plus, chauffeuring didn't include diapers, breast milk, or talk of lady parts.

"Is one of Auntie Lexi's babies yours?" Holly asked, looking up at him with her big brown eyes.

"What? No!" Trey nearly rammed the car in front of him, which earned him all kinds of honks and a stern headshake from the crossing guard.

The parking lot of St. Vincent's Academy looked like the starting line at a Formula 1 race. An endless queue of SUVs and minivans, each idling impatiently, each boasting luxury European emblems, and each displaying a placard with their child's name in the front window, wrapped around the school and down past the corner.

"Who told you that?"

"No one. Me and Chloe, she's the B to me and Lauren's FF, figured it out because Nonna said Auntie Lexi is big enough to birth a litter of DeLucas."

Holly snapped her seat belt, adjusted the chair, and went on as though Trey's life wasn't getting shittier by the second.

"Today was library day, and it went beginning letters first, and since I'm a D, DeLuca," she clarified and waited until he nodded in understanding before continuing, "I got to pick out my book almost first and we found one on baby kitties. Chapter one was titled 'The Retroactive Cycle of Cats' and it was about—"

"Yup, got it." Trey didn't bother to correct her, just like he didn't complain that when everyone else formed groups of "we," his life managed to spiral out of control.

"It said that a litter of kitties can have more than one daddy. So, we thought that maybe Auntie Lexi was going to have all of my uncle's babies."

Three blocks. That's all he had to do was get three blocks without female talk and he'd failed. The second his niece had scrambled in the car, tossed her backpack in the backseat, and started talking about the mating habits of domesticated animals—apparently her class science project—he knew he should have distracted her with candy. Only he didn't have candy.

Gabe would have had candy. He also would have known what to say.

"Want a breath mint?" Trey offered, reaching into his glove box.

"No, thanks. They can cause cavities," Holly said primly. "So if none of Auntie's babies are yours, then when are you going to have one?"

"Lexi is only birthing, um, having one baby. And it is Marc's," he clarified, and realized he sounded desperate and a bit shrill. Then he thought of what Gabe would say and added, "She's having Marc's baby because they are married and in love. And since I'm not married or in love, I won't be having a baby."

Ever.

Trey popped a mint in his mouth, cavities being the least of his worries, and once he exited the school parking lot, jammed the gas pedal to the floor. If he got to the studio fast enough, she wouldn't have time for follow-up questions.

"My mom wasn't married when she had me."

Right. Shit. Regan was a single mom for the first six years of Holly's life. In fact, Holly's birth dad, son of a bitch that he was, hadn't bothered to visit Holly since she was a baby.

"So, if you want your baby to grow up with mommies and aunties, then you better get on it."

Trey ran a hand down his face. God he was screwed. He was not only getting unsolicited advice from his brothers and sisters-in-law, now he was getting it from his niece.

"I have the book in my backpack if you want to look at it later," she offered, and Trey made himself two promises. One, to be anywhere but at Regan's house when later came, and, two, breast milk or not, next time he'd take the snot-monster.

At least she couldn't talk.

Sara hadn't panicked when she had, in a state of pure exhaustion, accidently sent out fliers advertising the wrong day for the Snowflake Princess auditions.

Not at first.

Not when Isabel Stark, PTA president who had dance-mom extraordinaire botoxed across her forehead, cornered Sara in the school parking lot with her daughter's headshot. Not even when Heather called to say she would try to be home by lunch—only it was way past lunch and she was still a no-show.

But as Sara raced back in the studio after school let out, a sullen Cooper in hand, and scanned the dance floor, the reality of just how crappy her day was going to get set in. The floor was already filled with her Tiny-Tappers class geared up and ready to go, and what could only be described as a herd of mini-dancers with stage moms in tow.

"But today is design day and Hive Commander Roman was going to help me finish sanding out my car, give it more muscle and less curves." Cooper frowned. "Plus anyone who doesn't have a finished car at Mighty Mites tomorrow won't get their wheels. It's the rule."

"I know, honey." Sara dropped to a knee, running a hand over his hair. "And I'm sorry, but Heather isn't home yet and I didn't want to risk being late for pickup."

"But with no wheels, I can't race," he whispered.

And with no car, Sara was running on empty.

"We'll get you wheels," Sara promised, having no idea where she was supposed to buy tiny wheels, only that she would make it happen. Somehow. Right after she figured out what to do with the three-dozen dancers who were already lined up for an audition that wasn't supposed to happen until next week. "And right after class, we will finish the sanding. I promise."

"Will it still look like Cinderella's carriage?" He was obviously repeating what some jerk had said to him about his car.

Sara had spent most of the past two nights helping Cooper on his car. No matter how hard she tried, it came out looking more VW Bug than NASCAR. But bugs were cool—right?

Cooper was a Mighty Mite, not a Mighty Mobile.

"I thought it looked like a big, bad bug." Sara gave Cooper her best bad-bug face, complete with fangs and claws and, what Sara thought, a pretty terrifying snarl.

Cooper just gave her a get-real look then toed at the floor, the wet rubber of his shoes squeaking against the hardwood. "Hunter Lock said his dad's been working on their car all week, and he still isn't finished, and he's done it like a million times."

Sara wanted to point out that it was Hunter's car, therefore it should be Hunter's handiwork, but she kept her mouth shut.

"He also said you'd probably paint it pink." His last words came out on a horrified little sob. Suddenly Sara had a pretty good idea why her son had been so quiet the past few days. "He says girls like pink and since I only hang out with girls, it'll be pink, and I should race it with the Lady Bugs. Then one of the dads said I should go with a more manly color."

Sara wasn't a vicious person, but she was ready to tell Hunter and that dad to butt the hell out. And then ask for a clarification on the hues of *manly*, since last time she checked that wasn't a color on any chart. It also wasn't a word Cooper had used before. Unfortunately, the truth hit home and the truth was that, between her and Heather and the studio, her son was almost always surrounded by women.

"A pink car would suck," Cooper mumbled. "I don't want it to suck. And I don't want it to look like a bug. I want it to be manly."

Sara's heart turned over. She knew that, although Garrett died before Cooper was old enough to actually miss having a dad around, he was smart enough to know what he was missing out on. Smart enough to understand what having a man in his life could mean. Days like today, Sara did too.

"I promise that tomorrow when you show up to Mighty Mites, you will have the best car in town," Sara said, turning around to see if her pants were on fire for that big lie. "No pink. No carriage. We'll make you a new one. Deal?"

He nodded and she ruffled his hair, sending drops of rain dotting the floor.

"Okay, now, go hang up your raincoat and grab a snack out of the back room. When you're done, you can help me sign in the new kids."

"Like be your assistant?" He didn't sound as thrilled as Sara had hoped. Then she looked around and realized that her son was surrounded by pink, pink, and more pink, with tiaras as far as the eye could see. No wonder he thought today was going to suck.

"You can hold the clipboard." Which was not pink. It was blue and gold—Chargers's colors.

His eyes went wide. "How about the permanent marker?"

"If you think you can handle it." Sara went for nonchalant, although there wasn't a nonchalant bone in her body. Cooper and permanent markers were a bad combination. If Sara needed a reminder of just how bad, all she had to do was look at the neighbor's cat, Avalanche, who was still wearing a blue Chargers's lightning bolt down his side.

"Awesome." Then he was gone, his blinking sneakers disappearing around the corner.

Sara was unbuttoning her raincoat when three more tutus and tiaras squeezed in the waiting room. She was cold, wet, and in desperate need of a nap, which was why, when her phone rang and she saw Heather's face flash on the screen, she nearly wept.

"Thank God, are you okay?"

"Sara," Heather's voice exploded through the phone. "You're never going to guess where I am."

"I hope the parking lot out back since the Snowflake Princess auditions start in ten minutes."

There was a long pause on the other end of the phone. "I thought they were next week, after the middle graders?"

"They were. But the fliers that went out to the schools said today, so please tell me you are walking through that door in two seconds."

"Um," was all she said, but it was enough to send Sara's stomach into a pirouette.

"Heather," Sara whispered, shifting so that she was facing the wall. "I really need you to be here today."

"I am so sorry, but there's no way I can make it. I'm actually on my way to New York. Can you believe it?" At the rate that her life was spiraling, Sara could. "They offered me the lead. As in permanent. On the condition that the chemistry between me and the male lead, who is totally hot by the way, is there."

"And is it?" Sara asked, forcing a little smile in her voice because Heather was okay. She was safe and excited and this was a huge moment.

"Scorching. As in call the fire department. And I know that this puts you in a bad spot, but I'll be back tomorrow night. They are literally flying me out to meet the rest of the cast and then back home."

"Okay." She could make it until tomorrow. It would be tough

and exhausting and she'd have to master the pinewood derby car in under twelve hours, but she could handle it.

"But Sara," Heather said and Sara pressed the phone harder to her ear. She tried to ignore the awful feeling in her chest, the one telling her that everything was about to change—again. "If I take the role, they'd need me back in New York on Monday. And it's a two-year contract."

That was when Sara panicked. It wasn't the quiet, dignified kind of panic that she used to be able to pull off. It was a full-blown, chest-closing-in, tunnel-visioned kind of reaction that had her sitting down—on the floor.

"Breathe, Sara," Heather said, her voice laced with concern. "I told them I had to think about it and talk to you. Monday is so soon and two years is a long time to be away. From you. And from Cooper."

Sara forced herself to calm down. She didn't want to ruin this for Heather. "What do you mean you told them, *you had to think about it*? You are taking this job, even if I put you on that plane myself."

"But you and Cooper—"

"Will come visit. This is an incredible opportunity," she forced out. Because really it was.

Heather couldn't stay in St. Helena forever. She was too talented to teach dance her entire life and deserved the amazing life that every dancer dreamed of.

"I called Madison. She had a huge falling out with her studio and already gave notice. She'll be free after March first and sounded excited about living in wine country," Heather said. "She actually wants to head up the ballroom program. Which is perfect if you ask me, since you hate teaching ballroom."

"I don't hate teaching ballroom." It just wasn't her specialty. Sara was a classically trained ballerina with several years of contemporary and jazz under her belt. Plus, ballroom classes were always at night when she wanted to be home with Cooper. "Even though she would be the perfect answer, I can't afford Madison."

Madison was a two-time grand-champion ballroom dancer who was beyond talented and great with kids and seniors alike. Only she'd cost a small fortune to hire.

"You can when you get that five thousand from the Garden Society," Heather reminded her. "And with all of the new kids the studio will get from the Gala exposure, you'll be able to focus on day classes, and Madison can handle all of the ballroom so you can be with Cooper. This is a great opportunity for you and the studio."

"It is, and you're right."

Hiring Madison would give Sara the freedom to be the kind of mom she'd moved to St. Helena to become and allow for the kind of life she wanted her son to grow up having.

The only thing she had to do was manage until March. Balancing her class load and Cooper would be hard enough, now that she had the Winter Garden Gala to add to her pile—and she couldn't mess that up.

Then there was Trey. Whatever, if anything, that even meant.

"Thanks for calling Madison. I wouldn't have thought of that, and," Sara swallowed, "about the role, I'm really proud of you, Heather. Garrett would have been too."

"Yeah," Heather whispered. "It's why I took the meeting, because I could hear him in my head lecturing me about going after my dreams, living life—"

"Balls out," they both said and started laughing.

"God, I miss him," Sara half choked, half laughed.

"Me too," Heather said, then fell quiet.

It stretched on for so long that Sara could feel it pressing down on her, but no matter how hard she tried, she couldn't think of what to say. It was Heather who broke the silence, but when she did, Sara wished they could go back to the quiet.

"I heard that Trey came to Swinging Singles last night and that you two had another moment. And you booked him for a private."

"How did you hear that?"

"Small town, remember? Please, tell me you're not going to 'think' yourself out of a great opportunity."

Too late.

She had thought about it. Almost the entirety of last night was spent weighing the consequences of saying yes. Like, they probably would do a whole lot more than dance. And that scared her. Trey scared her. Which was why she hadn't returned any of his calls.

He was sexy and gorgeous and so damn charming he brought up feelings that she hadn't dealt with since Garrett's death. He was also a notorious playboy.

"Before you tell me all of the reasons you should say no, picture his ass." Heather paused and Sara laughed. "Still not convinced? Then four words. Lipstick. On. The. Face. And you were glowing, Sara. Glowing. I haven't seen you look that happy since before Garrett died."

"I know, that's what scares me," she admitted.

"Why? Because you're attracted to a guy who makes you feel good?" Heather asked and Sara wanted to cry. "You're young and a total catch, and it kills me to think that while I'm in New York, you'll be in that big house, lonely and thinking about what could have been instead of what might be."

"I'm not lonely." Even as she said the words, Sara knew they were a lie. She went to bed early because it was easier than facing an empty house, and ate lunch at the studio since a table for one in a crowded restaurant was depressing. Sara had mastered being alone in a crowd of people.

Only she hadn't felt alone with Trey. She'd felt alive.

Problem was—she wasn't sure what Trey was looking for. Okay, she knew *what* he was looking for, she just didn't think it included working around the complications of a single mom. Or the timeline of a vulnerable woman who was easing her way into the shallow end of the dating pool.

Heather's voice softened. "You deserve to be happy, Sara. Really happy. I'm talking about the part of you that being a mom doesn't fulfill. Garrett would have wanted that for you. I want that for you."

Sara's hand went to her ring finger. It was still such a shock to find it naked. But the debilitating ache that usually followed hadn't appeared for months. It had disappeared around the same time that Sara realized love didn't have to hurt. That she could still love her husband, honor what they had shared, and find happiness.

"Trey's a gypsy," Sara said softly. She toed off her sneakers and pulled her ballet slippers out from under the desk. "From what I understand, he doesn't even have a place in town. He lives at his brother's hotel when he visits, which isn't often."

"So he's not good with permanent. That doesn't have to be a bad thing. Maybe he'll be around long enough this visit for you to get your feet wet. Then poof, he's gone and you've had your first fling."

"Or my next heartbreak." Wow, had she just said that?

"Not everything has to be considered in terms of forever."

She laced up her shoes and stood. Heather was right.

For a girl who knew exactly what she wanted from the time she could walk, there hadn't been room in Sara's life for anything that didn't have the potential of forever. There also hadn't been room for a whole lot of fun. Something she needed right now.

Sara thought about how she felt those few times she'd seen Trey, and found herself wondering if she could go through with it. If she could get past the fear and forever-itis and just go for it.

She looked at her watch. "I gotta go start class, but congrats again, and thanks for being the best sister-in-law."

"Right back at ya. Make sure to tell Cooper that I love him and I'll be there for the race this weekend. And, Sara, I love you, so promise me that you'll go for it."

"Love you too." Sara hung up and focused her attention on finding a sign-up sheet. If she couldn't solve the chaos in her personal life, at least she could get a handle on her studio.

"Is it just me, or are you always wet when I'm around?" a man asked, and Sara froze as his voice, low and smooth, sent little tingles of awareness shooting through her entire body.

"Oh my God," she breathed. *Man indeed.*

"I take that as a yes."

She let out a deep breath, braced herself for impact, and looked up. And good Lord, Trey got better looking every time she saw him. Not only was he giving off enough testosterone to cancel out all of the estrogen in the room, he could fill out a suit like nobody's business. A dark-gray suit that made his deep-brown eyes seem even more intense, if that were possible.

"Trey," she said, noticing that he too was wet. As in his hair was spiky with rain and his lips looked moist and delicious.

"I figured that since the line to your studio is down the street, and it's like a tutu convention in the waiting room, that you can't get lost right now." Setting two to-go cups on the counter, he flashed his perfect white teeth her way, which, with the whole suit-and-wet-hair thing, did crazy things to her heart. "So I thought I'd bring the lost to you."

"Yeah, it's kind of crazy."

She looked around the studio, and crazy didn't even begin to describe the situation. There wasn't a spare inch of space on the benches, and even the standing-room-only area was packed.

"I can see that." Although his eyes were too busy staring at her mouth to even notice the chaos behind him. "Is it always like this?"

She swallowed—hard. It had never been like this. Ever. Even with Garrett it had been a steady build. But with Trey, she felt like she was one wink away from going up in flames.

"No, um, the Snowflake Princess auditions are today. Only, today is Thursday, and I have a Tiny-Tappers class starting. Which is why I scheduled the auditions for next week. But I made a typo, and my assistant, as of five minutes ago, is moving to New York, so that means I have to teach a pole-dancing class that is in the middle of the only open private slot—"

She stopped because he was smiling. At her.

"That's why you're here, right? About the private?"

"Actually," he reached out and touched her hand, "I'm more interested in the private pole-dancing lesson."

So was she, which was the only excuse she had for not moving her hand. She was too busy noticing that his were huge and rugged and really warm. Suddenly her entire body was warm and all she could think about were his hands—on her. And just going for it.

He cleared his throat and she snatched her hand back.

"Your private would be for ballroom. The pole-dancing class is reserved for AARP cardholders only. So unless you want to watch saggy—"

He held a hand up. "I'll take ballroom with a beautiful lady, thank you." Then the easygoing playboy faded, leaving behind something more real. He slid a cup across the counter, the heavenly aroma of cinnamon and pumpkin filling the air.

Her stomach growled and her fingers actually twitched in anticipation. "What's that?"

"Coffee," he said with a smile. "Pumpkin-spice latte from the Sweet and Savory. I have it on good authority they are the best in town. Plus I get a family discount."

"Thank you." She took a sip and felt her face flush. Partly from the hot coffee, but mostly because he'd listened and the gesture was incredibly thoughtful.

"Now that we got the coffee portion of the relationship over with, let's talk about that dream date? I'm leaning toward one that starts with a twirl around the dance floor and ends with you in my arms."

She thought about what Heather had said, and considered just going for it. Then she saw Cooper over by the mirrors with his "carriage," as the girls were calling it. The growing crowd of pink pushed forward, and she felt every bit the single mom. "Can I see how tonight goes and let you know later?"

"Later, as in you'll call me?" Trey *tsked* as he leaned forward, leisurely resting his elbows on the counter, a tsunami of sexy-male swagger detonating with a single curve of his lips. "We tried that with the car and the coat, and I hate to say this, but I don't think telecommunications are your strong suit."

"How is the coat?"

"Ruined."

"I'm sorry."

"I'm not," he admitted. "It meant that I got to see you again. And if it takes *me* on a *pole* so that I can have my dance, then I guess I'd better get used to myself in a thong."

Sara laughed. Was it really that easy? Just say yes and everything would feel like it did right then. Light, fun . . . alive?

"A pink thong?"

"Hell, no." The second man in her life today to gag at the idea of pink. "I'd go for something more manly, black silk."

He flashed his killer smile, but Sara had a hard time smiling back. "More manly?"

He didn't answer; instead he reached across the counter and tucked a strand of her hair behind her ear. "I'm only asking for one dance, Sara. Tell me how I can make that happen."

The easy answer would be no. He'd leave, Sara could start her auditions, spend the night whittling a car out of wood, and go to bed early because the idea of one more night alone in that big house was more than she could handle.

Or, she thought, as she picked up his big, *manly*, made-for-sanding hands, she could live a little.

"How good are you with these?"

CHAPTER 7

Usually when a woman asked Trey if he was good with his hands, spending the night sanding and scraping a piece of wood wasn't what she had in mind. Yet here he was, at happy hour, sitting cross-legged on the cold floor in the back room of a dance studio, hanging with a bite-size kid while a bunch of little girls squealed and twirled on the other side of the wall.

"Wow! You're good at that," the kid said just as Trey rounded off the bumper. His mom made it easy since, from the looks of it, Sara had bought out the entire hardware store down the street.

His mom.

Trey released a deep, painful breath which pissed off his chest because Sara hadn't morphed into a pregnant woman in a wedding dress. No, she'd come stock-ready with a minivan future and an instant family. And she hadn't said a goddamned word about it.

Now, he had a thing for a single mom. And kids meant a whole new set of rules—rules that revolved around long-term and commitment, two things that were normally his cue to invent some reasonable excuse and get the hell out of there. Only this time, he couldn't think of what to say—or anywhere he'd rather be.

"Just make sure it's five ounces. The commander says that's the limit." Cooper held up his hand, all five fingers spread wide to emphasize his point.

"Got it." Trey kept sanding, forcing himself not to look at the mini-Chargers fan holding a screwdriver. He knew what he'd see— it would be the same look Trey had given his brothers when they would do something that was truly impressive. Which, if he were being honest, felt good.

Lately, Trey felt like the least impressive person on the planet, but hanging out in the back room of a dance studio, with another guy, building a car, was definitely the testosterone-infused environment he needed. So far, Cooper hadn't brought up diapers, babies, or reproduction of any kind, which he was thankful for. It was all cars and football while tossing back a few juice boxes, polished off by some impressive burping and sound effects.

"Okay, Coop, how do you want this bad boy to look?" Trey asked.

"Not like a carriage or a bug, and not pink. I want it manly with muscles," Coop said and Trey hid his grimace. He remembered Cooper from the other day when he'd picked up Holly from her Lady Bug meeting. Remembered telling him that pink was a wussy color. It was a joke. Obviously the kids took it seriously.

"Pink's not so bad," Trey said.

"For a girl." Yup, he'd said that too. *Crap*. "Hunter said the only thing that should be pink is a ballerina dress."

Trey agreed with this Hunter, but wisely kept his mouth shut.

"Then I told him I took ballet and I didn't wear a dress, and he said I was a ballerina and then everyone laughed." Trey bet by the wet eyes that Coop didn't laugh. "I tried to tell him that boy ballerinas were different, but I couldn't remember what they were called. Do you know?"

"Boy ballerinas, I mean, um . . . male ballet dancers are . . ." Hell, he didn't know, and any word he'd used to describe guy dancers before would probably get him in deep shit with Sara. "Awesome. Male dancers are awesome."

"You sure?" The kid was too polite to call him a liar, but the disbelief was thick in his voice.

"Damn straight," Trey said, proud of himself, until Coop's eyes lit with excitement over the bad word. "Do you know how strong they have to be to lift girls over their heads like that? In fact, someone needs to tell that Hunter kid that during college, some of my football buddies actually took ballet to increase their flexibility and balance. And strength. That sounds like awesome to me."

The kid smiled like he'd just said the best possible thing. "Are you a professional dancer?"

"I can spin a lady around the dance floor all right." Since that was not what the kid was asking, Trey picked up the sandpaper and mumbled, "Otherwise, no. Not really."

"Oh," Coop said, looking a little deflated. "A football player?"

"With my brothers on the weekend, but I was more of a baseball kind of kid growing up," Trey said, wondering why he was explaining himself to a five-year-old with a grape mustache.

Coop studied Trey, taking in his suit and button-up. After looking around the room and checking under the desk, he leaned in and, as though he were divulging a national secret, whispered, "A secret agent?"

"Nope," Trey said, grabbing another juice box. Then to end what would otherwise turn into an endless game of Twenty Questions That Confirm You're a Loser, he added, "I'm a salesman."

Coop looked as confused as Trey felt. "I sell wine. All around the world."

"Really?" Coop's eyes went wide with awe and Trey felt some of his swagger return. But the ego stroke was short-lived. "I sell lemonade. To all the people on my block. Last summer I made enough money to buy my own Tonka tank. It's camo and shoots lasers from the cannon and it's just like the kind my dad drives."

Of course his dad drove tanks. He was probably Special Forces too. Here Trey was, a wine salesman, trying to impress some kid with his mad sanding skills when his dad made weapons from sand and earwax.

"Your dad's a military man."

"Marine."

Explained why Trey was here and his dad wasn't. He didn't see a ring on Sara's finger and judging by Coop's good manners and impeccable hygiene, he'd bet that Sara had primary custody. "Is he stationed overseas?"

"Nope. He's with Grandma and Grandpa Reed."

"Where's that? San Diego?" Trey had learned that Sara had moved here from San Diego last summer.

"Nope, in heaven."

The last word hit Trey like a fist to the gut. His guess was divorce, not— "My dad was a soldier who fought bravely and died for his country."

And there it was. Coop's statement sounded more like something an adult would say, granted; it was likely what he had been told to say over and over again. Just like Trey had been told that his parents' death wasn't his fault. But no matter how many times something got pounded into his brain, it didn't make the reality any less . . . real.

"I'm sorry, buddy," Trey said, rubbing another long swipe along the car, breaking his earlier rule of not looking him in the eye. "That must have been hard on you and your mom."

Now it was Coop's turn to avoid eye contact. Searching through the bag, he pulled out a squeeze tube of army-green paint and paused right out of Trey's grasp. "Just cuz it's green doesn't mean it tastes like watermelon, so don't eat it. Mom will get mad. Oh, and don't lick the glue stick, it will make your belly hurt."

Trey stared. The kid was serious. "No licking or drinking toxic supplies. Got it. How about grabbing us another couple of juice boxes so we can get this thing ready for a paint job?"

"Thanks for the ride," Sara said as Trey pulled onto her street. He was not in the minivan. In fact, she learned that he didn't even own the minivan—the one she hit or otherwise. He owned a very non-kid-friendly sports car with bucket seats, a spoiler, and a backseat fit for a Chihuahua. But it had muscle.

"No problem," Trey said quietly, since Cooper was snoring away in the back, his legs pulled to his chest, his head lolled to the side on the leather armrest.

By the time her pole-dancing class had started, the rain had turned to a light drizzle, but it was dark and cold, and the streets were still slick from the storm. So while the first coat of paint was drying on the derby car—army green apparently fell into the *manly* category—Trey picked up a large chili from Stan's Soup and Service Station, with two spoons, and he and Cooper hung out and ate while Sara finished up so he could drive them home.

She hadn't had the heart to tell Trey that for her son, chili's ick-factor ranked right above cabbage and below squash of any kind, but it hadn't mattered. Cooper's need for guy time overruled his absolute conviction that things with beans could sprout in his stomach, and he sucked down two helpings. Just like the way Trey patiently guided Cooper through making his car, never once taking over when paint spilled or a corner got too sanded, overruled that little voice in Sara's mind, reminding her that sweet didn't translate into long-term.

Not for a guy like Trey.

"How did the Snowflake Princess auditions go?" he asked, sending her a sidelong glance.

"Crowded, chaotic, and totally amazing." Sara leaned back against the headrest and smiled. Her feet were sore, her head pounded from all of the giggling kids and chattering moms, but it couldn't have gone more perfectly. "I can't believe how many people your grandmother got to show up. I don't know if she was threatening or bribing."

"Probably a little of both."

"Well, I now have three classes completely booked and I haven't even had the middle-schoolers audition yet. If Monday is anything like today, I will have enough kids to have classes every afternoon, with younger siblings filling out my morning schedule, which means I can hire a full-time teacher and stay home nights with Cooper."

"It sounds like today was a complete success," Trey said, pulling into her driveway.

Sara waited until he put the car in park and looked over at her. "I have you partly to thank for that. I know that I kind of sprung Cooper on you." He raised a brow. "Okay, I totally blindsided you, but you deserved it. *Manly color.*"

"Regan asked me to pick up Holly from Lady Bugs, and one of the kids asked why I was wearing my sister's coat. Since I'd just gone a round with my brothers over the sparkly accents—thanks for that, by the way—I might have said something stupid to defend my masculinity. I never meant for Coop to hear it. Plus, you have to admit, that car was . . ." he looked over his shoulder at Cooper, who let out a sleepy Darth Vader breath-snort combo, but he lowered his voice anyway, "pretty tragic."

"I worked hard on that. It took us all week to get it done." She shoved at his chest. He didn't budge, except to trap her hand beneath his, making her next words come out breathy. "And I think it looked like a superhero's car."

"What superhero would that be? Lady Bug-ette?" Trey laughed and Sara felt all of the stress and struggles from the last few days disappear. It was impossible not to when he was smiling at her like that. "All it needed was pink polka dots."

"I understand my son is male. I wasn't going to paint it pink," Sara challenged while leaning in and trying to look intimidating. But it was hard to pull off when she was hyper aware of his hand still holding hers.

Unfastening his seat belt, he leaned in too. Only with his bedroom eyes and that cocky, you-know-you-want-me smile, he managed to actually pull off intimidating. And sexy.

"I'm male," he whispered, the space between them heated and crackled.

Male incarnate was more like it. The smell of crisp rain on his skin, the feel of his calloused fingers lightly running over her wrist, all of that sexy swagger he was expelling was proof enough. Then he smiled and her stomach flipped and, *whoosh*, all of the air left her lungs in one huge rush of nerves and excitement. "No arguments here."

"And yet you painted me pink."

"I like pink," she heard herself whisper.

The click of her seat belt echoed through the car as Trey leaned even closer, taking his time to study her neck, her lips, finally looking her in the eye. "I like *you*."

Sara liked him too. Enough to give her pause, to make her ask the hard questions, like if she was ready to move past Garrett's death, if she could see herself falling for Trey, if he was capable of breaking her heart. The answer to all was a resounding yes.

"I want to go to bed," a groggy little voice said from the backseat.

Me too, Sara thought, giving Trey one last look. *Me too.*

Thirty minutes later, Trey found himself pulling into Sara's driveway—for the second time that night. He grabbed the badass garage he'd fashioned from an old shoebox out of the backseat—one slightly sticky derby car inside—and strode up the stone walkway. The one-story, craftsman-style cottage boasted a charming garden and a wide front porch, complete with matching bikes and a wooden swing. It looked welcoming and so soothing, Trey nearly set the box on the doorstep, got back in his car, and drove to the hotel.

There was nothing temporary or staged about the house. Just like there was nothing temporary or staged about its owner. Sara Reed with her sunny smile and melt-your-soul eyes, was a card-carrying member of Families-R-Us, the one-stop shop to forever. Something Trey didn't do. Something he was willing to move six thousand miles to avoid. And yet there he was, paint stuck under his nails, bag of craft supplies dangling from his hand, knocking on her front door—hoping she wouldn't answer and praying that she would.

The door opened, and if Trey wasn't certain about his day before, he was now.

Definitely less shitty.

Sara appeared behind the screen. Gone was the bulky coat and dance clothes from earlier. Same with the tight little bun she'd worn on top of her head.

Now, her hair spilled in loose, dark waves, brushing her shoulders and framing that incredible face. She was dressed in a pair of faded jeans that hugged her hips and a thin cream sweater that in the light—*thank you, Jesus*—turned pretty much translucent, which meant that he could see clear through to the little cami she wore beneath. Also cream. With one of those built-in bra thingies that were invented to drive men crazy. The single thin strap over her almost-naked shoulder confirmed the former, and his dick the latter, because one tug of that strap and it was game on.

"Trey?" She opened the screen door and took a step forward, tucking her hands in the back pockets of her pants, which did stupid things to the front part of his pants. "What are you doing here?"

"Coop forgot this." He held up the box and bag. "I know he needed it for tomorrow."

"Thank you. That was nice of you to bring it back."

She reached for the box, but when he wouldn't let go, she raised a brow. "Be sure to not jar it. The paint isn't all-the-way dry." He meant to give it to her but couldn't seem to let go. Or shut up. "Which is why we couldn't finish the camo job on the car, but I put the black and gray paint inside the bag so you guys could do it tomorrow."

"I'll be careful, and I'll let Cooper know you stopped by." She took the box, looked inside—and then hit him with her smile. Going home was no longer an option. Neither was stripping her naked, since he'd bet Coop was snoring less than twenty feet away. But he could at least get his dance.

"I stopped by to see you," he said and Sara's smile lost some of its sparkle. She looked torn. So he took a giant mental step backward and went for friendly. "It seems you owe me a dance."

It didn't work; she still seemed uncertain. Especially when she looked over her shoulder toward what he assumed was Cooper's door. "It's late."

"A deal's a deal," he said, stepping forward and crowding her a little. He heard her breath catch, watched her eyes zero in on his mouth and—*hot damn*—she was nervous *and* tempted. *This* he could handle. Man, woman, needs, wants. Enough chemistry to ignite an electrical storm. This was his playground. "One dance lesson and I'll leave."

"Uh-huh," she mumbled but didn't sound convinced. Smart and gorgeous.

She looked down the darkened stairway, and back to him, hesitation in her eyes. He stuck out the box and gave his best scouts-honor grin.

"One dance," she said, and he knew he was in. She opened the door and stepped back, but didn't let him cross the threshold. "No poles, clothes stay on, and absolutely no touching below the waist."

Trey checked out her cami and shrugged. "I'm good with that."

She narrowed her gaze but let him in. He closed the door behind him and followed her down the hall, through the family room, and somewhere between the kitchen table and pantry, his eyes fell to her other tight buns and got stuck there. When a cold breeze smacked him in the face, he looked up.

"Are you kicking me out already?"

"No," she laughed. "I figured that the backyard would be the best place for a lesson."

"But it's cold. And wet. And—" Shielding his eyes with one hand from the floodlight she'd just turned on. "Are you trying to blind me?"

"It's either that or this." She clicked off the flood and turned on a set of twinkle lights.

Lining the shrubs and wrapping around the entire deck, hundreds of little lights flickered, casting a reflection on the wet wood of the patio floor, creating a soft glow that illuminated the backyard. The effect was incredibly romantic.

He could work with this.

"And since I'm going for a kid-friendly lesson," she said.

He took her hand and led her to the middle of the deck before she could ruin his mood lighting. "I already agreed to the rules. No poles, nudity, or touching below the waist."

She crossed her arms and glared. "No touching period, except where we have to for proper dance position."

"Nope." He placed his hands on either side of her waist, firmly in the fly zone, and tugged her close. "You can't go changing the rules now."

"I was adding an addendum," she said primly.

"That's like take-backs, not allowed." He took a step forward and pulled her to him like he was Fred Astaire and she was his Ginger Rogers. He smiled at his discovery—she was a Ginger after all. "Now, for my lesson."

"Fine. The proper hold for the waltz is closed position, so your right hand goes here," she instructed, her cool fingers wrapping around his wrist, raising his arm until his palm rested between her shoulder blades—instead of on the patch of bare skin between the small of her back and that luscious butt of hers, which he preferred.

"Where would my right hand go if this were an improper hold?" She glared at him. "What? I'm just saying it would help to feel the difference. You know, so that I *know* when I've got it right."

She ignored him and, resting her free hand on his cheek, shoved his face away from hers and sharply to the left. "Imagine there is a window over my shoulder. Try to look out of it."

Doing the exact opposite of what she asked, he placed a small kiss on the inside of her wrist, his eyes firmly locked on hers. "Why? This view is much more to my liking."

She snatched her hand back and he loved how easily she got flustered. "If you keep looking at me, you'll stumble into my space."

"That's a problem, how?" She let out a serious huff in combination with a stern brow raise, so he went back to being the good student. "Fine. Proper. Window. Got it."

"Good." She fiddled with his elbow, raising it to the correct place, explaining, "The goal is to keep your elbows from falling so that I can feel where you're leading me."

She sounded so damn professional. He took her hand in his, shifted his frame into the perfect closed position, and drew her to him until their hips were pressed tight, extinguishing any lingering doubt she may have of just how capable his leading abilities were.

"Oh," she whispered, her big hazel eyes looking up at his. They were more green than brown in the lighting, and wide with surprise and, *oh yeah*, she was looking at him as though she wanted him to kiss her. And he wanted to. Very much. But he knew if he did, she would kiss him back, and that would lead to touching—in the "no touchie" parts of their bodies, which would lead to a whole lot more—and he'd made a promise. Which had clearly been made in a moment of insanity, but it had been made all the same.

So he checked himself and took an aggressive move forward, leading her in long fluid steps, with the controlled rise and fall that made the waltz such an elegant dance. Nothing fancy—he was saving that for later—but enough that had her lips parting with surprise.

"You know how to dance," she said, and he couldn't help but smile at the utter disbelief in her voice.

"Yup." He didn't just know how to dance. He knew how to spin a woman around the dance floor until she felt safe and breathless. A powerful combination. "Careful, teacher, you keep looking at me that way and I will do more than invade your personal space."

She flushed and fixed her frame. "Right. Window."

He slid his arm around her back and pulled closer, closer than a normal dance hold required, but this time she didn't complain. In fact, she snuggled deeper into him and it felt amazing. She felt amazing. Even though she was a tiny thing, it was the perfect fit, as though she had been built specifically for dancing with him. Or maybe it was that he was the perfect fit for her. Either way, there was something about how her elegant hand fit snugly in his, and how their bodies brushed and swayed as they moved across the back porch, that had his heart pounding in his chest.

"You don't just know how to dance, you've taken lessons before," she said, a small note of surprise in her voice.

"Just not swing lessons," he laughed. "When I was eight, my dad decided he wanted to surprise my mom and learn how to waltz for the Winter Garden Gala. He needed a partner, so he took me. We drove into Napa for lessons every Thursday," Trey explained, remembering how much he'd complained. Dancing was for wusses, something his brothers reminded him every time he'd pack up his wing-tipped shoes.

"Was she surprised?"

"Yeah," Trey found himself smiling at the memory. "She was nominated for Garden of the Year, and when my dad whisked her out and started twirling her around the dance floor, she started crying. Said it didn't matter that she didn't win, with him she felt like a princess."

God, she'd been so happy. His dad had made her that happy.

"Your dad sounds like a great guy. A true romantic."

Like you, Trey thought.

"He always did things, small things, to let my mom know just how special she was to him. He used to tell my brothers and me that romance is the nurturing of love. I was too young to get what he meant at the time, but looking back on how he treated my mom, how insanely in love they were . . ."

He trailed off, unable to say any more without embarrassing himself. He hadn't talked this much about his parents in years. In fact, he didn't know why he was talking about them tonight.

Bullshit. He knew exactly why. It was her smile. She had a great smile, warm and understanding, and it scared the hell out of him. He knew the first time he saw her, and felt that unfamiliar flicker of something he'd thought long-ago buried, that she would be his undoing.

So he sent Sara out for a turn and pulled her back, making it clear he was done talking about his family. Only Sara didn't drop the topic, which was just like a woman.

"Did you dance with your mom too?"

"Yeah. She cried some more."

"That's sweet," she said, and he felt his ears warm. Damn, the woman had *him* blushing.

"Trust me, *sweet* is not something a ten-year-old wants to be called. Ever."

It had been embarrassing as shit and his brothers had harassed him for weeks. Although, hearing the word fall from her lips didn't seem to bother him all that much.

"Why did he take you to dance with him?" she asked. "I mean, I love that he did, and I think more fathers should, but most men think dancing is for girls and would enroll their sons in something more . . . *manly*."

"Point taken. I still have the paint under my nails to prove it." Trey released a breath and felt his body relax. "He took me because I'm the youngest and, until high school, the smallest." He still remembered the day when he'd finally outgrown Abby. "So I spent most of my life trying to prove myself. Do what my brothers did. When Gabe got into football, I made pads out of my mom's throw pillows and shoved him until he tackled me. When Nate started playing soccer, I demanded to be goalie." Trey shrugged. "My dad hoped dance would teach me that finesse could take me further in life than stubborn force."

Sara laughed. "Did it work?"

He didn't have to turn his head to know she was looking at him. He could feel it in the way her hips brushed his. But he turned anyway and . . . he was toast.

Trey couldn't explain what happened next, only that one moment they were dancing and the next they weren't. His hands, no longer in the proper hold, were resting just above her butt, holding her to him. Hers were laced though his hair.

"You tell me," he said softly, leaning down until he was close, temptingly close, their mouths only a breath apart.

She didn't pull back, and neither did he, instead waiting for her to decide. He watched her eyes as she fought the urge to rise up, but he held steadfast. Sara was a single mom, which was new territory for him—territory he wasn't sure how to navigate. The kiss at the winery had been one thing, but being here in her home was completely different—so the first move would have to be all hers.

And wouldn't you know it, Dad had been right. Finesse did work better than pressure. Sara rose up on her toes, tilted that pretty face of hers, and kissed him.

Right there on the patio, with the lights twinkling around them, and the glow of the tiny bulbs softly reflecting in her eyes. Her lips were soft and gentle, and as far as he was concerned, it was the sweetest kiss he'd ever had. Which was why he kept it slow, resisting the urge to devour her. A difficult task, since she was so damn soft, much softer than he'd expected.

And shy.

Even the way she tentatively nibbled his lower lip was a complete turn-on. So much so that he could go on kissing her like that for hours.

Problem was, in Trey's world, kissing always led to getting naked. But Trey knew women, and women like Sara didn't do sex on the patio, and then not regret it in the morning. Just like she wouldn't do private lessons if they slept together. And that wouldn't work because ChiChi was expecting him to pull off *Dancing with the Stars: St. Helena Edition.*

Even worse, he realized, he wanted more. And he wasn't just talking about sex. He wanted a month of dancing and teasing and just being with Sara—a thought that shocked him into pulling back.

"I'm sorry," she said, her fingers absently touching her lips. "I shouldn't have done that. I mean, you are," she waved her hands in the air in some gesture he had no idea how to translate, "you."

"And you are . . . ?" He asked because how the hell was he expected to take that comment?

"Not a one-night-stand kind of girl, no matter how much I wish I were," she clarified, but sounded disappointed by her statement. "My life is complete chaos right now, and I don't want to give you the wrong impression."

"It was a dance, Sara," he said, purposefully flashing his easygoing smile and trying to bring everything back to light and manageable. Though she didn't come off as the manageable type. "Followed by a kiss, a very brief, but very hot kiss. One which I wouldn't mind repeating."

"Me either, but . . ." she faded off and looked at the floor.

And Trey got it. He suddenly felt the third person in the room.

"Is this about Garrett?" When she raised a startled but confused brow, he clarified. "Coop told me what happened." Trey reached out and took her hand. "I'm sorry. That must have been hard."

"Very," she whispered and Trey felt his heart pinch, which was ridiculous. Trey didn't do complicated. Didn't have the time or interest. And there was nothing more complicated than a single mom who'd at one time been married to Captain America and obviously still loved him. Plus, Sara was the take-home-to-family kind of girl, and Trey avoided his home and family as much as possible.

"Are you still in love with him?"

"I think a part of me always will be," she said, looking him dead in the eye. No hesitation, no bullshit. "But I want to be happy again, maybe even find that kind of happiness with someone else. I'm open to dating, even open to more."

He liked the sound of *more*. Especially when her face turned the cutest shade of pink.

"But I need to go into this slow, feel my way through the dating pool. And I don't think you have a slow move in your body."

Normally, Trey wasn't in one place long enough to do slow. If he took his time with every woman, he'd never get laid. Not that sex was the only thing he was interested in. Not with Sara. Oh, he wanted to do the sweaty, naked tango with the girl next door, but he also wanted, well, he wasn't sure . . . but he had one month to figure it out.

First, he had to get her to agree to spend time with him. If that meant taking it slow, well, he was willing to give it a try. "Then have dinner with me. Saturday night. We can talk about anything you want, get to know each other."

"We have ballroom medley," she reminded him. "Mrs. Moberly has already asked if she could partner with you."

"How about lunch then, at the Sweet and Savory?"

"Cooper has his pinewood derby race Saturday," she said casually, but the way she searched his face told him that his answer here would make the difference between *more* and *there's the door*.

"So does Holly. The Lady Bugs have their race right before the Mites and since Gabe won't be back in time, I'm filling in."

That talk had gone well. Holly had been devastated that Gabe wasn't going to be there, which had Gabe considering rushing back for three hours to catch the race, which if you asked Trey was beyond ridiculous. Which no one had, but he'd said his piece anyway, which got Holly crying and landed Trey in the role of pit boss.

"I figure since we'll both be there, we could grab a bite after." He held his hand up before she could object. "I don't want to jump into anything serious. And with everything going on here at home and at the studio, I don't think you do either."

She shook her head. "Then what do you want?"

"I don't know," he admitted, slipping his hands around her waist and pulling her snug. "But when I'm with you, I get closer to figuring it out. I like being around you. You're funny and sexy and smart and . . . did I mention sexy?" She nodded her head, those big hazel eyes flashing up at him. "Have lunch with me, Sara. Saturday at the Savory. It is beyond kid-friendly so Coop will have a fun time. And since most of my family will probably show up to spy on us, it is as laid back as you can get for a first date."

"What about coffee?"

"Lexi usually has some on hand."

"No, I mean, aren't we supposed to go to coffee and make sure we are compatible before committing to a prolonged block of time?"

"Sweetheart, we already had coffee." He fit her against his body. "And our tasting proved just how compatible we are. If you want to take this slow, then a dimly lit café without chaperones isn't a smart move, since I bet we'll prove to be damn near combustible."

CHAPTER 8

S ara clung to her umbrella as she ran down the alley next to the
Sweet and Savory. A vicious wind blasted her the second she got
to Main Street, turning her umbrella wrong side out. Jacket
drenched, she pushed open the door to the bistro and stepped inside.

The restaurant was already overflowing with parents, excited
kids, and the sugary scent of heaven baked in pastry dough and, she
sniffed, pumpkin spice. Customers gathered by the front door, while
the line for the to-go desserts and hot concoctions was already fifteen people deep.

Lexi peeked out from behind the display case, a pink box in
hand, and when her eyes caught Sara's, she smiled. As always her
blonde hair was pulled back into a neat ponytail and she wore a
purple apron and enough flour and filling to make a dozen éclairs.

"Trey called ahead. Your table is over there." Lexi pointed to a
booth at the back, which sat right next to the dessert rack. Talk about
the way to a woman's heart. "Give me a minute and I'll be over."

"As long as you come bearing coffee," Sara said, sliding into the seat.

Lexi saluted and went back to helping Mrs. Kincaid with her heart-shaped bonbons to go.

Sara looked around at the restaurant and smiled. Last summer, Lexi had completely renovated the pastry shop. The over-decorated, kitschy feel that was synonymous with old ice-cream parlors had been replaced with warmer natural hues and earthy materials. Not a sequin or doily in sight. In fact, the only thing that remained was the cardboard cutout of David Hasselhoff, which stood by the cash register holding a plate that displayed the pastry of the day.

Today, however, nearly every rustic farm-style table had a car prominently displayed, and for a lucky few, it was accompanied by a trophy. A big, plastic trophy like the one Cooper, who as of 11:43 a.m. was an official St. Helena Pinewood Derby finalist, clutched to his chest as he burst through the front door of the bistro with Heather, back from New York, in tow.

"Mommy, look!" Cooper said, dropping Heather's hand and tearing through the restaurant, not stopping until he shrink-wrapped himself around Sara's body.

Looking completely huggable in his navy-blue uniform with the official Mighty Mites red kerchief knotted around his neck, he ran the car up her arm and down the other side. Even though he'd come in fifth place, the smile on his face said he felt like a champion.

"Hey, honey. I missed you." Keeping one eye on her son, and the other on the front door for Trey, she held Cooper tighter and placed a kiss on top of his head.

"Trey will be here in a few minutes," Heather said with an amused smile.

"Oh, I was just checking to see if the rain had stopped."

"Uh-huh," her sister-in-law said, not convinced. "I promised to help Lexi run the register this afternoon. And she promised to show me how to make her fig-almond bars since I can't get them in New York. Anyway, I guess Gabe thought it would be funny to e-mail Commander Roman and offer up Trey's services for the tear-down committee, which is what he is still doing. And since I was needed here, and Cooper couldn't wait to show you his trophy, he offered to escort me."

"Want to have lunch with us?"

Heather looked at the tempting desserts and sighed. "I have to be back in New York tomorrow and I don't think they will be happy if I come home five pounds heavier. So do me a favor and go wild for me." She leaned in and whispered, "And I'm talking about the hot date who couldn't keep his eyes off you at the race. I expect juicy details."

Heather disappeared behind the counter and Sara smiled. Juicy was a good goal.

An elbow in the ribs had her scooting over to make room for Cooper, who was sprawled out on her lap.

He climbed over her and plunked the trophy on the table. "It's real gold. I heard Hunter say so. Did you see how fast my car went?"

"I think I even saw smoke, it went so fast."

"It wasn't smoke," he said. The *jeez Mom* was implied. "It was pencil lead."

"Pencil lead?"

"Yup." He was back to making a racetrack out of Sara's leg. "Trey put pencil lead on the axle cuz it makes the wheels spin faster." Cooper looked up, his brow puckering in thought. "He did say we smoked 'em, so maybe that's what you saw. You know, the smoke?"

Sara had no idea what an axle was or how drawing on it could make it go faster, but she didn't care. This was the first time since she'd signed him up for Mighty Mites that Cooper seemed to fit in.

After he'd raced, his hive mates had gathered around, high-fiving him and wanting to check out his camo racer. And Trey had been right there in the mix, helping Cooper point out the cool parts, bumping knuckles when the other guys stood in awe.

"It's the lead. It greases up the wheels. Smart move, kiddo," Roman said, stopping at the edge of their table.

"Thanks, Commander Roman." Cooper beamed proudly. "It was Trey's idea."

Roman's smile became tight. "Well, it was a great trick. You were looking good today, Coop." Roman ruffled Cooper's hair, then he turned his attention to Sara—to all of Sara—and leaned in. "You too."

Sara smiled and looked at Roman. Really looked at him for the first time as a single, handsome, available man, because Roman would be the safe bet. He'd been married, had his heart broken, and knew the struggles single parents went through. And he was nice and patient and safe and—there was that word again. "Hey, Roman. It's good to see you. Today was great. Your hive did a great job."

Roman smiled and leaned in for a hug and Sara let him. She even rose out of her seat and pressed closer than normal, letting his hands rest on her back a little longer than necessary.

He was big and built and smelled all manly and—nope, nothing. Not even a little flutter of maybe.

"I wanted to see if you thought any more about this." He stepped back and handed a Mighty Mites–inspired flier to Sara. "Spots are filling up quickly and I would hate for him to miss out."

Sara looked at the bold, collegiate letters at the top of the flier and felt her heart sink. This was the Mighty Mites's annual swarm father-son campout that Roman had been telling her about the other night at dance class. It was just a few weeks away and her family was short a few of the necessary requirements—namely the father part.

Even worse, this year's theme was Make Fire and Burn Rubber.

"Especially since he placed so high today at the qualifier because the campout is where the kids will represent their hive in the final pinewood derby race." Which explained the "burn rubber" part of the campout.

Cooper scooted to the edge of the bench on his knees. "Me and Matt are bug-buddies, plus I get to show everyone how fast my camo car is."

"I don't know yet, honey," Sara said gently. "It's Sunday through Tuesday and with Auntie Heather gone, there's no one to teach classes."

Canceling classes would mean a huge loss in money. She'd already canceled two classes today so that she and Heather could be here for the race. She couldn't cancel more. Not so close together.

"He has to go," Matt said, his shocked expression matching Cooper's. "Cuz he's my bug-buddy and we can't go nowhere without our bug-buddy."

"I worked really hard and I won and all the kids who won get to race, it says so right there." Cooper divided his attention between the flier, Sara, and Roman, his eyes so bright with hope it just about broke Sara's heart.

"I'm sorry, honey, but I have to think about it." Sara placed her hand on Cooper's bony shoulder.

Cooper slumped back against the wall, pulling his hat down until his head almost disappeared, and flipped the car over in his hand. "But it's dad's car."

And if that didn't have her searching for a way to make this happen, seeing Garrett's name scrawled onto the bottom of the car did. She couldn't afford to close down the studio for three days, but maybe she could use some of the money from the Garden Society to fly Heather back for the weekend. "When do you have to know by?"

"I can hold the spot until next weekend, but Monday I have to send in the total head count to the regional office."

"All right. Let me see what I can do," she said.

Part of her was determined not to let Cooper miss out on something so huge. The other part though, the part that wanted to protect him from any more heartache and disappointment, knew that her son was smart, and the second they started building fires or burping the alphabet or all of the other manly things Sara had no idea how to do, Cooper would figure out that he was the only kid on the father-son campout minus the father.

If he didn't, then Hunter Lock would point it out. Of that she had no doubt.

Roman must have sensed Sara's hesitation, because he said, "Just let me know," then turned his attention to Cooper. "Matt and I invited some of the hive over for a campfire showing of *Cars*, complete with hot dogs, popcorn, and s'mores next Friday. A practice night under the stars. What do you say?"

"Can I go, Mom?"

"I don't see why not."

Cooper would have more fun hanging with his friends than sitting around the studio. Plus, it would give her time to catch up on all of the paperwork that had accumulated since the auditions.

"What time should I drop him off?"

"I can pick him up after school if that works," Roman said, looking at the vacant seat next to Matt.

Suddenly Sara wondered if she was supposed to ask them to join her. She had in the past and now Roman was looking at the table like he hoped she would again. Sara might not be current on the rules of dating, but she knew that asking another man to the party wouldn't go over well.

"If it makes it easier," Roman offered, "I can drop him off at the studio Saturday morning after breakfast."

Breakfast? As in sleepover? Sara wasn't sure if she felt comfortable with Cooper being gone for a whole night. The house would be lonelier than ever. Plus, he was barely five. Way too young to be away for an entire night. He'd only ever spent the night away with Garrett's aunt and that had been so Sara could plan the memorial service.

"I'm not sure about the sleepover." All the boys, including Roman, looked crestfallen, so she quickly added, "But I can always come pick him up when everyone's climbing into their sleeping bags."

"All right." Tears avoided for the moment, the two boys high-fived. Roman smiled.

"What about you, Sara?" A low voice whispered in her ear. "You up for a night under the stars?"

Sara looked over her shoulder to find Trey standing right behind her. He was holding two large coffees—and at least one was spiked by the smell of it—and a hot cocoa. And there was nothing "maybe" about the way her body took notice, or friendly about the way he was staring at her mouth. His gaze was so intense she could almost feel her lips throb.

Gone was suit-and-tie Trey, and in his place stood a rugged, sexy man. Not that she didn't appreciate him in a suit but—*wow*. Dressed in a pair of well-loved jeans that were loving all the right places, a long-sleeved, dark-blue T-shirt, and a ball cap pulled low on his head, the man looked beyond hot.

She looked at the puffy, pink letters painted across the bill of his hat and grinned. In fact, she'd been grinning since she first saw it that morning at the race. "Team Terrific?"

"I wanted Team Outta-Here, but Holly said it didn't have the right ring to it. Regan shot down Team Take That, claiming it was too confrontational." He shrugged. "And since the alternative was Team Tinker Bells, this didn't seem so bad."

"Trey!" Cooper said scooting everything over to make room for the newcomer. "You're here! Look, Mom, Trey's here."

"You think I'd miss this party? Never." Trey bumped knuckles with Cooper, who looked like Trey had just said he was taking him to Disneyland with the entire Chargers football team.

Roman, on the other hand, looked less than thrilled and a bit territorial. He crossed his arms as he took in the situation, no doubt putting two and two together and coming up with: Sara's on a date.

"Roman," Sara said, wondering what the etiquette for this kind of situation was, and flashing what had to be the most forced smile she'd ever conjured. "This is my friend—"

"Hey, Trey." Roman held his hand out and, as if it wasn't uncomfortable enough already, the two shook like old friends.

Of course they would know each other. St. Helena had two gas stations, one fire station, and enough wine to ensure that everyone knew everyone's business. And Sara would bet by the fifty sets of eyes riveted her way that everyone stationed within the bistro was, at the moment, interested in knowing her business.

"Roman went to school with my brother Marc, but we were actually all in the same Mighty Mites swarm," Trey explained, resting a pretty possessive hand low on Sara's back, which ticked her off. Or maybe that was what being turned-on felt like. It had been so long, she wasn't sure.

Sara blinked. "You were in Mighty Mites?"

"All of my brothers were. It's like a rite of passage here in St. Helena."

So they weren't just friends, they'd known each other since birth it seemed, and yet neither had spoken a word to each other at Swinging Singles.

"What?" Trey looked her in the eye. "Why do you look so surprised?"

"I'm not, I just—" *Feel completely out of my element and want to go home.* "I guess I took you more for a junior golfer kind of guy."

Roman laughed. Trey did not.

Instead he leveled Roman with a challenging glare. "I believe that I earned my knot merit badge before anyone in our swarm. In fact, I still think I hold the county record for mastering all eight knots." He turned that intense gaze on Sara, only the challenge held a different kind of heat, then he grinned. "Fastest fingers in the valley."

Sara looked at the drawstring on her pants and laughed. Trey got it. He got her. There she was, feeling nervous and unsure and kind of like she'd made a gigantic dating misstep, and Trey had somehow managed to make her laugh—managed to break the growing tension.

Bad idea or not, she liked him.

"Why am I not surprised?" she said.

He waggled a brow. "You should see my sheet-bend knot."

"Friend," Trey said as Frankie fought to open the door wide enough for him and the baby-mobile, complete with Baby Sofie, to enter Petal Pusher: Buds and Vines. A nasty gust of wind blew through the flower shop, sending a bunch of girly smelling petals into the air. "We're on a date, some other guy is sniffing around, and she introduces me as her friend."

What the hell was wrong with him? So she introduced him as her friend. To Roman Brady. So what if he rescues small children and animals for a living? Who the hell cares?

Except that he did. He knew what the "friend" maneuver was for, had used it many times before, and knew exactly what it meant—I'm into you, but I'm keeping my options open.

"Yeah, what was she thinking?" Frankie asked, her face serious as she picked up a pot with some bright-purple flowers sticking out the top. She smelled them, wrinkled her nose and set them back. "Roman is great with kids, single, and smokin' hot in that all-American hero kind of way. He takes classes with her regularly—"

"Regularly?" Trey asked. He had hoped that it was a one-time deal.

"Every Saturday and Monday night that he's not at the station." Frankie waggled a brow. And he believed her since Frankie's brother was also a local firefighter. "Not to mention, he was last year's PTA Fireman calendar's Mr. May, as in 'May I see those amazing abs once more.'"

"You're not helping."

"Yeah? Well, neither are you. If I wanted to spend today bitching and moaning and getting all touchy-feely, I would have brought one of the hormone twins." Frankie crossed the store, stopping at a rack that held an assortment of fresh-cut flowers.

It was obvious that if Trey wanted to bitch and moan some more, he'd have to follow. So he pushed Baby Sofie toward the back of the store, careful to give the big horseshoe-looking arrangement a wide berth since her chubby little hands had pulled free from the baby-blanket burrito.

A bad move, he quickly learned, because Sofie was in desperate need of something to shove into her mouth, which Trey's quick maneuvering denied her, so she let him—and everyone in the store—know it.

"It's just that one minute she's telling me she wants to take it slow, the next she is practically making plans to go out with a guy who is one date away from proposing," Trey said over Baby Sofie's cries.

He rolled the stroller back and forth like he'd seen Regan do, but it didn't help.

Frankie released an irritated sigh and spun to face him. "You're not going to help me until you bare your soul, are you?" Trey shook his head. "Maybe she is just nervous about getting involved with a guy who is moving in a month." Trey looked away and Frankie stopped talking, her mouth dangling open. "She doesn't know that you're moving?"

"Conversation hasn't come up." Hard to do when he hadn't seen Sara in two days. Okay, so he'd made a point to avoid her since that embarrassing pissing contest at the Sweet and Savory on Saturday. He'd acted like an idiot because, for the first time in his life, Trey had been jealous. Roman flexed his super-dad muscle in Sara's direction and Trey wanted to stake his claim and run like hell all at the same time.

And that freaked him out.

"Look, I have one hour to find the perfect flowers, so can we cut the crap?" Frankie asked. "Your problem is that you're too much of a pussy to be honest with her and yourself. So you like her, and from what I hear she likes you, sounds like a good thing to me. Except she's looking to start over here in town, and you're looking for a fun way to pass the time before you take off."

"It's not like that."

"Then, tell me, what's it like?"

"I'm not ready to start picking out baby names or anything, but Sara is more than just—" Trey stopped because he honestly wasn't sure how to finish that statement, just like he wasn't sure how to feel about his family thinking that he was the kind of guy to screw with a single mom because he was bored. "She's just more, okay."

Frankie leveled him with a stare. "Is this just you having your delicate man-feelings hurt?"

Trey thought about that, seriously considered if this was about ego, and finally shook his head. Nope. Unfortunately, what he felt for Sara went way beyond his delicate man-feelings. If it didn't, he would have walked the second he learned she had a kid.

"Your problem is easy then. Just give her more." She leaned down and picked up Sofie, who was babbling angrily. Frankie sniffed her diaper, shoved her in Trey's hands, then turned back around to study her options in floral accessories, leaving Trey with no option than to hold the slobber-monster, who immediately started gumming his tie.

Sofie was too busy ruining his clothes to be disgruntled. Too bad Trey's mood wasn't so easily pacified. "How do I do that? Give her more without giving her hope of, well, more?"

Trey could do a month—a month of flirting and dancing which would, hopefully, lead to a whole lot of sex before he left for Italy. Anything more than that wasn't a possibility. But Sara, she was different. She was the kind of woman who loved, and loved hard. It would only be a matter of time before she fell again. Her heart was too big not to.

Trey, on the other hand, wouldn't fall.

Whenever love entered into a relationship, things went from fun to complicated, and someone always wound up hurt. Usually someone other than him. And he didn't want to hurt Sara.

"Because what if she's lying to herself and she can't stop at just fun? Or what if she is being honest and I miss out on something great?"

Trey noticed that Sofie had given up on the tie and face-planted against his chest, her little lashes struggling to stay open. So he swayed gently and lowered his voice. "I like being around her. A lot. I even like hanging out with Coop and I don't do single-mom romances. Ever. But when I'm with her—"

"Why are you still talking? Do I look like Sara? No, I don't. So telling this to me gets you nowhere. Tell her," Frankie said, opening a giant refrigerator that spanned the back wall and pulling out a cluster of yellow flowers. "Walk into her studio tomorrow and—"

Frankie turned toward him and froze, her hands strangling an innocent bouquet of flowers. Chilled air and the scent of freshly cut stems slowly crept out of the open refrigerator but she didn't move. Eyes wide, lips parted, she kept blinking as though to make sense of what she was seeing.

"What?" Trey asked.

"Whoa," was all she said.

Keeping up a snooze-inducing pace to his sway, Trey looked over his shoulder but saw nothing. He turned back around and realized that Frankie was looking right at him.

"That," she said, gesturing to his entirety. "Go in there just like that with Baby Sofie strapped to your front, a bottle stashed in your back pocket, and harness the power of the man/sleeping baby thing you've got going on."

"Are you just trying to get out of babysitting?"

"Yes." At least she was honest. "And if you want to stand a chance against Mr. Smoking Hot, you need to show her you're a good, honest guy and more than a playboy looking for a one-nighter." She shook her head and smiled. "Trust me, you and Baby Sofie tag-teaming her? I give it two seconds before she's ready to listen."

"And that's it? Roman's out and I'm in?"

"What part of being honest and *listening* did you miss?" Frankie asked. "After she fusses over Sofie and how cute you look holding her, you spill your guts."

"Cute?" he choked.

"Trust me, on you it works. Tempers the frat-boy douche factor," Frankie said. "So you look her in the eye and say, 'Sara, I like you and I want to take you out on a date, mano a mano, and maybe, if this works out we can share breakfast tomorrow and for the next few weeks, and maybe you can wear my flower at the Gala. But before you say yes, I need to be honest with you, I'm moving out of the country—as in this can never be anything more than February. But I want to be all of your February.'"

"You really think it's that easy?"

In his experience, women never responded well to cut and dry. They needed flattery and seduction. Then again, he wasn't trying to sweet-talk Sara into one night.

"Yeah, I do. I think that honesty goes a long way. And if you don't tell her the truth before you sleep with her, when she finds out that you're moving, you'll be walking around with your nuts in your throat."

"Are you sure that isn't just what you'd do?" Trey asked, knowing that Frankie had a trigger-happy knee with a more than accurate aim.

"Nope, it's what all women would do. And if she doesn't, then I will. Single moms are a sacred breed and my boots are all polished and looking for action." Frankie narrowed her eyes, then, just like that, smiled and held up a grouping of flowers in each hand.

"Now which one do you like?"

CHAPTER 9

Frankie was right. Babies were a total chick magnet.

Trey had taken one step inside the dance studio with Sofie strapped to his front in the baby slingshot, and every woman in the room turned to look at him. Then smiled. Even the gapped-teeth little ones in pink tutus and fairy wings, but especially the ones in their mid-thirties whose lack of a ring hadn't diminished that internal ticking that made most men run.

Trey would have run, wanted to even, but figured if running with scissors was a bad idea, running with an infant was beyond stupid—and defeated his purpose for coming in here to begin with.

He was only holding the kid because Regan left him alone in the car, and an important client called, which of course woke up the rug rat, who started crying and Trey started sweating. So when the screaming had reached DEFCON 1, he'd sent the call to voice mail and slid the snot-monster into the harness. In tandem, they'd managed to make their way inside the studio—the very crowded studio.

And now he was ready to show his baby-man prowess and then signal Regan for the handoff.

Only Regan wasn't there, but his reason for coming along in the first place was. She leaned across the desk, shuffling through a pile of forms and checking the computer, while a little girl who had suctioned herself to Sara's leg wailed.

Trey had spent most of the night before thinking about what Frankie had said, and decided to go for the direct approach. If he told Sara he was leaving in a few weeks and she backed off, he would have successfully avoided a disaster. If, however, and this is what he was hoping would happen, he was straight up about what he was looking for and she was interested, then these next few weeks in St. Helena were going to be amazing.

Diaper bag slung over his shoulder, Trey made his way through the waiting room of moms to the desk. A three-foot-tall snowflake zigged by waving a wand and Trey zagged, narrowly avoiding Baby Sofie ripping it out of the girl's hand.

"Duz-duz-duz-dat!" Sofie screamed, her little legs pumping angrily, kicking Trey in the gut. A couple more inches and the kid would be long enough to do some serious damage.

"Mrs. Reed," the little girl whispered, wiping her nose on Sara's leg. "There's a customer staring at me. I don't like people staring at me." Which Trey assumed was part of the reason for the tears.

"If you're here about the Snowflake Princess performance, I'm sorry, but this class is already full," Sara said from behind the counter and Trey didn't bother correcting her. Not when she was bent at the waist, frantically digging through a stack of papers while the silky, very sheer, fabric of her skirt gave him an impressive view of her ass. "Actually, it's packed, but based on the level of dance experience, I might be able to squeeze one more into the Friday class."

"I have an impressively proper closed dance hold if that counts, but I'd really like to learn the improper one," he said, smiling while he waited for her to straighten and meet his gaze.

Several amusing seconds later she did, and her face was a charming shade of pink.

"Will it be covered in Friday's class or should I book a private?"

"I didn't know you were still interested." She smiled but it didn't really ring true. That was when Trey realized she wasn't merely frazzled, she was nervous. "In lessons. I didn't think you were still interested in lessons."

No wait, make that vulnerable and a little hurt. Exactly what he'd been trying to avoid.

"I'm very much interested." Trey refused to let his gaze travel over her bust-hugging tank top or her lush mouth, instead focusing on her eyes. "And I'll take the dance lessons too."

Sara glanced down at the little munchkin sprouting off her calf, who was watching them with big curious eyes. "I saved you a spot in ballroom medley Saturday night and last night's Waltz and Rumba Infusion, but you didn't show up. Or call."

Her tone was pleasant and her words were polite and he got it— little prying eyes. This was not the time or place for this conversation.

Keeping it G-rated, he explained, "I'm sorry about last night. Regan asked if I could entertain Holly while she bathed Sofie, which turned into an evening of me with a pillow shoved up my shirt for a never ending game of maternity dress-up."

Which was a half-truth, because even if Regan hadn't called last minute needing his help, he would have found some excuse not to go. Not until he figured out what he was doing.

"Maternity dress up?" She grinned, real and bright and, god-damned, he was in trouble. "And Saturday?"

She went back to focusing on what he could now see were new student applications, but not before he saw a flash of disappointment in her eyes.

"Saturday, I was—" he stopped and remembered what Frankie said. Straightforward.

Taking a breath, he moved his hand so that their fingers were barely touching. Even that simple contact was enough to send his heart pounding. "Saturday I wasn't sure if you were with Roman, under the stars, so I kept my distance."

She looked up at him, her expression startled. "Oh."

Without breaking eye contact, she reached behind her, grabbed a sheer lavender scarf off the back of her chair and draped it over the little girl. "Okay, Mia, invisibility cloak in place, you can go take your spot on the floor. Just make sure that the other girls hear you coming."

With an excited giggle, the invisibility cloak scurried out from behind the desk and took off, leaving them blessedly alone—except for a grunting Baby Sofie.

"About Saturday, Roman showed up and . . ." She exhaled and so did Trey. "He's just a friend."

"He wants to be more." She didn't look surprised at his comment, only resigned, which meant that she knew that Roman was into her, and yet she'd invited him to join in on their date. "But I guess you already know that. So my question is, what do you want?"

"With Roman?"

He nodded.

"I just want to be his friend."

He raised a brow. "You called me your friend and I know what you taste like."

Sara's gaze dipped to his mouth and her body swayed a little closer. Even though the counter—and a very disgruntled Baby

Sofie—were between them, Sara's body language was loud and clear. She wanted a repeat of the other night, and damn if he didn't want to give her that.

Only they were surrounded by munchkins and nosy moms. Her phone was ringing, the clock said he had seven minutes until class started and—*sweet baby Jesus*—what was that smell?

"Oh my." Sara wrinkled her nose and, hand securely over her mouth, took a giant step back—thanks to the poop-machine.

"You going to help me or stand there laughing?"

"Neither, I'm going to answer the phone and think fondly of you as you deal with that." She paused. This was not how he imagined the day going. "Unless you need me to get Regan. She's just in the bathroom."

A place that Trey learned pregnant women spent a lot of time visiting. "Nope, I got this."

With his hands under the kid's pudgy little arms, he pulled the ejector cord on the sling and held Baby Sofie up. The pantsuit thingy she was sporting looked a little fuller in the back than it had when he'd put her in the harness.

"So much for being my wing-girl," he accused, flipping her around to face him. She smiled back, mighty content with herself.

"Doo-doo-doo-doo-dat!"

"Yeah, yeah you did that, all right. Right when I was trying to impress the lady." Trey leveled the baby with a look. "You and I are going to check this out, but if it looks as toxic as it smells, we're finding your mom."

Sofie squealed and started pumping her legs.

Sara just smiled. At him. Fully amused. "Scared of a little dirty diaper?"

"Hell yeah. And man enough to admit it." He walked around the counter, backing Sara into her closet so that they were hidden from view. "For the record, there's nothing little about anything going on here. Including this."

Shifting Baby Sofie to one arm, he leaned in and kissed her. Hard and fast and with enough promise that by the time he pulled back, they both knew that it was game on. Ball was in her court.

"Tap and Barre School of Dance," Sara sighed into the phone as she pressed a shaky hand to her lips and watched Trey walk toward the restrooms. Heather was right: the man knew how to fill out a pair of pants.

Beneath the fancy suit and silk tie, Trey was an adventure waiting to happen. An adventure, she thought while appreciating the way his slacks hugged that very fine butt of his, she desperately wanted to happen. It had taken everything she had not to purr and rub up against him when he came in, baby in hand, looking like Uncle of the Year.

"Hey, Sara," Roman said through the phone, cutting off her thoughts. The clipped inflection in his voice had her body going on high mommy-alert. "I'm calling because we had a little incident at Mighty Mites and I need you to come pick up Cooper."

Incident?

"What happened?" She was already reaching for her purse. "Is he okay?"

"He's fine," Roman said in that steady, reassuring voice. The man was a rock.

"Are you sure?" Sara's voice caught and she forced herself to swallow back the tears. "If everything was fine, you wouldn't be calling me."

Crying wouldn't help, but Cooper was so small for his age, and extremely sensitive. Fitting in had been a challenge for him and sometimes it seemed no matter what he did or how hard he tried, a few of the bigger boys took pleasure in giving him a hard time—boys like Hunter. Sara had tried not to baby him, to step back and give him space to work things out on his own. But maybe she should have stepped in earlier.

"I know what you're thinking, and he's fine," Roman said, and all she could think about was what Garrett would have done to those boys. He would have scared the crap out of them. "He just had a little altercation with one of the other kids."

Sara froze. "An altercation?"

Even the word sounded violent. What kind of mother raised kids who could cause an altercation at age five or six? *A bad mother, that's who.*

"No one is hurt, except for maybe a few feelings, but Hunter's mom is making a fuss and brought up the zero-tolerance policy."

"Zero tolerance? You make it sound like Cooper instigated it."

Roman was silent for a long moment. "He shoved Hunter Lock into a mud puddle."

"He what?" Sara said a little shrilly.

"I'm not sure who started it, but the result was two crying kids. And the rules state that both of them have to be sent home. I'm really sorry, Sara."

A strong hand settled on her shoulders and Sara looked up to find Trey standing there, holding a partially naked Baby Sofie and the confidence that he could make everything all right if she'd just let him.

He studied her face and then gently asked, "Everything okay?"

"No, Cooper got into a fight." She ignored Roman in the background stating that it was a not a fight, but a minor altercation.

Then he was going on about ballerinas and football. "They're sending him home. He's going to be so upset because today was his day to show off his trophy."

"I can go get him if that helps," Trey said and any hope she had of holding it together flew out the window. All the smooth lines and swagger were gone, replaced by something genuine and real. And all Sara could think about was how she had almost missed this side of him. "You take the pooper until Regan gets back and I'll go get Coop while you teach class."

The girls. She'd completely forgotten.

Sara rose up on her tip-toes and stared over Trey's shoulder. Way too many eyes stared back. She took a breath and started counting: *Two . . . Four . . . Nine . . . Thirteen . . Sixteen . . . A full class.*

Last week she had five kids, and today she had a full class of excited little dancers who could fill up a dance floor and charm the elderly. Not to mention, a flock of dancers whose parents paid tuition that would help her afford an assistant. But today Sara had no assistant and no way to just up and leave. She didn't even have a car.

What she did have was a no longer altercation-free son who needed a ride home—and most likely a hug. Or maybe it was Sara who needed a hug. Regardless, there was going to be a hug-fest.

Rolling back down to the pads of her feet, she looked up at Trey and whispered, "What if he needs me?"

He cupped her cheek. "I'm sure that he will. But since the idea of a few dozen little girls in tutus terrifies me, and you going in there all mama-bear would only embarrass him, I think the best solution is to let me take him home. We can watch Sports Center, toss back a couple glasses of apple juice, and talk guy-to-guy. Then you can swoop in after dinner and give him a hug."

Sara thought about what Trey was offering, about how great it would feel for just a moment to not be in this alone.

"What about work? Don't you have work?"

"Some conference calls and phone interviews, nothing I can't get done at your place."

"You sure?" she asked, as though her heart wasn't in serious danger of rolling over and waving the big, white surrender flag. She was pretty sure if he said yes, her crush would turn into something much deeper . . . that didn't have an expiration date.

"Oddly enough, I am." He dropped his free hand to her hip and pulled her close. "Especially if payment comes in the form of a private dance lesson."

Oh boy.

With a nod, she hit speakerphone so Trey could hear. "Hey, Roman, Trey DeLuca is going to head over. He'll be there in five minutes, and I'm giving my permission for him to sign Cooper out and take him home."

"Trey?" Roman said, and Sara could almost hear the guy's head thunking against a hard surface. "Hey, you know what? Don't worry about it. I can keep Cooper with me and then drop him by the studio after the meeting."

"No need, buddy," Trey said, sliding the BabyBjörn carrier over her body, his hands brushing the sides of her breasts as he secured the straps. "I've got it handled."

Handled indeed. In fact, at that moment, Sara realized that there wasn't much that Trey couldn't handle or that she wouldn't mind him handling—especially if it entailed his palms cruising over every inch of her. And he was looking at her as though he knew exactly where he wanted those big, capable hands of his to start.

But him handling her was not dependent on him handling this mess with Cooper. And she needed him to know that. It was one thing to help her son make a car with her one room away. It was another to expect him to be chauffeur, chef, and story-time supervisor.

"I can always call ChiChi," she offered, giving him one last out. "She and the Foxy Ladies have watched Cooper before."

"It's a few hours of bro time, Sara. How hard can it be?"

By the time Sara was ready to close up shop for the night, she had a permanent pounding behind her left eye. The costume company had sent out the wrong sizes, so instead of twenty delicate snow-flakes flittering across the stage, she wound up with enough snow-balls to cause an avalanche. And although she knew that Cooper had arrived home safe, she still hadn't a clue as to why he was sent there in the first place.

To make matters worse, she wouldn't be able to find out until her last client of the day showed up. She had tried calling her "spe-cial" client, but hadn't managed to connect and cancel, so she was tying up the loose ends of her day and waiting for him to arrive.

Locking the front door, Sara shut off the main studio lights and powered down her computer. Thankful that at least Stan had returned her car earlier, she grabbed her dance bag and purse and walked down the hall toward the back room, which was behind the main studio floor. She reached around the door to click off the lights and—

"Holy shit," Sara shouted. At least she tried to, but her throat closed in on itself, making the cry for help more of a squeak that was further muffled by the sound of her bags crashing to the floor.

She clutched her hand tightly to her to keep her heart from exploding—right out of her chest—when three frosted heads turned to look at her in surprise.

The Foxy Ladies sat on the sofa, glasses low on their noses, alarm high as they peered over their rims at her. Well, all of the ladies except for ChiChi who, dressed in a black pantsuit and frosted helmet hair, stood next to the wall, her ear pressed against it.

"What are *you* doing here?" Lucinda scolded, and Mr. Puffins, who was dressed in a camouflage rain slicker and matching hat, opened one eye to let out a low, throaty meow. "Gave me the palpitations."

When Sara's pulse had returned to a somewhat normal rate, she glanced toward the back entrance. Relieved that her last client hadn't arrived yet, she stepped inside the room, a bad feeling forming in the pit of her stomach.

"I have a private in ten minutes," she explained, that bad feeling getting worse.

What used to be her spare studio, used for pole-dancing classes and privates, now looked like CIA headquarters. In the middle of the normally empty space, between two of the floor-to-ceiling silver stripper poles that Heather had insisted they needed to "push the limits of their studio," sat a makeshift desk with a computer monitor, a bottle of angelica, and enough petits fours and finger sandwiches to supply the Garden Society for their monthly high tea.

"Your turn. Why does my studio look like the set of Batman?"

Sara's question didn't seem to settle well with the senior section of the room. Neither did Sara's dinner when her eyes fell on the security camera secured to the upper corner of the wall. It was facing the wrong way—and attached by a black cord to the computer screen. Only, they weren't watching *Jeopardy*.

"Is that Petal Pusher's back room?"

The ladies exchanged a serious look, then Lucinda spoke. "When you became an honorary member of St. Helena's Widowed

Warriors, we took a vow to protect you and yours. That protection goes both ways."

"You make it sound like we sacrificed a chicken and then swapped blood," Sara laughed, because good Lord, these women and their theatrics. The grannies, though, looked dead serious. "We played quarters."

"With my angelica," Pricilla said.

"And we let you win," Lucinda added, in a very Corleone fashion.

"Fine," Sara threw her hands up in defeat. She needed to get them out before her private showed up, not stand there arguing. "We're connected for life. Now would you please tell me why you are here so I can finish up and get home to Cooper? He's had a hard day."

"All those secret meetings you had where Deidra was being agreeable, she was playing you," Pricilla whispered.

"We met for a bowl of soup today at Stan's. It wasn't a 'secret meeting.' She offered to help find an MC, which she did, and I paid for lunch. No conspiracy there." All three women gasped, and Chi-Chi made the sign of the cross. Twice. But Sara kept going, "You guys found the band and helped with the advertisements. How is that different?"

"Because the MC is the only one besides the mayor who has access to the envelope that contains the winner's identity," Pricilla said, her face wrinkled with more worry lines than were healthy for anyone who wasn't in the process of being mummified. "They can read off whatever name they want and no one would be the wiser."

"Except." Sara tapped her chin once. "The mayor."

"Who is Deidra's second cousin twice removed," Lucinda said.

"Deidra is a cheat, plain and simple," ChiChi snapped. "I don't mind losing if everyone's playing by the rules."

"And this right here is proof she's a cheat," Pricilla said turning on the monitor.

Sara crossed the room to watch Deidra flitting around the back room of her flower shop.

The Sunroom, as it was known, usually functioned as an indoor patio with wicker tables and wire-back chairs, where customers could enjoy a cup of tea and talk about flowers and trimmings and all things green. Deidra also held classes throughout the year to teach locals about indigenous plants, gardening tips, and how best to prune a rosebush for winter survival.

In the video, the tables were shoved together in front of the floor-to-ceiling glass walls to make one large seating area. Deidra was circling the room in a flowing mango-colored gown and plenty of bling, dropping flowers into a vase in perfect synch with the light hum of music—that was wafting in through the vent?

"Wait, is this live?" The Tap and Barre shared its west wall with Petal Pushers, which explained the backward-facing camera and ChiChi's fancy stethoscope. "Did you drill a hole in my wall so you could use my security camera to spy on my neighbor?"

"Deidra doesn't do democracy," Lucinda said, as though that made up for the gaping hole in her wall. "She's mad that you won the coordinator position and is out for blood."

ChiChi's eyes went hard. "The nominations were heard, the board voted, and yet she's still trying to get her way by asking for a recall, claiming that you're too busy with your studio to focus on all the small details of the Gala."

"She's staging a coup d'état." Pricilla clasped her hands together.

"Only she's calling it a tea party," Lucinda stated. "I was picking up some salmon for Mr. Puffins at the market when Marilee Craver pulled me aside. She doesn't take well to sneaky behavior and there is a whole lot of sneaky going on in this town these days."

Sara glanced at the Deep Throat situation room in front of her, but wisely kept her mouth shut.

"She was at the library talking to Mrs. Moberly about those love books she likes so much, when Peggy came in saying that she wouldn't be able to make it to tea at Deidra's because her shop was getting a shipment of studded collars in that day and she'd have to sign for them."

"I assume the collars are for the dogs and not Mrs. Moberly and her love books?" Sara joked, but she was the only one who laughed.

"Mrs. Moberly doesn't read those books—Marilee does—stay with us, child," ChiChi said, shooting Sara a reprimanding look. "Mrs. Moberly and Peggy are on the Garden Society's board."

"And they both head up Winter Gala committees," Pricilla added.

"So does Connie Larson, and she said that Deidra's been meeting with the Garden Society's board members in secret, convincing everyone that you're in over your head, coming to her begging for help. We think that she's going to try to override the vote," ChiChi said.

"Friday. Right next door," Lucinda added.

"Why would she hold it next door if she doesn't want you to know about it?"

"Because she knows we'll never set foot in there," ChiChi explained.

"Well, if she thinks she can petition the board to take over your slot, and no one will be there to veto it, she's got another thing coming." Pricilla gave a firm nod.

"Plus we already set foot in her store," Lucinda said proudly. "Last night we swapped out some of her Earl Grey with powdered ex-lax and added a dash of cayenne pepper for kicks. They won't stick around long enough to vote."

"That's a terrible idea," Sara said. "Someone could get sick."

"Don't worry." Pricilla patted her knee. "Some of those ladies need a little help loosening up."

"If Deidra gets her way and wins Garden of the Year . . ." Chi-Chi faded off as though someone had poked a pin right through all of her fury. "She says that she'll make it so only the winner would get to waltz instead of making it the traditional finalists' waltz."

"And she'll win since she's using dye in her water," Pricilla added quietly. "No one can get pansies that color without using dye."

"I won't get to dance, unless you walk into that meeting Friday and prove that you are the woman for this job."

Sara didn't like the idea of getting in the middle of this battle, especially if it involved the Garden Society, which oversaw the distribution of funds—funds that would help her hire a new dance assistant. If she made a mistake, even a small one—like, say, let it slip that her dance school was doubling as spy central—she could lose her position as entertainment coordinator. And the five thousand.

Then again, if Deidra convinced the board to side with her, Sara's studio might be cut from the roster altogether.

She needed the money. It changed everything for her. Plus, she loved the Foxy Ladies. With Garrett's parents no longer alive and Sara's mom living in a different state, these crazy ladies were the closest thing to a grandmother that Cooper had. And they were her friends when she'd desperately needed some.

"What do I need to do?" she asked.

"It's easy," ChiChi said. "You go in there on Friday and tell them that you have arranged the entertainment for the entire night. And really play up the kids and how excited they are."

Sara opened her mouth to argue but ChiChi kept going.

"You won't have to have the girls dance the entire time. Explain that you have set up a schedule that includes time for social dance, which encourages all of the people of St. Helena to participate."

"They'll eat it up. They love jargon like 'community' and 'bridging the generational gap,'" Lucinda added with a snort.

"It will set the mood for your big finale." ChiChi's fists exploded like fireworks, her fingers twinkling over her head. "The Winter Garden of the Year Finalists' Waltz, a three-minute moment in time where all of the nominees can come together and celebrate the town's history and beauty."

"And true love," Pricilla whispered, her eyes a little glassy.

"If I do this, then you have to promise to take down the highly illegal operation you have running out of my studio. And swap her tea back."

ChiChi gave a defiant tut, so Sara crossed her arms and sent them her best on-the-count-of-three glare.

"Fine, but only if you promise to mold my Trey into one of those television dancers," ChiChi countered. "I don't want to dance that waltz, I want to live that waltz."

Sara thought of how Trey's hands felt skimming down her back and wondered just how improper they could get in one lesson. When she realized that in order to catapult him to *Dancing with the Stars* level that they'd have to partake in several privates, right there in the pole-dancing room, her lady parts warmed up and got ready to tango. "I'll work my magic."

ChiChi narrowed her gaze on Sara, giving her a thorough examination that made swallowing hard. With a smile, the older woman patted Sara on the arm and said, "I bet you will, just remember he is a good Catholic boy, dear. Now, don't forget to lock up."

And with that, the ladies gathered up their bags and left. Sara looked at the security camera and computer, and decided she'd take care of it in the morning.

"Sorry about that," a gruff voice said from behind her. "She can be stubborn."

Sara turned around just as Charles Baudouin hobbled out from behind a giant plastic cactus which was standing in the corner of the prop closet. Charles was Lucinda's brother, the patriarch of one of the founding families of St. Helena, and a man very much in love.

Somewhere in his mid-eighties, he wore a vintage three-piece suit, wing-tipped shoes, and a dashing head of silver. He also relied heavily on his cane to walk, part of the reason he'd been taking lessons in private. The other part was too romantic to resist, which was why Sara found herself in this situation to begin with.

"That's all right." She let out a breath and shook off the last five hours of her day. "They're just doing what they do best, getting into everyone's business."

"Do you think they saw me?" he asked, his face pinched with worry.

Wouldn't that solve everything?

"No, I think they were too busy playing secret agent to Deidra's villain to notice." Sara stopped, taking a moment to really study Charles. He was charming and regal and had a way of making Sara laugh, but beyond what Heather had told her—which wasn't much—what did she really know about him? "Can I ask you a question?"

"Depends on the question." He smiled and Sara could see how, back in the day, he would have been a charmer.

"When Heather moved, she begged me to take you on as my client. And since I'm as hopeless of a romantic as her, I agreed." And because no matter how big he smiled, there was a deep sadness surrounding him. A sadness that reached out and sucked Sara in, because she knew that kind of pain. It came from losing your entire world and being forced to keep moving. "But you are so secretive about our meetings, hiding in the closets, coming through the back door. I have to know, who are you trying to impress?"

"Impress?" Charles let out a breath and slowly lowered himself to the couch. "I am trying to recapture some forgotten memories, remember happier times, and maybe find a way to prove to ChiChi that an old coot like me might still have a few new tricks left in him."

And wasn't that the perfect thing to say. Sara felt her eyes start to burn. If this man wanted to recapture a happier time, remember what it was like before losing out on love, then who was Sara to stand in the way?

CHAPTER 10

"Y ou want to run that by me again?" Trey asked, but even as the words left his mouth, he knew he was screwed.

"Hunter said I wasn't going to the campout cuz I'm a ballerina," Cooper said. Trey could hear him sniffle every few words through the window. "I told him that I wasn't a ballerina, that boy ballerinas are called awesome, and then he laughed, and the other guys laughed too, except Matt. He never laughs at me."

"Get to the point where you punched him," Trey said, leaning his head back against the locked car door and staring blindly up at the stars, because the more Cooper spoke, the more Trey had to admit that a replay of him and Sara on the patio was not going to happen.

"I told him that dancers were stronger than football players, just like you told me to—"

He was so screwed.

"—and when he didn't believe me, I shoved him and he fell. In the mud. Then he cried." And now Cooper was back to crying. "I didn't want him to get his uniform muddy. I just wanted him to stop laughing."

"I know, buddy. Accidents happen."

"His mom used a different word. It started with an *A* but sounded different."

Trey sat up straight and turned to face Cooper through the side window. He looked so small, sitting there in the driver's seat, his legs pulled to his chest, his muddy shoes firmly planted on Trey's leather. He rolled his racecar back and forth across his knees, down his calf rollercoaster-style, and flipped it for a smooth landing on the passenger seat. "Altercation?"

"Yeah, then she got real mad and made Commander Roman call Mommy and Hunter said you came cuz she's too mad to even look at me."

"Your mom's not mad, Coop. She was just worried. And I'm worried, so why don't you open the door?"

When the kid didn't answer, Trey hit the unlock button on his key.

Click.

And *Clunk.*

Cooper immediately locked it back, as though he hadn't just trapped Trey out of his car—again—and kept talking, "Hunter said I'm not allowed to go back, so I'll never be a full Mite."

"You get to go back," Trey said for what must have been the fifteenth time over the past hour. "You just have to take a, uh . . ." What did Regan call it? "A time out."

Silence. Trey turned back around and resumed his seat on the wet asphalt. Cooper scrambled to the window and pressed his face to the glass. After a quick check to make sure Trey was still there, the kid went back to playing Indy 500.

Trey hoped Coop did better at playing racecar driver than *he* had at playing hero.

God, he'd completely blown it. Day one into his role of Manny of the Year and his charge had sucker punched some punk kid, gotten suspended from his after-school care, and locked himself in the car.

And just when he thought the night couldn't get any worse, his phone rang. It was Sara.

Trey held the ringing phone over his head and in clear view of the driver's side window. "Hey, buddy, it's your mom. You want to come out, or do I get to tell her that you barricaded yourself in my car?"

"Eeerrrn . . . *Smash!*"

"Right." Trey pressed talk. "Hey, Sara."

"Hey there," she said. Everything came to a crashing halt at the sound of her voice. Sunny and warm and so damn sexy he found himself smiling. His butt was wet, the take-out pizza cold, his leather seats scratched to hell and he was smiling. No wonder he had a momentary lapse in sanity and offered to babysit. "How did the day go?"

Trey lifted himself up enough to crane his neck and peer in the window. Cooper was blowing raspberries at the rearview mirror and downshifting with the straw of Trey's soda, which sat perspiring in the cup holder, the ice probably all melted by now. He sat back down and closed his eyes.

How hard can it be? Trey blew a mental raspberry of his own. "It's going."

"Did I tell you today how amazing you are for helping me out?"

"You might want to refrain from counting the ways until you get home."

The phone fell silent while Sara, smart as she was sexy, started piecing together all of the possible scenarios—and most likely berating herself for allowing a guy who couldn't properly secure a diaper to an infant to look after her son.

With a sigh that sounded more resigned than pissed off, she said, "Car or bathroom?"

"Car." Trey's eyes snapped open. "Wait? He's done this before?"

"Not in a long time," Sara admitted.

"Define long."

"Not since Christmas break when he colored the neighbor's cat." She skated right over that one. "He tends to hide when he's upset. Or when he's in trouble." *Like say for punching some kid out?* "And with Heather moving and him being sent home today . . . He mostly sticks to the bathroom though. Your car, really? Interesting."

Yeah, what was *interesting* was that he had a real-life Houdini on his hands and she hadn't bothered to mention it. Nor had she bothered to mention that five-year-old boys were nothing like grown boys. In three hours, the kid had gotten in a fight over nothing, made a mess of Trey's suit, and locked himself in a car to avoid confrontation.

Trey tried not to think of Roman and how he wanted to shove him into a big mud puddle for suspending Cooper—or saying he'd call Sara later to explain everything. And yeah, so he was moving halfway around the world to avoid disappointing his family, but he'd never lock himself in Marc's car. Minivan or not, a man's car was a man's car, and therefore off limits.

"Have you tried unlocking it?" she asked as though he hadn't already thought of that. As though every time Trey got mid-click, the kid didn't somehow manage to relock it.

Click.

Clunk.

"Your son has quick trigger fingers."

"I blame video games. How long has he been in there?"

"Almost an hour. We went for pizza, I got out of the car and he stayed inside . . . with dinner."

Sara got quiet again, and this time Trey felt the concern waft through the phone. "Did he drink a lot of soda before his self-imposed lock in?"

"I might not babysit much, but I know better than to load a kid up on caffeine before bed. He had a small strawberry lemonade." Which Cooper had spilled even before they left the restaurant—all over Trey. He looked down at the big red glob on his shirt and sighed. "And I had a—"

Trey stood up and looked in the window. The kid was sitting in the driver's seat, holding Trey's super-gulp soda, looking back. "Are you telling me he isn't potty trained?"

Sara laughed. Glad someone could find humor in this situation. "He's a boy, not a dog. And, yes, he knows how to use the potty. It's just that . . ."

Trey watched Cooper wrap his little lips around the straw and take a long swig. "It's just what, Sara?"

"Sometimes he has accidents."

Trey closed his eyes and banged his head against the driver's window. Cooper laughed then took another long swig. Kid couldn't suck it down faster if he had a funnel.

"Define sometimes. And please don't tell me, not since Christmas break." She didn't answer. "Sara?"

"You said please so I'm not telling you."

Trey took another look in the car and noticed that the super-gulp was so big, Cooper had to use both hands to hold it. Meaning that they weren't anywhere near the door lock. Smiling, Trey turned the phone to speaker and set it on top of the car, slyly grabbed his key, hit unlock and—

Click.

Clunk.

Fuck!

Cooper sat on the leather seats, soda balanced in one hand, Trey's valet key gripped in the other, sucking down that soda like he was a man with a mission. Maybe if he reasoned with him.

"You gotta take a wiz, buddy?" Trey asked and—*thank you, Jesus*—Cooper shook his head.

"Uh-oh, bad move," Sara said through the speaker. "Now he is going to be thinking about it."

"You either have to go or you don't," Trey reasoned.

Except Cooper was no longer shaking his head. He was looking at Trey all panicked as though he'd had to go for days and was only now realizing it. The cup was back in its holder and his little hands were now grabbing the front of his pants.

"Ah, shit, he has to go," he said to Sara, then, "Come on, Coop. Open up and I'll take you to the restroom."

"No!"

"He's tired," Sara said as though that was a strong enough reason for a man to pee in another man's car. "Just talk to him, I'm almost there."

Trey didn't think almost was going to cut it. Coop was shifting back and forth, the rubber of his soles making marks on the seat, looking at the super-gulp, and holding himself as though he was about to spring a leak.

"Look, buddy. You know that camo car of yours that we made? The one that won you the trophy?" Cooper nodded. "How would you feel if I up and wizzed all over it, huh?"

Cooper's face went slack. Now Trey was getting somewhere.

"Well, that's how I'm going to feel if you go in my car. Understand?"

Click.

Thirty minutes, a dunk in the bath, and three bedtime stories later, Cooper was fast asleep, doing his best Darth Vader impression as Sara made her way down the stairs. She walked into the kitchen and froze at the doorway.

Trey stood at the sink, sudsy sponge in one hand, Superman plate in the other, his jacket and button-up hanging on the back of the chair. Sara watched as he rinsed the plate and moved to place it on the drying rack, the thin cotton of his undershirt doing some stretching of its own—right over his broad shoulders and muscular back.

The man was beautiful, built, and, *be still my heart*, doing her dishes. No man had ever offered to do her dishes. Talk about a single mom's naughty dream brought to life.

"You didn't have to clean up," Sara said, but didn't make a move to stop him, because really, this was the most action she'd had in years. Well, except for that sensational kiss earlier today. And the one last week, which she was hoping to relive tonight. "I would've just loaded everything in the dishwasher later."

"Dishwasher is already full and if you'd seen the mess before . . ." Trey rested his palms on the edge of the sink and looked over his shoulder. "Pizza was plan B."

Forcing her gaze from him, she grabbed a juice glass off the table and walked to the sink. One side was overflowing with more pots and pans than Sara even owned, and the water was so black it looked inky. "What was plan A?"

"My nonna's lasagna." Which explained the sauce pot, double boiler, and copper deep-dish pan. "When that didn't work out, we went for good old macaroni and cheese."

He held up a scorched casserole dish and Sara grimaced.

"You know it comes in a box. You boil water, add milk, and," she wiggled her fingers, "voilà."

"I was out to impress."

"Cooper's a kindergartener. The absence of anything green on the plate is impressive. Neon-orange, superhero-shaped noodles might just win you Babysitter of the Year."

Especially since a meal that came from a box was a rarity in the Reed house.

"I was trying to impress you," he admitted, flashing a tired smile.

In fact, everything about Trey tonight looked tired and a little worn. Even his eyes, which were usually lit with humor and excitement, were dim around the edges. He looked wiped out and disappointed.

"I'm sorry about today."

"I'm not," Sara said quietly, taking the dish out of his hand and setting it on the drying rack. "You told my son that he was—what was the word he used when I tucked him in?—oh, yes, awesome."

That got a small smile. "I got him suspended."

"There is that," she said, bumping him with her hip and picking up the dish towel.

She should be irritated at Trey, stressed out over what she was supposed to do with Cooper for the next two weeks while he rode out the suspension, but she couldn't. Although she would never, under any circumstances, condone fighting, Hunter had it coming and she was proud that her son finally found the confidence and the words to stand up for himself. She just wished he'd kept it to words and forgone the physical display of awesomeness.

"I'm being serious." Trey rested his palms on the counter and sent her a look so male, her nipples took note of just how well his serious side worked on him. He looked brooding and open and so adorably miserable, it took everything Sara had not to hug him. "I opened my mouth and said the wrong thing, and because of it, Coop got in trouble."

"So you said the wrong thing." She shrugged.

He handed Sara a clean pot, which she dried and hung on the rack above the kitchen island.

"And now you have to live with the mess of managing both work and Coop without after-school care."

"You were trying to make a little boy feel good about himself. It wasn't your fault he misunderstood," Sara said, turning back around, only to stop dead in her tracks.

Trey leaned a hip against the counter, looking at her as though he didn't believe her, as though he couldn't believe her. And damn if her heart didn't roll over for him.

"Things happen. People make their own choices, Trey. It wasn't your fault."

Something raw and vulnerable flashed in his eyes at her statement. It could have been the best thing or the worst thing to say in that moment, she didn't know, but something between them shifted.

"And to answer your earlier statement, you do impress me. Everything about you impresses me." The way he cared for his family, took a genuine interest in her and her son's lives. How he managed to make her feel safe and challenged and adored all at the same time.

He cocked a brow and folded his arms over his chest.

Sara became aware of two things simultaneously. First, the movement caused the thin material of his shirt to pull taut across his firm pecs and bulging arms and, second, he'd had some trouble with the spray nozzle because the front of his clothes were soaked to the point of translucency, sticking to his body and making her wonder just how far down the water dripped.

And, once again, Heather was right. Sara needed the kind of happiness that went beyond being a mom—the sweating and gasping-for-air kind of happiness that only Trey could provide.

Trey cleared his throat and, great, the amused look on his face spoke volumes. She was caught checking out his goods.

"Let me help you."

"Okay," Sara breathed. Trey didn't just fill out a pair of slacks to perfection, he was nice and funny and made Sara want things she thought long ago lost. And he was hot.

So hot she was already thinking that Friday was the perfect night, if she could make it that long. Cooper would be at Roman's, the house would be blessedly empty, and they'd have three hours after her last class and before she'd have to pick him up. Three hours was enough time, right?

God, she needed to get her legs waxed and stop by the Bolder Holder for something adventurous. Maybe even get some candles for her room. Unless of course, she thought, looking around at the crayon pictures on the refrigerator and the Batman action figure stuffed in the fruit basket, he'd want to meet at his suite.

"I can pick up Coop after school and bring him home, then just finish my work here. I mean if that's okay with you." He shrugged. "If not, I can work at night when I get home."

"What?" she asked, because how did they go from sex to Cooper's schedule?

"What, what?" He looked just as lost as she did.

"I was talking about Friday," she explained.

"Oh, well, Roman said that Coop can still go to movie night since it is an unofficial Mites gathering, but he can't return to hive meetings until a *week* from Friday. So I figure, until then, Coop and I can hang out and do guy stuff while you're at work."

"You want to *manny* my son?" she asked. Was she hearing him right? Trey, man-of-the-world, wanted to spend the next two weeks sitting her kid?

"I want to help you," he amended.

That should have been the end of the discussion, because having a short fling with him was one thing, mixing Cooper up in this situation was a bad mommy move. Then she thought about the way Cooper's face lit up when Trey said he'd stay for pizza, and how proud he'd been introducing Trey to his hive at the race.

It was obvious in the way he watched other dads and sons around town that Cooper needed a male figure in his life. And here was the perfect specimen of one, offering to fill the role. A role that she was sure had an expiration date.

She didn't know how much Trey traveled, but based on his living arrangement, she'd guess he'd raked up some pretty hefty frequent-flyer miles.

"You're going to be busy with the Gala and your new classes, and with Heather being gone, well, I figure he'd rather hang here with me than spend all day at the studio."

That was the understatement of the year. Cooper would rather hang with Trey than drive around the track in Indianapolis with Batman as his co-pilot. She knew what it was like to spend every day before and after school in a studio, doing homework while her mom taught class. And she didn't want that for Cooper, especially since he was still upset over getting suspended from Mighty Mites.

"Pretend I say yes, what do you get out of this arrangement?" Sara asked, because she knew what she'd get out of this: short-term help that she desperately needed. What she didn't understand was how Trey would benefit.

"I get to work in a place that my nonna and sisters-in-law can't find me, which means I might actually stand a chance at meeting my deadlines, and I get uninterrupted access to the hottest dance teacher in St. Helena."

"Are you saying we barter? Mannying for lessons?" She walked toward him, her shoes clicking on the hardwood floor.

"Yup." His gaze slid down her body, lingering on all the right places and sending her into sexual meltdown. "Guy-time in exchange for some woman-time later."

Stopping right in front of him, she looked up into those deep brown eyes and stuck out her hand. "Deal?"

Trey took her hand, but he didn't shake it. Instead he held it palm up and placed a kiss right in the center, his eyes never leaving hers. "Deal."

"You know," she said a little breathless, "I would have given you lessons, even if you didn't offer to sit Cooper."

"Even after today?"

"Especially after today," she whispered.

Trey studied her face, so intensely that she suddenly felt shy. Sara, widow and a single mom, would have looked away, but the new Sara, the one who wanted some excitement and was tired of being alone, stared right back.

Trey shook his head. "What am I going to do with you?"

"What do you want to do with me?" She had several ideas, and if he didn't say something, she wasn't above listing them.

"Sweetheart," he whispered, the word sliding over her skin. "Talking's never been my strong suit, I'm more into showing."

Just like a man, Sara thought, but that was all she could process before his mouth came down on hers, and focusing on anything other than the way his lips languidly explored hers was impossible. Not with the way he was teasing and tasting—and then his tongue got involved and thinking wasn't an option. All she could do was feel. And, God, it felt good. He felt good.

Another thing that felt good? The way his hands gripped her waist, spinning her around so that she was trapped between the counter and a solid package of muscle and heat. Then things got out of hand, or maybe it was that his hands knew all the things her body craved, because he was touching her as though he couldn't get enough, couldn't decide what he wanted to touch first.

Sara had some specific requests, one was north and the other just a few inches south, but she was too caught up in his body to articulate. So she decided to take a page from his book and show instead of tell.

Her hands slid down his chest and over his abs and were just about to reach the promised land when he shifted and pulled back enough to look at her.

Not sure how to progress, she tightened her fingers—which happened to be wrapped around his belt—and tried to speak. Not an easy task when she'd just had the best kiss. Of. Her. Life.

"Why did you stop?"

Not that she was open to rounding third base with Cooper asleep just down the hall, but a few more nibbles would have been nice.

He rested his forehead against hers, his breath coming out in harsh bursts. "Because I like you."

"You're stopping because you like me?"

"Yeah," he began, then shook his head. It was good to know that she wasn't the only one confused. "A lot. And, don't get me wrong, seeing you naked is all I can think about. In fact, seeing you naked ranks third on my bucket list."

"What's number one?"

"Seeing you naked in my bed. Often," he said in a low, gravelly voice that sent her nipples into party mode. "Which is closely followed by seeing you naked on that pole."

Before she could comment, or tell him that she wanted that too, he tried to back up and put space between them. So she tightened her grip and held him to her.

With a low sigh, he gently cupped her face between his palms and looked her in the eyes. "Before we go there though, I need you to know that I don't do permanent. So you *need* to be sure that you're good with casual, short-term. Because that's what I am, Sara."

"I can barely think past what Cooper is having for lunch tomorrow, let alone a serious relationship," she admitted, although the idea of an end date had her heart spinning. Or maybe that was the idea of her naked with him on that pole. "I already did the whole love and happily-ever-after track. I'm not looking for that. At least not right now."

He studied her, really studied her, then as if he still wasn't convinced that she understood, he said, "I'm in town until the end of February, beginning of March at the latest, and I would love to spend that time with you. But then I'm moving to Italy and I don't know when I'll be back."

"Italy?" she asked, giving herself a moment to process that bit of news. "Your brothers are moving you to Italy?"

"I'm moving myself. I needed a home base and Italy seemed the best fit." There was something about the way he said it, as though Italy was the logical choice, only he wasn't sure if it was the right choice.

"St. Helena wouldn't be a good fit for a home base?"

He shrugged a shoulder, but there was nothing casual about the expression on his face. "I can't stay here forever, and home is a little crowded right now. Plus most of the clients who need my attention are in Europe. It makes sense."

No it didn't. Not to her. She'd kill to have a family like his: loving, supportive, so intertwined that no one ever felt alone. And yet he was just walking away.

"If that doesn't work with what you had in mind," he said quietly, "I understand. It won't change the promise I made to you, and I will still help out with Coop. I just wanted to be honest, because, well, I like you."

And weren't those three of the most romantic words she'd ever heard. Unable to help herself, Sara wrapped her arms around his middle and held on tight. "I like you too."

Already too much, she thought. Trey was no longer the sexy stranger who was exciting to flirt with and made her laugh. He was the guy who had helped her son carve a car from wood, and cleaned her kitchen just because. He was also the only person in her life to be honest and up-front about where they stood.

Trey's arms slid around her, his fingers doing some sliding of their own, down her spine to rest temptingly low on the small of her back.

"Does that mean yes?" he whispered against her neck, his hands taking that final plunge south and cupping her butt. And if she had any lingering questions about how serious he was, the hard proof pressed against her stomach. "Please tell me that it means yes."

Sara wasn't sure what she had expected. Maybe a hot fling with a steamy send-off when Trey traveled for business, then they'd pick up when he got back. Or not. But there would have been the choice.

But Italy? As in a permanent move? Could she do it?

The people in Sara's life never managed to go the distance. Whether by choice or death, it seemed as though she was determined to live in a cycle of love and loss, which always ended with her going it alone. First her dad, then her grandmother, and finally Garrett.

At least with Trey, he was being up-front about the relationship, clearly stating that there was a hard stop, an end that she could see coming and prepare for.

"It means I have to think about it," she said and Trey exhaled so hard she felt sorry for the guy. He was tense, rock hard, and ready to go, and she'd just slammed on the brakes.

Instead of pouting or taking that as a cue to cut out, Trey's hands turned gentle, understanding, and he pulled her close, tucking her head under his chin. "Fair enough."

She relaxed against him and took in a deep breath. He smelled like pizza and dish soap and sexy man. And he felt like he belonged—in her kitchen and in her arms. Maybe not forever, maybe not even tomorrow, maybe this hug was all it would ever be.

But right here, right now, he was hers.

CHAPTER 11

Three days later, Trey pushed through the revolving door of the Napa Grand, pausing to enjoy the crisp air. It was a perfect winter day. The storm had finally passed, leaving behind the fresh scent of rain and rich soil, while Main Street, which looked like it had been hit with a Valentine's Day confetti blaster, was bustling with locals and a few courageous tourists.

Old wine barrels lined either side of the street, overflowing with bright-red camellias and clusters of pink pansies. Heart-shaped fliers hung from every storefront announcing the Winter Garden Gala was only a week away. And his brothers were still AWOL.

True to her word, Sara had made time for a private lesson each night when she came home. And true to his word, Trey hadn't pressed her for an answer on where they stood in the getting-naked department. Instead they'd had civil conversations about Cooper's homework, the performance for the Gala, how his interviews were going—anything to avoid the fact that both of them were solely focused on getting down and dirty.

Sara couldn't even say the word "pole" without blushing.

Trey shifted the case of wine to his other arm and made his way toward Petal Pusher. The Garden Society was having an impromptu meeting to finalize the wine selection for the Gala, or so ChiChi claimed, and since he still was officially the Ryo wine rep, it was his duty to go.

He could have argued that Abby was coming home early next week, giving her ample time before the Gala, and could therefore handle it herself. Or that his presence had more to do with hijacking Deidra's secret meeting than wine selection. But ChiChi was determined, and Sara's cute little backside had shimmied into the flower shop not too long ago, so he decided to play the doting grandson, packed up a generous selection of Ryo's best, and went to work.

Opening the front door, Trey rounded the heart-shaped pansy display and made his way toward the sunroom and the sound of arguing. With a deep breath, he stepped through the French doors and found what could only be called, Family Feud: the Mad Hatter Edition.

A long table stretched the length of the room, covered in a red seasonal themed cloth with coordinating arrangements going down the center. Trays of finger sandwiches and little tea pots with matching cups were strategically placed for maximum affect. But instead of a bunch of old ladies nibbling crumpets while talking about their grandkids, the table worked as a dividing line, with Deidra and her supporters on one side, and ChiChi and her comrades on the other. At the head of the table, barely visible over a vase of roses with dead twigs sticking out of it, stood Sara.

"Now, one more word like that and I will put you all in time out," she threatened and Trey found himself smiling.

The normally patient Sara was frazzled, and she looked like she meant business.

"But she's trying to make this the Deidra show," ChiChi argued, standing up, her hand strangling a linen napkin.

"I am just saying that the winner should receive the honor of having the first dance. Alone," Deidra countered.

"This isn't a wedding," Sara reasoned but no one was listening.

"The first dance is the finalists' waltz," ChiChi yelled, her face going red.

"Why are you so scared, Chiara?" Now it was Deidra's turn to stand. "Afraid that your pansies aren't—"

That was all she got out before Pricilla shoved one of those tiny sandwiches without the crust into Deidra's mouth, ending the argument. Deidra's eyes went wide with outrage and she started mumbling a blue streak of accusations. Even though the mouth full of bread and cream cheese made it difficult to understand what she was saying, the intent behind the threat was clear.

Sara let out a long, tired breath. By the looks of things, they must have been going at this for a while now. And were getting nowhere fast.

"Sorry, dear," Pricilla said quietly. "But a person shouldn't talk about a woman's dead pansies like that."

And there went the sign of the cross.

"Afternoon, ladies," Trey interrupted, flashing his most charming grin. It worked wonders on women and had an 89.9 percent effective rate with disarming the retired sector. And if that didn't work, well then he had wine.

Everyone in the room went silent and looked his way. Sara, however, didn't just look his way, she looked him up and down, taking in every inch and releasing a little sigh when she met his gaze.

He'd take that sigh and raise her a moan. She looked great, better than great. Today she was in a fitted tank top that was the same color as her skin and did crazy things for Trey's imagination.

She also wore a flowy skirt—light yellow—that barely covered her butt, and blessedly tight leggings that hid nothing.

Trey loved her dance skirts, she owned one in every color. All of them were sheer, and all of them had played a special role in his fantasies as of late.

Best of all, she looked happy to see him. Something that made him flex as he set the case of wine on the table.

"Thank God you're here," she said, and something else altogether flexed. "Wait, why are you here?"

Not as good as the first, but better than if she were to ask him to leave. He tapped the top of the wine box. "I come bearing wine."

"But the tasting was scheduled for Tuesday," Deidra said. "Today is the tea party."

"My mistake. I saw everyone gathering and assumed it was for today." Trey upped the watt-factor of his smile and shrugged. "I can come back."

Mrs. Moberly, the town librarian, looked at her still-full cup of tea and grimaced, before zeroing in on the wine. "I think there is room in the agenda."

"What agenda? I got invited to a party, not a meeting. And I think this young gentleman just brought the party," Connie Larson, the rescue half of St. Helena Hardware and Refurbish Rescue, said, her gaze landing on Trey.

He sent her a little wink.

She smiled and pulled out the seat right next to hers in offering. "Why don't you and that box come over here? I'm sure we'd all love to see what's in the package. Right, ladies?"

Excited murmurs filled the room and Sara let out a little laugh. She had a great laugh. It made her eyes sparkle and his mind go fuzzy.

"Thank you," he said, picking up the box and making his way to the front, right next to Sara. Mrs. Larson let out a disappointed *tut* but rallied when he turned his back to the room and set out the bottles one by one. Taking his time to line them up, bending over when needed, he smiled when the women started commenting on his "display." Mission accomplished.

Turning back to face his audience, he locked gazes with the host of this non-meeting and asked, "Deidra, would you mind helping me out? I'm in need of an assistant for the tasting and since Sara is heading out, I was hoping you'd volunteer."

ChiChi mumbled something crude and crossed her arms.

Deidra beamed.

And Sara blinked up at him surprised, and relieved. "I'm leaving?"

"Yes, dear, you are," Deidra said, hands on Sara's back about to usher her through the door and out of the way, when Trey intercepted.

Draping an arm over Sara's shoulder, he pulled her to his side, noticing that her breathing had taken on a labored effect. "But before she leaves, I want to say how thankful I was when I heard she had agreed to step in as Entertainment Coordinator for this year's Gala. Just thinking of my niece, of how excited she is to participate in one of the most treasured St. Helena events, reminds me of how special our town is."

All of the board members exchanged a guilty look and Deidra scowled. Wanting to make sure that Sara wouldn't lose the stipend, he added, "So if there are no more questions for Sara, I say we let her get back to teaching this new generation of St. Helenians how important participation and community service are."

When no one spoke, except to thank Sara for her time and effort, Trey said, "Deidra why don't you set up the glasses while I walk Sara out?"

Trey didn't wait for an answer, just like he didn't waste any time hustling Sara through the door. It wouldn't take much before the grannies found another feud-worthy topic that he'd have to arbitrate.

Just like it wouldn't take much to fray his already unraveling control. Especially when Sara stood there, looking up at him like he'd saved her universe—again—and that his intentions had nothing to do with getting him laid.

Okay, so maybe it did have more to do with getting laid. There was a warm quality about Sara that tugged at his chest, drew him in, even when he knew it was better if he walked away.

"That was incredible," she breathed, her eyes lit with excitement. Trey closed the French doors behind them. "You opened your mouth and started talking, and before I knew what was happening, they were all rapt, too mesmerized to even talk, let alone argue. It was as though you knew exactly what they needed to hear so they could feel comfortable saying okay."

Trey shrugged, not sure how to take her comment. Was she saying he was good with words, or a smooth talker?

Then she placed a hand on his chest and looked up at him through soft eyes, and he was too busy feeling to think about anything.

"You have a good heart, Trey." And damn if that didn't make his chest tighten. "And here I thought your plan was to get them so drunk that we could roll them home, and when they woke up, they'd be too hungover to argue."

"No, my plan was to . . ."

Was to what?

He couldn't remember. She licked her lips and dropped her gaze to his mouth and, poof, not a damn clue as to what he was saying.

He knew what he should be doing though. Saying his good-byes and seeing her to the door before he screwed this up. He promised he'd give her time to think on things, and even though he knew with one well-practiced move, her answer would be a big resounding yes, it wouldn't be yes to the kind of guy who deserved the hero worship she gave him moments ago.

Only she swayed closer, her hips gently bumping his and, again with the poof, he didn't have a damn clue as to what he was feeling. Except that it was crazy, and scary, and so right he had to kiss her. A little brush of the lips to show her how special she was.

So he did and she kissed him back. But gentle went out the window when she gave a throaty moan and ran her hands up his chest and into his hair. Without breaking contact, she walked him backward until a wall or a shrub hit his back and she pressed herself tightly against his front.

Always up for spontaneity, he went with it.

Sara tugged his head down, gripping his hair and—*Jesus*—that mouth of hers was so soft and generous, he almost forgot that there was the entire St. Helena grapevine right on the other side of that door. And that Sara still hadn't made up her mind.

He wanted to help her make up her mind. And quick. As long as her mind was in sync with his, then come tonight, when Coop was at movie night, Trey would be having his own private party under the stars. With his own personal dance teacher. Because her sexy little moans and flimsy tank straps were driving him insane. One tug and the entire top would fall to her waist and he'd—

Be. That. Guy.

With one last kiss, he pulled back and found breathing uncomfortable. Hell, standing was uncomfortable.

"We're stopping again," she whispered, looking up at him with enough heat to scorch.

"Unless you're done thinking," he said and when she looked away he added, "Then yeah, we're stopping."

"If you put your hand here and move your hips like this, she'll be putty in your hands," Sara said, showing Charles how to dip his secret crush—aka ChiChi—and not hurt his bad leg.

Charles tried it with Sara in his arms and the man actually grinned.

"She'll feel like the belle of the ball," she added after Charles righted her.

Charles had grown on her. His gruff, hard exterior covered the tender heart he kept hidden from the world—and his family. In fact, he was fast becoming her second-favorite student. Her first was Trey, and the lessons they shared would have to go down as the hottest dance classes in the history of the world. He never once pushed for her to hurry up and decide, or tried to seduce an answer out of her. But the way he looked at her let her know that as soon as she was ready, they'd get down to business. And when they did, it would be intense and consuming, things Sara hadn't felt since Garrett. And that made her nervous.

"What if she was taller than me?" Charles asked, staring at the mirror as though it was staring back.

That gave her pause, and a stomachache. ChiChi was definitely *not* taller than him. If anything she'd come up to his chin. Deidra in heels? That was another story.

"How tall are we talking?" Sara asked, crossing her arms.

"Oh," he said, rubbing his chin and still avoiding eye contact.

After a few moments to speculate, he lifted his hand a good two inches over his head, "About yea-high. And stubborn. I don't think she'll take well to being led. Anywhere. Especially from me, but I'd like to be able to make her feel like a princess on her wedding day."

Sara's throat closed. She didn't know the whole story behind Charles's falling out with his grandkids, but she knew enough to understand that he was lonely and full of regret, and her heart hurt for him. As far as Sara could tell, he didn't speak to anyone in his family, aside from his sister Lucinda. Although they seemed to spend most of their time arguing.

"Do you want me to help you come up with a dance for Frankie's wedding?"

"Her dad passed away when she was young and as far as I know, none of her brothers know how to dance." He shrugged. "We aren't really close. My fault, not hers." He paused to make sure Sara understood. "So I wouldn't blame her if she didn't invite me, but if she does, and they have the daddy-daughter dance . . ."

He faded off and Sara teared up. So did the older man when he added, "Every girl should feel like a princess on her wedding day."

"I agree," Sara said decisively.

If she had been onboard to make Charles the smoothest dancer before, then she was aiming for Fred Astaire now.

"How about we focus on you sweeping ChiChi off her feet at the Gala, and then afterward, we can continue the lessons three times a week until the wedding?"

"Thank you," he whispered and took out a handkerchief.

"As long as it's ChiChi we're sweeping away."

"It's ChiChi," he said with a laugh. "It's always been ChiChi. From the time we were kids I knew."

"What about your wife?" Sara asked over her shoulder while she walked over to the stereo and flipped through the songs, looking for the right one. She needed the perfect song for the perfect courting.

"Evie?" His voice held a reverence that warmed Sara's heart. "Prettiest girl I had ever saw."

"You might want to leave that part out when you're charming your way into ChiChi's arms," Sara warned, pressing play. A smooth jazz song filled the studio, and Sara didn't know if it was perfect, but it fit the mood.

"ChiChi was never a girl," Charles laughed. Hooking his cane over his forearm, and taking Sara into his hold, he glided her across the room. Bad leg or not, the man had moves and was a daredevil on the dance floor. "She was born a woman with opinions and sass, much like she is today, only shorter."

Which explained so much, Sara thought. "So what happened?"

"By the time I got around to telling her, she was in love with someone else." Sara didn't know what to say, so she kept her mouth shut and let him lead. "He was my best friend and looking back, he deserved her. But I never stopped loving her."

Sara stumbled a little, but gained her balance. "Even when you married?"

Charles didn't stop moving, even when Sara fixed his frame and back-led him through a complicated turn.

"Evie was the love of my life. We raised a family, made it through the rough years together, always reminding each other to laugh. But ChiChi," Charles looked down at Sara and she could see the love there, so raw and intense she had to look away. "She's my true love."

Sara did stop this time. Even though he wasn't making sense. "I don't understand. How could you love ChiChi and Evie?"

Charles moved her through a series of reverse turns into promenade. "You say that like your heart only has enough room for one person."

"Because it does." She loved Garrett so much she couldn't imagine loving another person with the same fierceness.

"I fathered two children and three grandchildren and I love them equally. Differently but equally."

Sara shook her head. "That's not the same."

"I used to think so too, but I was wrong," Charles looked at her softly. "ChiChi is all spit and vinegar, full of so much passion and vigor she makes me feel alive."

That's how it was with Garrett. He was wild and spontaneous and vowed to live life on the edge, forcing her to leap, for the first time in her meticulously planned life, without a net. They jumped from one thrill to the next, never slowing down, taking chances that, even when she landed on her butt, she never regretted.

Looking back, she realized, those years had prepared her for single motherhood. She knew how to love and nurture, but Garrett taught her how to rebound and move forward—take things in stride.

"Now, Evie," Charles said softly, and even his movements became more fluid, less showy. "She had this gentle spirit, a quiet quality about her that softened me as a man, allowed me to be the kind of husband and father I needed to be. When she died, I thought she took that softness with her, but I was wrong. For years I had it all wrong. It's been inside of me all along. It was her gift to me."

Trey was fun and sexy, but when they flirted and danced, she felt warm and desired and utterly adored. He challenged her in a way that felt safe, as though she could leap without fear of falling because he'd catch her.

"But you don't think that loving ChiChi diminished what you felt for Evie?"

"I am who I am because of both of them. If Evie were here, I'd be dancing with her instead of trying to court ChiChi. And I would be the happiest man alive."

Sara believed him. Every emotion he felt toward his late wife was on his face for Sara to see.

"I don't know what I did to deserve a second chance, but I'm not going to let love pass me by again because I'm too busy being angry and living in the past." Charles gently turned them. "ChiChi may have prepared me for Evie, but in the end Evie prepared me for a great love with ChiChi."

The song stopped and so did Sara's heart. Trey made her feel things she hadn't felt in years. He also made her feel things she had never felt before. Taking a risk on a guy who was leaving the country, knowing that he could shatter her heart, was terrifying.

Then again, taking risks was Garrett's gift to her. Maybe Trey's gift was to be the next big adventure of her life.

After a beat of silence, "At Last" by Etta James poured through the studio. Charles took Sara gently in his arms and she allowed him to lead.

"Now, this is the perfect song for a waltz," Charles said and Sara had to agree.

This thing with Trey wasn't love, but it was something. All she needed was the courage to leap.

Trey had finished up his last interview of the day, finalized the Garden Society's wine order for the Gala, and was about to order up some dinner when he heard a tap at the door.

Dropping his feet to the floor and his tie on the back of the sofa, he padded over, hoping it wasn't one of his sisters-in-law in need of a Hubby-for-Hire, and praying it wasn't ChiChi with another one of her schemes that would end with him playing assistant to Deidra Potter and her wandering hands again.

It was neither.

It was the exact the person he wanted to see. Needed to see. Just looking at those big trusting eyes made his hellish day circle right back to where it should be—easy. It was as though with one smile, she could make all the BS disappear, and turn him from stressed-out sales guy to someone who didn't have to struggle just to breathe normally.

"Sara?" he asked, unable to help the grin that overtook him. "I thought you had class."

She shook her head, then nodded, the confusion sending her long hair spilling over her shoulder. "I do, I did, but—"

"What class?" he said his gaze running the length of her. "Because if that's what you wear when teaching, sign me up."

She was dressed in one of those silky dresses that clung to her body and was held together by two flimsy little straps, which tied around her neck and were designed to make men think about sex. Which, point to Sara, that was all he was thinking about. Sex. With her. In that dress. Especially since it was red and hit low enough to display an interesting amount of cleavage and high enough to show off those legs.

"It was a private, and I ended it early so I could go home and wash up, because I realized that we didn't have our lesson today." She flung her arms out to the side, fingers wiggling. "So I changed and, here I am."

Indeed, here she was. Trey forced his gaze off of her legs and back to her eyes. Only that was worse because she was gazing back—clearly unsure and trying hard to muster the courage to state why she was really here.

"What kind of lesson are we talking about, Sara?" he asked, because he could see the heat flickering in her eyes. He just didn't know if she was ready to follow through yet.

"The improper kind," she whispered, following up with a grin that, according to his dick, was 100 percent trouble. She looked around the room and took a step forward, the hem of her dress brushing his thighs. "Only it seems that we're short a pole."

Holy Jesus, she was serious. And he was one lucky bastard. Just picturing her in nothing but a pink thong—he looked at her dress—make that a red thong, her back against the pole, legs wrapped around his waist as she reached for his pants—

"I wasn't sure if you still needed time to think," he heard himself say as she rested her hands on his stomach and slowly pressed him further in the room. She was too small to move him, but he let her because—*fuck*—this was really happening. "Please tell me I gave you enough time."

Instead of taking the kid-free day to get caught up on paperwork and find his domestic sales replacement, Trey had spent all of his time picturing what he wanted—Sara naked and moaning out his name.

"You did. And thank you," she whispered, her fingers traveling slowly up his chest, pushing him further and further into the room. "I've decided that maybe we both need to start checking things off our bucket list."

"You want me to wear the thong?" If wearing a thong meant he got to see her in one, Trey was game. Even if it cost him his man-card.

She smiled. "Maybe. But before anything happens, I need you to understand that we have to set some ground rules so no one gets hurt."

"Agreed." He slid his arms around her waist and slowly tugged her against him. "I'm into conventional, unconventional, pretty much any scenario that involves you naked, and I could be persuaded to experiment with role playing, with or without the thong." He sculpted her ass, to get a better idea of what she was wearing under the dress. "I'm particularly interested in the dance teacher and student angle. But I draw the line at animal costumes and bondage."

She raised a brow.

"I could be talked into bondage, but my hard limit is animal costumes." He flashed a wicked grin. "We'll need a safe word."

She smacked his chest, but didn't push him away. "I'm being serious, Trey."

"So am I."

"I meant that we have to be careful around Cooper. He needs to think that you're just his sitter and I'm just your friend. I don't want him to jump to the wrong conclusion, thinking he's getting a daddy only to have you leave."

Trey pulled back. "I would never hurt Cooper. Or you."

"I know."

Two words. Two simple words. But they were spoken with so much confidence that Trey felt them resonate through his entire body.

"It's just that for Cooper to believe it, then the town needs to believe it. Which means we'll have to, um, be creative when it comes to meeting."

His heart slammed against his ribcage and refused to move because she was looking at him like she was starved and he was what was for dinner. And dessert. If this went well, maybe even breakfast.

Please let this go well.

"As I already mentioned, I can do creative." He could do anything if it meant she was saying yes. "And what we do or don't do is nobody's business but yours and mine."

"Okay," was all she said.

And then, without further explanation, she dropped her hands and walked through the French doors to the veranda off the main room of the suite.

He took a minute to enjoy the view, swaying perfection encased in red silk and a beautifully bare back that left his hands sweating, and then followed her outside.

Sara stood at the railing looking over Main Street as the breeze blew her hair across her back and a light mist stuck to her bare skin. The sun had set and the clouds had moved in, leaving St. Helena lit by only the soft street lamps below. But even in the dim light, he could see that she was nervous. And that Santa had come early, because there was no way she could be wearing a bra.

"You okay?" he asked from the doorway.

"Just needed some fresh air."

"Second thoughts?"

She nodded slightly and he moved closer, wrapping his arms around her from behind. She hesitated for only a moment, then her body relaxed into his. He felt her release a deep breath before turning in his arms and whispering the five words he'd been waiting to hear since he first saw her at the hospital. "Will you be my February?"

Trey didn't answer, afraid that something stupid would come out. Something like, *How about February and maybe the first few weeks of March?* Which would lead to wanting to cross off the rest of winter and all of spring, only he wasn't going to be here in spring. He'd be in Italy. Alone with his freedom and a hard-on. And Sara would still be in St. Helena, out there in the dating pool, probably making nice with some steady, reliable guy.

Like Roman.

Fuck!

So instead he kept his mouth shut, mentally gave himself until March first, and then grabbed Sara and pulled her to him. If his non-verbal form of communication fazed her, she didn't show it. In fact, her hands were threaded in his hair before his lips even made contact. But when they did, *aw man*, it was mind-blowing.

She was soft and pliant and so damn welcoming. Then she moaned—no, it was more of a groan—and before he knew it, his hands were back on her ass, a place he'd spent every waking moment dreaming they could be, but reality was even better because she took that as a green light to wrap one of those toned and silky legs around his thigh and shimmy even closer. Which he had no problem with because it caused her skirt to shift, and with a little negotiating, his hands slipped down and under and, *thank you, Jesus,* she was wearing a thong and his life was complete. .

Except there he stood, upstanding guy that he was, with his hands up her dress while she was clinging to him and panting against his mouth, on the patio where anyone could see.

Even though there was no one on the street, he'd promised a secret affair and he was determined to pull through.

"Inside," he said.

Improper dance hold in full effect, he spun her around and through the front room until he felt the couch behind him. He sat back and took her with him, loving how her skirt rode up her thighs almost as much as he loved how she felt straddling him.

"I thought me naked in your bed was number one on the bucket list?"

"It is, but number three was you naked and often," he said against her neck. "I figure the best way is to start at the bottom and work our way up. But first things first. Stand for a second."

She did and he reached up to grab the little bow at the back of her neck, the one that had been teasing him to distraction, and gave a light tug. The straps untwined and the entire top of her dress slid down to pool at her feet, and that was all it took for fucking Christmas in February.

CHAPTER 12

Sara didn't move as she watched breathlessly while Trey's gaze slid ever-so-slowly from her breasts down to her stomach. By the time he got to her red thong, she was shaking with want.

"Come here," he said, a low rasp to his voice that made her shiver in the best way possible.

He palmed her hips and drew her toward him, spreading his thighs to make room for her. She rested a hand on his shoulders and used the other to take off her shoe.

"Always so proper," he *tsked*, his strong fingers wrapping around her wrist and stopping her. "Improper rules clearly state that the shoes stay on."

"Oh," she breathed, resting both hands on his shoulder. She'd never done anything improper in her life, but she was ready to be courageous. Improper smile in place, she willed the nervousness in her voice to relax. "Then where do my hands go? You know, so that I *know* when I've got it right."

"Right here." He threaded them in his hair. "Hold tight, sweetheart, because you and I are going to be gasping and moaning all up in each other's space."

And then he was threading his own fingers through the back of her new silk undies—*thank you, Bolder Holder*—molding them to her butt, and pulling her so far into his space she could feel him hard against her thigh.

He smelled delicious, and felt even better when he leaned in and pressed a languid, wet kiss right above her belly button. She liked improper. A lot.

"That feels . . ."

"That feels what, Sara?" he whispered against her stomach, his gaze meeting hers through his thick lashes.

She swallowed, not sure how to explain. All of the loneliness she carried with her was gone and that empty space, the one in her chest that ached so bad it'd gone numb, was warm and full and felt, "Nice. That feels nice."

"I see we have some work to do, because I know we can do better than nice." She felt him smile against her skin. "The question is, where do we start?"

She had a few suggestions, some ranked higher than others, but before she could tell him, he moved. It happened so fast she barely saw it coming. One moment she was standing in front of him, the next she was sprawled out over the coffee table and he was leaning over her.

"How about here?" Then his mouth covered hers.

It was startling and moving and she felt lost and found all at the same time. He kissed her as though he couldn't get enough of her, as though he could never get enough. And that worked just fine for her. Trey was a kissing God and his hands—masterful. They were everywhere all at once, and driving her out of her mind.

So her hands got busy too, working on the buttons of his shirt. She stopped kissing him long enough to slide it off and yank his undershirt over his head. But when he settled over her again, he didn't fuse himself to her mouth. Oh no, he rested a hand at the small of her back and pulled her so that she was arched off the table and then without warning he kissed the undersides of her breasts, moving up until—time literally stopped.

So he did it again, pulling her deep into his mouth, and scraping the tip of her nipple with his teeth.

"You like that?" he asked against her breast. She wanted to scream *yes,* but he did it again and—good God, why had she gone so long without sex?

He looked up into her eyes and smiled. "I'll take that as a yeah." Sara nodded. It was all that she could manage. "I'd like to change it to a fuck-yeah."

She wasn't big on talking during sex and had no idea what a fuck-yeah could be, but she wanted to find out. Desperately. So she swallowed and said, "Please."

"Such manners," he whispered as he slid to the floor and kneeled between her legs. "We'll work on that."

He scooted her to the edge of the table, his mouth inches away from her number one choice in fantasy destinations. Her stomach trembled with anticipation and she found that she couldn't look away, especially when Trey smiled up at her right before he placed an open-mouthed kiss in the center of her silk. And this time she did scream.

"Yes!"

"Now, that was better, but still not what I was going for. Maybe if I tugged these down." Her undies were gone. "And went a little more like—"

"Oh my God!" she groaned, her back tearing off the table as the slide of his soft tongue covered her entirely.

"Closer. But still not quite there."

"Yes, there," she moaned, her hips pushing forward until his tongue was pressing on the little bundle of nerves. "Right there."

"Bossy," he mused but got down to business. He didn't rush her, didn't even pull back when she squirmed on the table, pressing up to get the right amount of pressure. The man was all patience and practiced grace and he led her closer and closer toward the most sensual experience of her life.

She still wasn't sure what a fuck-yeah was, so she gripped his head and tried to hurry him along. Which of course only made him go slower, which only made her hotter.

Then, without warning, he slid a finger in and she was beginning to understand. When another finger joined the effort, he picked up the pace and she knew without a doubt that her fuck-yeah was right there, just out of reach. All he had to do was move a little to the left and up—she shifted her hips—and yeah, right there, right there where—

"Oh." Her head went fuzzy from every nerve in her body giving a standing *O* and a high-five at the same time, and, "Oh. My!"

"What kind of 'Oh my' are we talking?" He wanted to know.

It was an, *Oh my, you're magic and don't you dare stop because I'm almost there*, but she couldn't breathe let alone speak. So she just opened her legs further, inviting him closer and he got the picture.

"Yeah, me too," he whispered against her, his breath on her hot skin.

His fingers were heaven, the way they stroked and pressed. Then his tongue was back in play and her orgasm took her by surprise, everything inside her tightening to the point of pain and suddenly shattering. "Oh my . . . *Yeah!*"

Holy moly, she understood what he'd been talking about. Only she couldn't process it quite yet, because her body was still riding out wave after wave of pure Trey-induced bliss, with her half in and half out of consciousness when—

"Oh, fu—" was all she was able to get out when Trey gripped her hips and pushed himself fully inside of her, all of him, stretching her beyond capacity. She didn't remember him getting undressed or locking her legs around his waist. But there they were, and he felt so good. So good that *fuck yeah* didn't cut it, but even if it had, all she could do was moan.

"Closer," he affirmed, and the roughness in his voice brought her as close as a girl could get without spontaneously combusting. "But still not all the way there."

No, but she wanted to be. She almost was, but he stopped moving and started talking, which was driving her insane. He just stared at her, building the anticipation as he slowly lowered his head, making her heart pound and her body strain to get closer.

"Let's see what we can do about that, shall we?"

She went to nod but he took her mouth, stroking and teasing her and—*wow*—the man could kiss. She gave a little moan of approval, because this was what she was talking about. Less lip flapping, more tongue action.

With a deep groan, he gripped her hips and gave a little squeeze. Okay, a lot of squeeze, possessive and hot, and it had her going up in flames. He slid one palm up her side, brushing the edge of her breast, before slipping it under her head. His other hand headed south to caress her butt, pulling her toward him, until she felt so full, so complete.

She swallowed hard. "This is . . . Wow."

She didn't know how else to explain it. The way he held her, touched her, kissed her, made her feel adored and treasured—like this moment was as special to him as it was to her.

Trey pulled back, his eyes heavy with lust, but his expression one of awe. Neither of them moved or spoke. She lay on the coffee table naked except for her red heels, which were digging into his ass, her hair a mess and his fingerprints all over her as he took in every detail.

"I know," he whispered and pressed a gentle kiss to her forehead.

And just like that, casual went out the window. The way he was looking at her shook her entire being and, *oh boy*, this didn't feel like short term.

Nope, with him, Sara felt alive and somehow whole. A feeling she had missed, and now that she'd found it again, she desperately wanted to cling to with everything that she had.

Afraid that she'd say the wrong thing and scare him—or herself—Sara swiveled her hips and clenched, relieved when his eyes rolled into the back of his head.

"Jesus, Sara," he breathed. "Slow down or I'm not going to be able to—" she rose up, shoving closer, pulling him in deeper. "Fuck!"

"More?" she panted.

With a smile he said, "Fuck, yeah."

That did it. She squeezed with everything her legs had left, molding herself to him as he crushed her between the hard wood of the coffee table and the even harder plains of his body. His lips, however, stayed gentle, melting Sara's heart, as they slowly traveled down her neck to her shoulder until the past two years fell away and all that she could feel was him and the incredible friction.

She lost herself in the slow withdraws, and even slower thrusts. She loved that sex with Trey was like a steady climb, not a sprint to the finish. He wasn't the kind of guy who could be rushed, he wanted her to enjoy every moment, ride out the pleasure for her. But then he whispered her name, almost absently as though he hadn't meant to, and that, combined with the weight of his body on hers, inside of her, pushed her over the edge, his name exploding from her lips.

Trey rocked a few more times and then followed her with an explosion of his own. His entire body was still shaking when he rose up on his elbows and, oh God indeed, he was breathing as hard as she was.

"So?" He grinned, breaking the spell and lightening the mood and, most important, making her laugh. Which was a whole lot better than what she felt like doing: crying.

"I thought it," she admitted.

"I guess then we need to move this lesson to the bedroom so I can really work my magic." He raised a brow. "Since you were *almost there*."

Sara's hand flew to her mouth. Had she said that out loud? The smug factor in his expression told her that, yes, in fact, she had screamed it.

Trey leaned down and playfully nipped her fingers. She had barely moved them when he snagged her lower lip between his teeth—and a phone rang in the distance.

With a defeated huff he collapsed into her, burying his face in her hair. "Is it too much to hope for that my family would leave me alone for one night?" He lifted his head and pouted. "Just one night."

She leaned up and kissed him. "I think it's my family."

"Let it go to voice mail." His lips were back on her neck.

"It could be Cooper," she said, shoving him until he rolled off of her with a grunt.

Giving herself a second to get her land legs back, she grabbed her purse off of the couch and pulled out her phone. *Great.*

She walked to the kitchen area before answering. "Hey, Roman."

Trey sat up, his gloriously naked chest puffed out, and his pout turned into a full-on frown. On his feet, he quickly disposed of the condom—at least someone had been thinking—and stalked naked toward her. She shook her head and held out a hand to stop him.

She was so busy taking in the full-frontal view, admiring the delicious contours of his body that she almost missed what Roman had said.

"What?" she said, taking one last look at Trey and his pecs before mommy-mode went into full effect. "Cooper's sick?"

With a single nod, Trey began gathering up her things.

"I think it was too much pizza and roughhousing, but yeah, you should come and get him," Roman said into the phone.

"I'll be there in ten minutes." Sara ended the call and found Trey in front of her, fully dressed in a pair of dark-washed jeans and a long-sleeved T-shirt.

"Here." He handed over her dress, which was wrinkled, and her purse. No underwear. "I'll have my car brought around. We can be there in five minutes. Tops."

Sara tied the straps to her dress and caught his hand before he could pick up the hotel phone. "You don't need to do that."

"What? And drive your car?" He smiled, but it was tense. "I still need time to regroup from the minivan before I drive a station wagon."

"You can't come."

"Why?" He sounded genuinely concerned, and confused. So was Sara, but this was the hard part of their arrangement. The part that was going to save her heart—and Cooper's.

"We promised to keep this between us." Sara placed a hand on his chest. "You showing up with me dressed like this on a Friday night doesn't say friends without the precursor of benefits."

Trey released a long breath and stared at the ceiling. His defeated expression proved her point. Even though it shouldn't sting, it did. The truth was, as long as he was leaving, friends with benefits was all that they could ever be.

"We could say that your car broke down and I happened to drive by."

"Used that with Heather and it was true. She still didn't believe me." She leveled him with a gaze to show just how serious this was, but he was too busy staring at her mouth to notice. "Plus, you what? Drive me there to grunt at Roman, pick up Cooper, and then go back to my house where three minutes after Cooper falls asleep we wind up on the couch? Naked?"

His hands slid around her hips and he let go a lethal grin. "Works for me."

"And when Cooper comes out asking for a glass of water and, whoops, sees us, *you'll* spend next week explaining the mating habits of humans to him, because I'm not ready for that talk yet."

Trey released a breath. "Right. Just be careful. This could be Roman's way of getting you over for his 'night under the stars.'"

"Even if it was, I wouldn't do that." Sara rolled onto the tips of her toes and pressed a gentle kiss to his mouth, then put some serious heat behind it. "*You're* my February, Trey. And as long as you're here, the only person I want to spend time with is you."

By Monday afternoon Trey had wrapped up the last interview and narrowed the fifteen candidates down to a solid three. And just in time. Gabe and the rest of the DeLuca delegation were due back Wednesday afternoon and, if they could agree on the new sales manager by Friday, Trey could begin training next week and be in Italy come March first.

The same exact day Sara would be free to date someone else. Someone who wasn't the manny, and therefore wouldn't need to be kept a secret, he thought as Cooper came racing down the hallway, a blue cape flapping behind him.

The kid leapt into the kitchen and struck a pose with his legs in attention and his hands on his hips. "Suited up and ready to go." He stopped, his smile faltering. "Where's your costume?"

"I'm wearing it," Trey said, smiling at his cleverness.

Today was superhero day at Mighty Mites, the one day a month that every kid looked forward to. With Cooper still on suspension, Trey had suggested that they have their own superhero day, which earned him a high five and a hug that, if he was being honest, got him a little choked up.

Cooper was dressed as Batman. Trey, short one costume, and refusing to wear a pair of blue leggings left over from Sara's dance recital, went with Superman's alter ego. A good thing since a shopping run was in order. They needed eggs and cupcake mix for the bake sale tomorrow at Cooper's school.

Trey straightened his tie, channeled Superman, and said, "I'm Clark Kent."

Cooper took in Trey's suit and frowned. "But he's not a superhero."

"Sure he is." He grabbed his car keys off the counter and pocketed the short grocery list he'd made while Cooper had been getting his superhero on.

"He's the paperboy." Cooper swayed back and forth on his feet, taking his sweet time to inspect Trey's costume. "Which would be fine if you have a bicycle. Do you have a bike?"

"I have a car. A fast car. With a sun roof."

"Well, that's not a bike, now is it?"

And wasn't that just his life. Always right skill set, wrong party. Hell, a mini-man in spandex and plastic boots was taking pity on him because he couldn't tell the difference between two wheels and four.

"Nope, it's not," Trey said scuffing his way to the door. "But Clark Kent has a job, which means he makes money. Lots of it. Enough to buy cupcakes."

"Uh-huh." Cooper didn't believe a word Trey was spewing. But he wanted cupcakes so he wisely followed Trey out to the car.

By the time they reached the baking aisle at Pickers Produce, Meats, and More, Trey realized that he should have ordered a dozen cupcakes from Lexi.

Who knew there were so many choices in cupcake land?

"Can we get these?" Cooper asked, waving two packages of candy Batman decorations. "We can make the icing blue like Mommy does and then put these on top."

"Sounds like a plan." Trey dropped two boxes of cake mix into the basket, and then dropped in two more. Because Clark Kent was also the brains of the operation and, like any good superhero, was always prepared, he added four tubs of icing: two chocolate and two vanilla. "Now we need eggs."

"And popcorn?" Cooper asked, beaming up at him. "For the movie? Mommy always pops popcorn. With extra butter on it."

Cooper's stomachache caused him to miss the movie part of Roman's campout. With Sara working until eight and Trey wanting to make Coop's night a little special, he promised him their own campout and screening of *Cars*. After they accomplished a decent batch of cupcakes.

"Sure," Trey said, heading toward the chip and snack aisle.

"This is going to be the best movie night ever." Coop tossed the candy Batman symbols into the basket and slid his smaller hand into Trey's.

"What are you doing?"

Coop kept walking. "Holding your hand."

"We're just walking to the snack aisle, it's only right here," Trey pointed out because the kid's hand was warm and sticky and—Trey bent down to sniff—smelled like glue. "Not like we're crossing the street or anything."

Coop looked up at Trey as though they were back to the two-wheels-versus-four conversation. "Sometimes it's just better to hold hands."

So Trey held Coop's hand, smiling as he led him down the aisle toward the back of the store, his plastic boots clomping against the floor and sounding like a storm trooper sweeping the area. When Trey saw the selection of snacks, he knew that popcorn wasn't going to cut it. Not if tonight was going to be the Best Movie Night Ever.

Between the two of them, they loaded up the basket with a variety of chips and three different dips, and they added a box of graham crackers and some kind of chewy-fruity snacks that Trey would bet his fast car with a sunroof didn't contain a single drop of fruit. Rounding the girlie-aisle, Trey spotted the coconut-scented lotion Sara liked so much and, remembering that she was almost out, dropped it into the cart.

At the produce aisle Cooper picked up a banana. Trey had no idea what it was for, but the way Coop held it to his chest instead of dropping it in the basket said that it was important. Which was why, since the kid was practically strangling it, Trey grabbed another one—just in case.

"Matt," Cooper said, jumping up and down and pointing to a three-foot-tall boy who stood at the meat counter dressed in all green, looking more like a miniature Jolly Green Giant than the Green Lantern. Then again, Trey was in a suit trying to pass as Superman.

Trying being the operative word, Trey thought ruefully, taking in the six-foot-three behemoth of a man standing next to Matt and holding a full rack of ribs. Dressed in a costume that was all kinds of badass, complete with a flowing cape and enough rippling abs and bulging biceps to intimidate even the real Superman, Roman was ready to save the world and get the girl.

Trey looked down at his loafers and admitted that he should have worn the blue tights. At least he wouldn't have looked like he was ready to push papers and audit someone into boredom.

"Hey fellas," Roman said, guy-next-door charm in place. "Good to see you, Batman."

Cooper beamed.

Roman took a dramatic step back and shook his head in mock surprise. "I mean, Cooper. Wow, for a minute there I thought . . ." Again with the head shake. Coop ate it up . . . and dropped Trey's hand. "You look just like him. Spitting image."

"Thanks, Superman," Coop said with hero worship in his eyes.

"Who's your buddy? No wait, let me guess." Roman sent Trey a sly wink, as though he didn't know to play along. "007."

An international spy was way more impressive than a paperboy. He drove fast cars. And *always* got the girl. Why hadn't Trey thought of that?

"Oh, wait, James Bond isn't a superhero." Right, because of that. Not to mention Bond never stuck with the same girl. "I know, Commissioner Gordon?"

Giggling, Cooper shook his head. "Nope, this is Clark Kent. Paperboy. Only he doesn't got a bike."

"Not paperboy. He works at the paper," Trey said.

Cooper shrugged.

There Trey stood, paperboy extraordinaire with coconut-scented lotion and cupcake mix, looking up at a guy who drove a big, red fire engine with a siren and had enough steak and ribs in his cart to impress an army of real superheroes.

Trey sighed. Roman was also the kind of guy to impress the girls because he had stable, selfless, and husband-material sewn into the back of his cape. Oh, and he was only looking for one girl.

"Good to see you, Clark Kent," Roman said, shaking Trey's hand. "Making cupcakes?"

"For the bake sale tomorrow," Trey said, feeling like Manny of the Year.

Roman leaned in, as though imparting a great and ancient wisdom. "If you add a little pudding mix to the batter they'll come out extra moist."

"Yeah, it's already on the list," Trey said, wondering if he meant dry pudding or the already-prepared kind in the cups. Then made a mental list to buy both.

"We're having a movie night," Coop volunteered, slipping his hand back in Trey's in a sign of little buddy support. "With popcorn and candy. In a fort!"

"Sounds great." Roman looked at Trey, and he really meant it. Proving that the guy was also selfless. "Matt and I were going to practice knots Saturday, to prepare for the merit-badge test. If you want, you and your mom are more than welcome to join us after she closes up the studio."

Selfless but interested in Sara.

The guy was politely throwing his hat into the ring, and suddenly being Sara's secret didn't feel all that great. He wanted to say that Sara was already wearing his hat, that in fact she had put it on the other night in his suite and it wasn't coming off—well, not until March, which even sounded lame in his head.

So Trey kept his mouth shut, even resisted the urge to remind everyone that *he* was the reigning knot champion in town and, if anything, Roman could learn a few things from him.

"Can we have a sleepover after?" Matt asked.

"I don't see why not," Roman said, smiling at Trey. "I'll talk with Sara about it."

Matt's face went wide with excitement and he started jumping up and down chanting "Sleepover!" Roman's grin said he was chanting the same thing.

Coop, however, looked about as excited over the dual family sleepover as Trey did. "I don't know if I'll get my merit badge at camp cuz the application is still on the fridge and Mom keeps saying, 'We'll see.'"

Which Trey knew meant "no." He also knew that Sara was doing everything she could so that her son wouldn't have to miss out, but in the end, the result would be the same. There was no way she could take off three days to go camping with Coop, not with Heather being gone.

"Tell your mom I can hold off for another day or two," Roman offered.

Coop just shook his head, his plastic boots scuffing at the floor. "That's okay. I didn't really want to go."

Trey almost asked him if he felt his nose growing, because he may have only been sitting Coop for a week, but the kid only ever talked about three things: cars, superheroes, and the Mighty Mites campout. The trembling of his lower lip had Trey tugging him a little closer.

"You sure, buddy? It's the big race," Trey said quietly and Cooper nodded.

"Hunter said that because he don't got a daddy, his mom would take him," Matt informed the group. Trey's jaw clenched to keep from saying something that would get him—and most likely Cooper—in trouble. "And then he'd have to sleep with the Lady Bugs, cuz it's no girls allowed."

"When did he tell you that?" Roman asked.

"At movie night," Coop whispered, which explained the stomach-ache and early phone call.

Trey couldn't help it. He set the basket on the ground and squatted down, getting eye-level and taking Coop by the shoulders, like he'd seen Gabe do with Holly a million times.

Coop looked up and what Trey saw in his eyes reached out and pulled him in. All the way in. Any plans he had of keeping it fun, simple, of not getting involved, vanished. He knew—just *knew*—what that look meant. And it brought back every messed-up emotion and insecurity he had, reminding him of how hard growing up without a dad around could be on a boy.

At least he had his brothers to show him how to rebuild a car-buretor or round second base. And there was always someone to partner him in the annual father-son baseball game or help him out with guy stuff. But Cooper had no one.

"You won't have to sleep with the Lady Bugs. Hunter was just being an as—" Roman coughed and Trey wisely changed direction. "You worked hard on your car and deserve to race."

"He's right. You earned your place, Cooper." Roman looked down at Cooper, who was starting to sniffle, and gave a nod. "I was going to talk to you about this on Friday, but you went home before I could mention that if your mom can't make it to the campout, Matt and I were thinking it would be cool if you wanted to sleep in our tent. You know, hang with us for the entire weekend. Be part of Team Blaze."

Coop's eyes went big with awe. "Really?"

"You bet. Would you like that?"

"That would be," Coop looked at Trey and back to Roman, "awesome."

Trey resisted the urge to point out that *awesome* was their word. And saying it with the enemy went against every law known to man. It was almost like going to the big game with someone who's rooting for the other team. It just wasn't done.

But Roman was offering a solution that made everyone happy. Well, everyone except Trey, which made no sense at all. The last place he'd want to spend one of his last weekends in St. Helena was with a bunch of grimy kids in the middle of a field. Not when he could be at home, with a very naked Sara, having a campout of their own, with him demonstrating his knot skills with a scarf and the bedpost.

"Actually," Trey said, wondering what the hell he was doing, "if Sara couldn't get the time off of work, I was going to take Cooper."

CHAPTER 13

"You promised him what?" Sara asked, doing her best to keep her voice down. She didn't want to wake Cooper and she didn't want to ruin her good mood.

After a fabulous rehearsal, Sara arrived to find Cooper clean and ready for bed with a cape over his race-car pajamas. He was also huddled under a makeshift fort, hugging a bowl of popcorn, and snoring. The sight of her little guy, smiling and content, melted her heart.

The sight of the sexy guy next to him melted something else altogether. Trey had ditched the suit for a pair of green jogging shorts that hung dangerously low on his hips, a fitted black T-shirt, and a yellow cape. His hair was sticking up in the back, he had popcorn stuck to his chest, and when he sent her a sleepy smile, Sara almost forgave him for making a promise to her son that he had no right to make. Because he had turned what could have been a disappointing day for Cooper into an evening her son would never forget.

"You sound upset," Trey said from inside the fort and Cooper fussed a little in his sleep. "Are you upset?"

"No. I'm not—" Sara broke off because, one, she was upset. Mad that Trey had offered to take Cooper to the Mighty Mites campout without bothering to consult her. And two, her voice caused Cooper to flop over on his side, sending popcorn all over the carpet.

Trey put a finger to his mouth, then shimmied out of the fort—backward. And what a view—yup, squeeze-a-licious. It was hard to stay mad at a guy with a flowing yellow tablecloth for a cape and an epic case of bed head. But Sara tried her best.

"In here." He laced their fingers, which felt way too good, and led her to the kitchen, which was an even bigger disaster than the front room. Dirty dishes lined the sink, batter was stuck to the ceiling, and—Sara lifted her shoe—there was a thin dusting of a suspicious white powder all over the floor.

"Flour?"

"Powdered sugar." Trey pointed to a tray on the table holding two-dozen beautiful Batman cupcakes. "Cooper asked if he could make the cupcakes 'winter' when I got a phone call. I came back and realized what he meant. I'll clean it up before I go."

But Sara was too busy admiring the cupcakes to answer. They were amazing. Like DC Comics hired Martha Stewart to come up with the perfect Batman cupcake. There were twelve Batmans and twelve Robins, but no dusting of snow. "Did you have to make a new batch?"

"Four batches, actually," Trey admitted. "Then I gave up and called Lexi. She dropped these off about an hour ago."

"You didn't have to do that," she said, turning around to face him.

"It was either that or run the risk of burning the kitchen down." He walked toward her, stopping so close she had to look up at him.

"I'm sorry I made you mad," he whispered. "That wasn't my goal."

"I know. And I'm not—"

"Mad?" He ran his hands down her arms and laced their fingers and gave a little squeeze. "Yeah, you are."

She squeezed back. "I just wish you would have talked to me first, because I could have told you that Cooper hasn't slept a single night away from home, so starting with two doesn't seem smart."

"You're right," he said carefully. "I should have. And maybe we can have a trial run. I can have him sleep over at my place or we could set up the tent in the backyard."

"I don't know." Trey looked at her like she was some psycho helicopter mom who never let her kid out of her sight.

"We can give it a try," he said all reasonable, which made her want to hit him. "Look, Coop really wants to go and show off his car and get his merit badge and do guy stuff with his buddies. I know that you can't take that much time off. So when Roman said that he could share his tent and I—"

"Please tell me you didn't do this because you think I'm interested in Roman."

"No."

She raised a brow.

"Okay, maybe a little. Roman was wearing a Superman costume and carting around slabs of beef and I was all 'Clark Kent *is* a superhero and look at my lotion.'" He smiled. She did not. But it was hard. "Mostly, though, I did it because Cooper would have had fun with Roman and his kid playing campout. Until he figured out that he was the add-on. The kid who didn't have a dad. I've been there, Sara, and it sucks. I didn't want that for him."

Neither did Sara. And it was really hard to stay mad at Trey when he looked so upset and was only trying to save her son from disappointment. But his plan had the potential for complete heartbreak if they weren't careful.

"Did he tell you that he came home sick Friday because that asshat Hunter was giving him a hard time for not having a dad?"

"No," Sara breathed through the pinch in her chest. "I just don't know if your taking him is the best solution."

Trey studied her for a long moment. "So you'd rather him not go, than to go with me?"

His voice nearly broke her heart. Trey was a great guy, who was trying to make a little boy's dream of going to camp a reality. But what he saw as merely a few days of fun Cooper would see as a new best friend.

"No." Sara wrapped her arms around his middle and looked up so that he could see the truth in her eyes. "I trust you, Trey. You are great with him and I know that you'd be Cooper's first pick. With you, I know that he would be safe and have fun. Too much fun."

"This is where you deliver the 'but' clause," Trey said and Sara wondered how many times he'd been told he wasn't the right guy for the job. In this case, he was the perfect guy for the job, only he wasn't applying.

"You're offering a temporary buddy, when he's looking for a daddy. There is nothing about that situation that could end well."

Trey gave a single nod, but it was full of disappointment. At her or himself, she couldn't tell, but either way, it didn't make sense. He was the one who made it more than clear that he wasn't a long-term bet.

"I don't want him to miss out on going, Trey." He had worked hard. And deserved to go. "But I also don't want him to lose out when March rolls around and you leave. He wouldn't understand."

Sara barely understood. She was already a mix of intense emotions after just one night, she could only imagine what Cooper would feel after a fun-filled guys' weekend away where everyone was palling around with their dads. Cooper was smart, he'd make the connection. And when he did . . . Sara didn't want to go there. The mere idea hurt her heart.

"I don't want to confuse him," Trey said, pulling her against him and resting his cheek on the crown of her head.

"And I don't want to have to tell him he can't go," she whispered into his chest, loving the way he glided his hands up and down her spine.

"Then don't." He pulled back and the look he sent her spoke to every womanly part of her body. "Let me have a talk with him. Explain that I'm moving to Italy and this is just a couple of guys hanging out, racing cars, and building fires."

"Fire and racing are not two words that make a mom feel all warm and cozy. And," she paused taking a brave breath, "what if something goes wrong and I'm not there?"

Because that was what happened to her. People left and never came back. Her father had craved freedom, Garrett adventure, and her grandmother peace in her old age. All of them had their reasons, but the result was the same—Sara had lost another person she loved. She would give anything to go back and tell them that she loved them, beg them not to leave her.

Sara knew that she was overprotective of Cooper, but life had taught her to hold tight to what she loved. Because once they were gone—it was forever.

Trey stared at her for a long moment, saying nothing, the fierceness in his expression radiating through her entire being and cracking open something inside of her.

He got it. Trey understood the pain of loss, it was there hanging heavy in his eyes. He might be a runner, Sara thought, but he ran for a reason. It was the same reason she clung so tightly to her world.

Fear.

"It's two days, Sara," he reasoned. "A lot can happen in two days."

"Not with me there," he whispered. Against her lips. "Just give me a chance to make this right."

"As long as you promise me he won't be crushed," she whispered back, praying he was true to his word that he wouldn't disappoint her.

He nodded and since their lips were right there, a breath apart, he kissed her. Soft, and reassuring, and everything she needed in that moment.

Sara allowed herself to float for just a moment before pulling back. "No blurring the lines, remember?"

"Lines," he repeated. Against her throat, her neck, and lower. "Where is that line again? Nothing below the waist, right?"

"Wrong rule," she breathed, loving how he could make her let go of the stress from the day, the bad memories that always seemed to linger, and enjoy the moment.

"That's your problem. Too many rules." Trey covered her mouth with his completely. This time his lips were hot and hungry and—

"Mmmmm. You taste like frosting."

He was laughing when he pulled back. "Cooper's specialty."

"Graham crackers with frosting?"

"And bananas. You didn't get a good enough taste, come here."

He went for her mouth but she smacked his chest and pushed back.

"Here is the line." She drew an imaginary line around her body. "No crossing it. Not with Cooper down the hall."

"That was a box, not a line. And you said we had to be creative." He took a step forward, caging her between the counter and his body. "Sex in a man-made snowstorm counts as creative if you ask me. We could even lie down and make naked snow angels." He trailed a finger between her breasts. "You go first."

Sara warmed. He was even charming when he argued. "How about you help me clean up the snow? Then tomorrow at ten fifteen I come to your hotel room and we get creative. In that bed. I have a forty-five-minute break between classes."

"No good," he said. His finger grazed over her nipple, "Five minutes to change your shoes," down to her stomach, "another five to lock up," around her belly button, "and five to get to my suite. And another ten to get you back." His hand stopped right at the hem of her dance skirt and his gaze met hers. "That only gives me twenty minutes to be creative, and sweetheart, I need every second for what I'm planning."

"Then what do you suggest?" she asked, not sure if she could wait much past tomorrow to kiss him again.

"I'll come to you," he said. "And we can mark that pole off my bucket list."

The sun was actually shining when Sara pulled into her driveway. Because of a last-minute Garden Society meeting, most of her senior ladies had called to say that they wouldn't make the Waltz and Rumba Infusion class—leaving only Stan and Harvey. When both refused to partner the other, Sara called it a night.

Grabbing the pizza from the passenger seat, she went in the house excited to surprise her guys. Only when she reached the kitchen and looked out in the backyard, she was the one who found herself staring in awe.

Heart in her throat, Sara crept out on the back porch, careful to stay beneath the shade of the overhang so as not to interrupt the male bonding that was transpiring on the lawn below. Trey and Cooper stood over what appeared to be every bit of Garrett's old camping gear, and some she didn't recognize, cataloguing it.

Both were dressed in well-worn jeans, ball caps, and matching camo T-shirts. Only Trey's shirt was dangling from his back pocket. He must have been at this for quite a while because even in the chilly winter air, his skin was slick with heat, which made her slick and hot. And when he picked up a tattered looking tent and began unrolling it on the flattest part of the lawn, muscles that Sara had explored just yesterday during their pole-dancing lesson bunched and flexed as he moved, and she had to remind herself to breathe.

"Can you see if there's a mallet over there?" Trey asked, dumping out the contents of the tent bag. Six metal stakes, a bundle of rope, and some kind of supports fell to the grass.

"There's a metal one and a rubber one," Cooper said, his head stuck in a giant metal tool box. Garrett's toolbox.

"The metal one's a hammer, the rubber one's a mallet," Trey explained. "Both will work, but the mallet will sting less. Take your pick and bring it over so we can drive the stake into the ground."

Cooper looked back and forth as though this were a trick question, which would ruin their fun day if he got it wrong. Biting his lip, he settled on the mallet, then ran over to Trey, dragging the tool the entire way.

"Good choice." Cooper beamed at the praise. "And if you ever find yourself out in the middle of nowhere and forgot your tools, you know what you do?"

Smile gone, concentration face on, Cooper shook his head.

"You grab a big rock."

"You want me to grab a big rock?" Cooper asked, already scouting the backyard for the perfect rock.

"Let's use the mallet first."

He must lift all of those cases of wine he sells, Sara thought as Trey grabbed a stake and muscled it into the ground. Then he turned to Cooper and, instead of taking the tool and getting the job done quickly, Trey patiently explained how to properly hold the mallet and even steadied the stake while Cooper took a few swings—not a single one made contact.

"Try holding it a little higher on the handle, like a baseball bat."

Cooper's face fell, because he didn't play baseball. Sara didn't even think he owned a bat. She was about to step forward and explain when Trey moved behind her son and fixed his grip, doing the first swing in tandem. The mallet made solid contact and Cooper looked up at Trey stunned. Then a big smile spread across his face.

"See how that felt?" Trey took a step back. "Now, you try."

Cooper did. And the thud of the contact threw him a little off balance. Not that he noticed, not with the way Trey gave him a big manly fist bump as though he'd single-handedly driven the stake through the earth with one swing.

Sara swallowed, so overcome by the wonder of her little guy having fun and bonding with such an amazing man, she decided to not focus on the fact that Trey was leaving. At least not for today. Because right here, right now, Trey was exactly what her son needed.

He was also what she needed, her heart whispered.

They made quick work of the other stakes and Trey helped Cooper thread the rope through the top of the tent and, after a thorough lesson in square knots, they secured it to each of the poles.

"Hey guys," she said, leaning over the rail.

Cooper looked up and his eyes went wide. "Mommy! Look! We're making a tent."

"I see that," she said right as Cooper launched himself up the three steps to the porch and into her arms, clinging to her legs like a koala. She gave him a squeeze, only he was already wiggling back to the ground.

"And I malleted the stake into the ground and even tied the rope with square knots, just like the ones for my merit badge test. And we're going to do pretend campouts in the tent, like boot camp."

"Boot camp?" Sara looked at Trey whose gaze, dark and heated, tracked right to her skirt, and a shot of hot need pulsed through her body.

Sara had been so excited for the unexpected night off that she hadn't bothered to change before closing up the studio. Or at least that's what she'd told herself. That wearing it home had nothing to do with the fact that, earlier that morning in the studio, Trey had slowly peeled it off her body—with his teeth.

Trey cleared his throat and made his way up the steps toward her. He was all bare-chested and sweaty. It was hard for her to focus.

"I was talking to Coop about the campout and he said he had never slept in a tent, so I figured that he and I could set one up and for the rest of the week, take naps in it." Trey shrugged. "You know, test it out."

"Trey said that even soldiers do a test run so that they don't get to the base and have the other soldiers make fun of them cuz they don't know how to make a tent." Cooper tugged at his ball cap.

"That was smart." And thoughtful. And so incredibly insightful. Sara felt herself fall a little more in like with him.

"And look." Cooper yanked at the bottom of his shirt and pulled it snug.

"Team Bro," Sara read, her eyes rising to meet Trey's, and something much more than desire hummed between them. Something warmer, and gentler, and—

Something that was not going to happen, Sara told herself. So what if he was funny and made her legs turn to mush? They'd made a deal. And when that calendar page changed, he'd be gone, off on another adventure that didn't include her. Or Cooper.

Stay strong.

"Uh-huh," Cooper went on. "You know like Team Brady or Team Lock, only since we don't got the same last name and we're best bros, Trey had them say this. And look." Cooper turned around and pointed to a mission statement written on the back. "'A unit based on friendship, fast cars, and juice boxes.' And we're going to wear them every day at camp."

Yeah, so much for staying strong.

"Why don't you go get washed up and throw on your jammies? I was thinking we'll eat dinner while watching a movie." Sara tugged the bill of Cooper's hat up to see his face. "I brought home pizza."

"Pizza?" Cooper hooted. "Did you know Trey's moving to Italy? They invented pizza and the Ferrari. And he's going to go to the factory and send me pictures. Isn't that awesome?"

"Awesome," Sara repeated what was fast becoming his favorite word. He used it in reference to dinners that lacked green, when his favorite show came on, and almost every time he talked about Trey. And Sara would have to agree, Trey was pretty awesome. "Actually, why don't you wash up then bring the pizza out here and we can all eat in the tent?"

"You sure?" Trey said, sending a pointed glance at Cooper, who was already hustling through the back door. "I can just order room service when I get back."

"Please stay."

Trey groaned and looked up at the sky. She knew he wanted to stay, just like she knew that if he did, things could get real messy, real fast. Which was why he was fussing with his hat and looking perplexed.

She rose up on her toes and placed a gentle kiss on his cheek.

"What was that for?"

"For making my kid feel," she smiled up at him, "awesome. And for making everything okay. No, better than okay." She kissed the corner of his mouth. "And for putting him first."

"We put up a tent." He shrugged self-consciously and Sara found it odd that for such a confident—often bordering on cocky—man, Trey had a hard time taking a genuine compliment.

"It wasn't what you did. It was how you did it. You included him, made him a part of the process, made him one of your pals."

"Coop was scared that the guys were going to laugh at him because he'd never been camping, and I know how bad it is to be the smallest or the youngest or the odd man out."

"I imagine it was hard being the youngest in such a large family with so many boys." It would have been exceptionally hard after they lost their parents.

"Sometimes it was great," he explained, taking her hand. "There was always someone older to help me out. But other times . . . Man, it sucked being the baby."

"You wanted to prove that you could hold your own?"

He met her gaze. "I wanted to prove that I belonged."

Which explained so much.

He tilted her hand so it faced palm up and absently traced the patterns. "I remember the first time I was old enough to go camping with my dad and brothers, I was so nervous that I would screw up or get scared at night that I wanted to throw up the entire ride, but I would have rather died than let my brothers know. Or my dad."

He looked up again and there it was, that boyish grin that Sara loved.

"He figured it out as soon as we got to the campsite. He sent my brothers to collect firewood and showed me how to set up a tent. By the time my brothers got back, all the tents were up and my dad said that since I set up camp, I got to sleep with him. And hold the special flashlight."

"What made it special?"

"My dad said it was."

"Is that the tent?" She nodded toward the yard.

"Yeah. I found it when I was looking through ChiChi's garage for my sleeping bag. I didn't find my sleeping bag, but came across the old tent. I told Coop he could have it after the campout, if that's all right with you."

"Won't you need it?"

"I haven't gone camping since," he cleared his throat, "my parents died."

Sara bet that there were a lot of things that he stopped doing, stopped feeling, after his parents died. And maybe, like her, all he needed was someone to remind him what it felt like to live.

"Want to give me a tour?" she asked, stepping closer, and for the first time, feeling closer to knowing the real man beneath all of that guilt and drive.

"What I want is you," he said, bringing her fingers up to his mouth to take a little nibble. "But I promised not to make this harder on you, and if we go into that tent—"

He didn't finish. He didn't have to. Cooper was in the house washing up. Trey was still in his glorious half-naked state, which worked for her. The tent—she peeked over his shoulder—had a zipper. And because she had a pretty good idea of what he would do once they got there, but wanted to be certain that his ideas matched up with hers, she said, "And I want to see the tent that a little Trey conquered."

Trey went very still. "But Coop—"

"I know, it will have to be a quick," she smiled when his eyes went heavy, "tour."

"You sure?"

"Oh, yeah."

Then with a growl that made her nipples hard, Trey took her by the hand and dragged her to the tent. He went in first, giving her a spectacular, up-close-and-personal view of his fine ass when he bent over to fit his massive body through the tiny hole, which was followed by an even more intimate get-to-know-you with his abs when he yanked her inside and turned around.

Neither spoke as she zipped closed the flap. But the air between them caught fire as they stared at one another, him silently daring her to make the first move. She was on her knees, he was on his butt, and she was going to break her own rule. The no-kissing-in-the-house rule. Although, technically they were in the yard, not the house. And Cooper would be at least another five minutes since he'd have to shimmy into his pajamas.

She looked around the tight quarters and then at Trey, amazed that such a small space could contain that much male perfection. "I think we should add this to the bucket list. You can teach me how to pitch a tent and then we can spend the night admiring my handiwork."

"Come here."

He reached out and hauled her against him, so tight she had the choice of straddling him or falling over. And since straddling him had been on her mind ever since their pole-dancing lesson, and it would give her hands a chance to explore his abs, she figured it was her lucky day.

She meant to tell him that, only he was already kissing her. Hard and potent, and by the time he lifted his head Sara's whole world was spinning. Her lungs were burning. And her hands were gliding along his six-pack to his flat stomach—on a collision course with a really bad idea.

His hands, however, were moving north, going a long way toward making this the best camping trip ever.

"What exactly would your entry on the bucket list entail?" he said.

More of that. Through the thin cotton of her shirt his hot hands finally arrived, making her nipples hard and sending shivers across her entire body.

"I don't know," she breathed, her fingers getting into the spirit. Yep, he definitely hand-carried his client's orders. "I have some ideas, but I need another minute for them to solidify."

"Take your time," he said and then that talented mouth was against her neck, his teeth gently raking down to her shoulder. "I've been solidified since I walked out of your studio this morning."

She was about to melt into him and forget that this was an adventure, forget that he was temporary, and forget that she wasn't supposed to feel like this.

"Mommy, I can't find my Batman undies."

Trey pulled back and they were both breathing heavy. She looked down at the bulge in his jeans and smiled. "I think I already got the tent-pitching part down."

CHAPTER 14

"Can you slow down? This isn't a race."

The hell he would. Trey's hands gripped the wheelchair handles and he glared down at Lexi. She was glaring back.

If he had known before he parked that Lexi was going to get all woozy on him, he would have insisted on pulling up to the patient drop-off area. But Lexi had said she was fine, that the walk and fresh air would do her good, and then she stumbled. Right into Trey's arms.

"And stop panting in my ear." Lexi crossed her arms over her enormous belly. "You're gasping like you're pushing a tank uphill." She turned back around in her chair, her expression one of complete horror. "It doesn't feel like that, right? Like I'm a tank?"

"Nope," Trey lied. "Can barely feel you."

If there was one thing he'd learned over his two week stint as Hubby-for-Hire, it was that women were sensitive. Pregnant women? They were unpredictable and, when provoked, went for the jugular— or into hysterics. Neither one was something Trey was open to at the moment. Not with his brothers arriving home today. Which was how he found himself pushing Marc's first unborn, and all of his wife's weight, up the steep drive to St. Helena Memorial, for her twenty-four week Fit-Mama appointment.

Lexi had assured him that there would be no needles or womanly photos of any kind, but that he could count on her asking questions. Lots of questions. None that had to do with the sex of the baby, since it was to remain a secret—she'd made that more than clear.

What he hadn't counted on was Lexi having to stop three different times to use the bathroom on their seven-minute ride to the hospital, or that her appointment started at nine, instead of the eight o'clock pick-up time she had requested. Which meant that if they didn't get a move on, he'd miss his short window with Sara. Something that had quickly become his favorite pastime.

"Are you okay?" she asked as he pushed her through the doors, not stopping until they were in the elevator.

"We're in a hospital," he replied, watching a nurse push an old man on a gurney—right toward them. Trey didn't want to be rude, but he also didn't want to be stuck in a tight-ass box with a dying man and swinging IV bags. So he punched the close button. Five times.

"What are you doing?" Little Miss Do Gooder asked, pushing the open button and inviting the needles in.

Wheels rolled. Feet shuffled. And the elevator filled.

Trey focused on the floor, and away from the deathbed on wheels that strolled inside—oh God, was that blood in the bag? Trey gagged a little.

"You're looking a little green. Want to come lie down in my office for a few minutes?" the nurse asked.

"She'll be fine, she's sitting down," he said to the floor—which was moving, odd since the doors still hadn't closed.

"I was talking about you, Trey."

Trey looked up and—*ah Christ*—maybe he did need to lie down. There was no way his luck could be this bad.

Kayla stood on the opposite side of the gurney in a pair of scrubs with a special smile just for him. Normally he would have taken that smile and the wicked promise that went with it, but she didn't do it for him. Not anymore.

"I'm fine," he lied, stepping closer to the wall—just in case. He hoped Kayla didn't notice the sweat beading on his forehead or the way his hands were shaking. The last place he wanted to be was in a hospital.

"Yes, you are," she said with a more than welcoming tone to her voice. Lexi didn't even bother to hide her amusement with the current situation. "I thought you'd be long gone by now."

Where he should be is back in his suite. Getting ready for his morning private with his favorite dance teacher. Today they were tackling the Argentine tango. The idea came to him when he found one of her costumes in the prop closet. It consisted of a pair of strappy black heels, fishnets that stopped mid-thigh, and a miniscule dress with a slit up to her bellybutton—and no panties.

Trey watched the elevator buttons change as they slowly ascended, then looked at his watch. He was sweating—but for a whole other reason. Because, honestly, there wouldn't be much in the way of dancing. They'd get three seconds in, she'd do one of those fancy toe flicks, and he'd flick right back—until the top of her dress was around her waist and her legs were around his middle. Then she'd kiss him as though she'd been craving his touch as much as he had hers.

"Actually, Trey is in town until the end of the month," Lexi supplied ever so helpfully. And to keep the conversation flowing during the longest elevator ride of his life, she added, "He's even going to the Winter Gala."

That got Kayla's interest. And it was Trey's signal to leave. If it hadn't been for the old man moving his arm, causing the clear tubing attached to his hand to pull and Trey to see spots, he would have moved faster when the door dinged and opened on the fifth floor. He managed to move out of the elevator and into the hallway. Just not fast enough to avoid Kayla and her double Ds calling after him.

"Hey, Trey?"

He wanted to keep moving, pretend he didn't hear. But Lexi pulled the brake on the wheelchair, leaving him with no option but to turn around. Which pissed him off, but amused his sister-in-law to no end because, once again, his past was catching up to him. Only this time Trey had no interest in revisiting it. "Yeah?"

Kayla leaned over the edge of the gurney, far enough for Trey to know that she was a big fan of bright-purple lace, and make the old man's day golden. "If you're looking for a partner for the Gala, I do love to kick my heels up and shout."

"Thanks for the offer, but unfortunately, I already have a date."

She shrugged. "Maybe next time."

"Maybe," he lied. There wouldn't be a next time. Not with Kayla or any of the dozens of women from his past who were just like her; stacked, ready, and didn't give a shit about anything but a good time.

Marriage might not be in the cards, but neither was floating from one shallow hook-up to the next. Not anymore. Not after Sara. He wasn't looking for forever, but he couldn't keep moving through life without connection.

"You have a date?" Lexi said over her shoulder. "To the Gala? This is news."

"No news." Trey wheeled her toward the waiting room at the end of the hallway. And before she could say something else about who he was going with, what his date would be wearing, or why he felt the need to keep secrets, he added, "Just an evening with Nonna. Short stick, remember?"

"Oh, Regan and I thought you were going to ask Sara." Lexi looked disappointed. And damn it if he wasn't right there with her.

"Well, I'm not. We're just friends."

Based on the rules Sara set, there was no way he could take her to the dance and be discreet, especially when there was nothing discreet about the way he was feeling.

Trey considered parking her facing the wall, then realized that she'd talk more because she'd get bored with nothing to stare at, so he spun her around and aimed the wheelchair toward the fish in the tank. Without a word he walked over to the reception desk, signed Lexi in, then walked back and sank into the waiting-room chair.

"You could ask her, though," she said. "If you wanted to."

Trey ignored her.

"Don't you want to? Unless . . ."

He caved and opened one eye.

"Well, Marc told me about your mom and the dance. I remember that Gala and, um, we just figured that since you are already going, maybe it would be nice to go with someone who makes you smile."

"Why would you think Sara makes me smile?" he wanted to know. Because they'd been careful. Or tried to be, at least. And once upon a time, not so long ago, that would have been enough.

Before domestication, Trey would come to town, take care of business, and get out. No one said a thing or gave him grief or asked endless questions about where he landed on the smile scale. Then his brothers had fallen in love. And, God help him, he had two sisters-in-law, and a third one on the way, and he couldn't even dream about a quiet night in his suite to unwind without one of them thinking there was something wrong.

"You mean, Sara, who never misses coming in on her forty-five-minute break to chat and get her coffee fix, yet she hasn't shown her face since Monday."

"Maybe she's just busy with the Gala."

"Maybe." Lexi smiled and Trey knew that they were caught. "But that doesn't explain why you left the hotel at nine fifty-five exactly, to disappear down the alley behind her studio, only to reemerge forty minutes later—"

"Dance lessons."

"—with your suit all wrinkled and your hair finger-combed. *Smiling*."

"Are you spying on me?"

"Small town, Trey. Just being neighborly." God, she even sounded like Marc now, especially when she gave a low whistle and sized him up—more than a little accurate. "Same time, same place. That's a pretty big commitment for a guy like you. And a pretty big smile for a foxtrot."

"Yeah, well, smile or not, I'm leaving as soon as the paperwork is ready to be signed." He even sounded bitter to his own ears.

Lexi slipped her arm around him and rested her head on his shoulder. "I know. Marc called me from the airport and told me that they got the land. And that you agreed to live at the villa until construction is complete."

"It's a perfect location," Trey said, repeating Gabe's earlier sales pitch. "The house is less than an hour from an airport, it is central to most of our European clients, and I can oversee the construction when I'm home."

"This is Marc and Abby's deal. Why isn't one of them overseeing the construction?"

"Marc?" Trey sat back and looked down at her belly, giving her a get-real look. To her credit she didn't even blink, just held her ground. "*That* isn't an option. And Gabe just got Abby home. Plus, she can't spend more than a week away from Nonna and her nieces, so forget a year. Nah, Gabe wouldn't let her go, and even if he did, she'd be miserable."

"Then hire someone."

Trey laughed, but it was heavy and hollow. "A DeLuca needs to be there, to make sure everything is handled. Plus, I was already moving anyway. This is the easiest solution for everyone."

"For everyone but you," she said quietly. "I know what it's like to constantly be the one to hold it all together. To give up what you want to make sure that everyone else's life runs smoother. And I also know that no matter how hard you try or how much you tell yourself that it's all right, that you're all right, it's hard. It's awful and exhausting and eventually it will drain you."

Lexi had been stuck for years in a marriage that was doomed even before they traded *I do's*. She gave up her family, her dreams, everything, to make her husband's life easier, to make their marriage work. In the end, she'd been left with nothing—but a fresh start. Which she'd made with Marc.

Italy was Trey's fresh start. It would allow him to be the kind of sales guy DeLuca Wines needed, without the daily reminders of how his selfishness cost them nearly everything.

Trey pulled her in for a side hug. Looking at her was too hard. "I'm good, Lexi."

The minute the words came out, he realized that they were true. For the first time in years, he was beyond good. Only he was afraid that the second he stepped on that plane, the happiness would fade and the big void that had defined the past thirteen years of his life would return. And his time with Sara would end.

She wasn't the kind of girl to take weekends here and there, and he wasn't the kind of guy who could offer more. Not with this new project.

"This is what I want."

"You are so full of it."

Maybe she was right and moving didn't have the appeal it used to. But the project put a justified six-thousand miles between him and—everything in St. Helena.

"And since I know that the DeLucas would rather die than admit their well-intentioned plans were rapidly spiraling out of their all-powerful control, I'll tell you what I told Sara." Lexi smiled and damn if he didn't find himself checking the clock again. "Marc and I are babysitting Holly after the Gala. We're setting up a tent in the middle of the suite for a mock-campout. It sleeps four, so we have one space open, if Cooper needs a sitter."

"What did Sara say?" With his suite being just across the hall from Marc's it would be the perfect practice run. Cooper would get to do a sleepover, and Trey would get some kid-free time with Sara. Kid-free time that allowed for a very adult breakfast in bed.

"Oddly, that she didn't need a sitter. It seems no one has asked her to the dance so she is going it solo." Her mouth curved slowly in challenge.

"She's going to the dance solo because she doesn't want a date."

Lexi leveled him with a look that clearly meant, *you're kidding, right?* "Every woman wants a date on Valentine's Day, Trey. It's in our DNA. If she is saying she doesn't want one, then it is because she is afraid you won't ask."

"It's more complicated than that."

"And yet you're still around," Lexi pointed out.

Yeah, he was. Until he was needed somewhere else. Which could be any day now, and when he got the call, he'd have to go. And Sara would stay. And that was going to suck. Big time. But right now, he had a unique opportunity to spend an entire evening with her, talking and dancing and, yeah, getting naked was on the top of the list. So was waking up with her in his arms.

All he had to do was ask.

"She needs a sitter," he said.

"Good. Then Marc and I will handle getting the kids home and fed after the opening ceremonies, if you are comfortable handling, well, everything else."

"Alexis DeLuca," a nurse with a mop of gray curls and teddy bear scrubs called out. She met Lexi's gaze and smiled. "The doctor will see you now."

She went to stand and Trey pushed her down. "Sit. Marc will kill me if I don't go in with you." He rolled her toward the nurse and added, "And Lexi, there isn't anything I can't handle."

"Uh-huh." Something about the way she sounded had his guy-dar kicking in, telling him to cease and desist. Turn that wheelchair around and get the hell out of there.

"Good morning," the nurse said, flashing them a sunny smile. "I hope you had a chance to review the information that the doctor sent home with you last visit."

"I did." Lexi pulled out a stack of pamphlets and her list of questions. "I was excited to talk about the benefits of breastfeeding over formula, and what kind of pump I should put on my registry. I brought my brother-in-law here to take detailed notes."

Sara hung up the last of the silver-flocked tutus and felt herself breathe a little easier. Everything was falling into place. A new order of snowflake costumes had arrived that morning, right sizes, right number, and right in time for their dress rehearsal this afternoon. Then, tomorrow all forty-seven—forty-seven!—of her dancers would meet at the St. Helena Community Park for a final run-through to get acquainted with the stage and mark their positions.

On the home front, Cooper had mastered the square knot and, with Trey's help, was well on his way to earning his merit badge. She was still uneasy about him going away for two whole nights without her, especially with Hunter being their elected hive captain, but after Trey sat him down and explained that he was moving to Italy, how could she say no? Especially when Cooper was more excited about Trey living in the birth country of the Ferrari than he was upset about him moving.

Sara was upset about him moving. The Ferrari just didn't do it for her. She went into this knowing that he was going to leave, but even having the advance warning to prepare wasn't going to help. Nope, Sara thought as she slid on her fishnets, she liked him way too much for that.

She'd just walked behind the counter and slipped on her tango shoes when the bell on the door jingled and in burst Trey. His hair was windblown, his clothes wrinkled, and he was breathing heavy. The way he normally looked *after* their meeting. He was also holding a pink box with a little white string, which could only have come from the Sweet and Savory, and spoke right to her heart.

"Hey," he gasped, resting against the door and leaning his head back to take in deep breaths. "Sorry I'm late. Lexi. Pumps." With his free hand, he made a billowing gesture in the general direction of his chest. "So many choices. Ran late."

Sara looked at the clock. One minute until ten. Maybe that "like" problem went both ways. Or he was overly excited about their tango lesson.

"Actually, you're right on time. And what happened to coming in through the back door?" she asked, stepping out from behind the counter, the click of her slinky heels echoing off the hardwood floor.

"Because I came here to ask you a question. One that is deserving of a front door entrance and—*Jesus.*" Trey looked up and went still. His eyes riveted on her body.

As long as they got to the naked portion of the visit, and soon, she was fine with a little staring. She liked the put-together, business Trey, but him in a pair of dark-washed jeans and a long-sleeved sweater that showed off his incredible pecs? And abs? And that flat stomach that rippled under her hands when she—

"A question," his voice was thick and husky, "that if you keep looking at me like that, I'll never get to."

"Sorry," she whispered. "I know I just saw you last night, but—"

"Yeah, me too." He pushed off the door and met Sara in the middle of the dance floor. "And we'll get there."

"When?"

"Soon." He slid one hand down her waist to her bottom—then lower, past the hem of her skirt until he reached the top of her stockings. She moaned at the sensation of his fingers tracing the edge where fishnet met bare skin. Moaned even louder when he stopped. "I want to do this right."

"You were doing it right," she protested.

"I want to give you these and I can't until you say yes."

Eyes on Sara, he slowly untied the string and opened the box. Instead of a cake or pastry, he pulled out a bouquet that—best day ever—was made entirely of mini-cupcakes. Chocolate ones, red velvet ones, even lemon drop ones, all frosted to resemble different kinds of flowers and each attached to sticks wrapped with shiny green ribbon that were bound in a cluster. The result was beautiful and mouthwatering.

"So I only get the cupcakes if I say yes?" She put a hand on his chest and leaned in to get a better view of the selection. So what if her hands wandered a little? Cupcakes and Trey in the same room made her body hum and her hands daring. "I have a better idea. You ask me your question, then we do a little swap. A bite of yours for a bite of mine?"

At her offer, his eyes lit with wicked intent as he enjoyed a leisurely once over, taking the time to appreciate every inch of her costume. Spending twice the amount of time on the inches that weren't her costume.

Then his gaze met hers and everything shifted. His stance, his body language, even the way he held the bouquet.

"I'm not here to ask you to the Valentine's Gala," he began and Sara's heart nearly exploded right out of her chest. "Because that would be a date."

"And it would violate the 'just friends in public' rule." It would also put her in intimate proximity to a man who she was halfway in love with, on her wedding anniversary.

"So many rules," he murmured, his finger back to work on the hem of her fishnets, reminding her of just how many rules they'd broken yesterday during their pole-dancing lesson. And then last night in the tent. How many rules they were going to break in just a few minutes.

Could she break one more?

"I figured since you will be there and, small world, so will I, what's the harm of a stolen tango or two between friends?" His fingers turned soft and his eyes went serious. "And maybe, I could take you home when it's over and kiss you at the front door and try to charm my way in for a nightcap."

Trey swallowed, then shifted on his feet and Sara wondered if he had ever asked a woman out—not back to his hotel room, but out on a date that was about more than sex.

"That is, if you're not too busy for a non-date."

Suddenly, the idea of staying at home, eating ice cream alone in her bed after spending an evening surrounded by love and romance made her want to cry. She didn't want to spend another Valentine's Day alone. She wanted to spend it with Trey.

"I want to say yes."

"Then say yes."

"But—"

Trey held up a silencing finger. He placed the cupcakes in the box, put the box on the floor, and his hands were immediately on her butt. He hauled her up against him and the intimate contact scrambled her brain and melted her limbs.

"Let's get back to the you saying yes part," he whispered, his hands sliding up her back to pull her into the most improper dance position known to man, then he started swaying gently.

They stared at each other before she wrapped her arm around his neck and molded her body to his as he glided her across the room. They fit perfectly, his thighs pressing into hers, his hand low on her back, leading her so that they moved together as one. He felt so secure, so sure of himself, so incredibly right, Sara was afraid she'd follow him anywhere.

"You can't stay the night," she whispered, already giving in, wondering how they could make this work. "Cooper wakes up at an ungodly hour."

"I have an idea."

Sara felt herself tense. Last time he had an idea she ended up agreeing to let her son go to overnight camp without her.

"I talked to Lexi today. She said she'd already talked to you too. She and Marc are doing a mock campout for Holly and they offered to take Cooper for the night. I told her I'd have to talk to you."

She looked up at him and couldn't help but smile. He'd listened to what she'd said and was trying to abide by her wishes.

"What if he gets scared and wants to come home?" she asked, because that was what she was afraid would happen.

"We can stay at my suite, right across the hall. It is a two second walk to get him." Trey stopped and dipped her, the move both unexpected and thrilling. His lips were a mere breath from hers. "If not, we get him after breakfast."

A whole night with Trey. No watching the clock. No sneaking in kisses between bath time. No more wondering what it would be like to fall asleep in his arms. To wake up beside him.

"You've thought of everything," she said when he pulled her back up and into his arms. "This could really work."

The only thing left to do was decide if she wanted this to happen. She'd asked for adventure and he was offering her one. All she had to do was remember that this little make-believe romance she agreed to was nearly over. And that if she wanted to truly experience all that he was offering, it was now or never.

"I took care of everything because I *want* this to work, Sara. I want this to work with you."

Suddenly, any hopes she held of not falling in love with him vanished with that one statement. One night or a hundred, it didn't matter. She wanted this to work more than anything, and the idea of never was something that Sara couldn't stomach.

CHAPTER 15

Trey slid into a vacant seat just as the last Snowflake Princess took the stage. He was supposed to be in the holding area behind the rose-covered arbor, waiting to escort ChiChi onto the floor when the MC introduced the seven finalists for Best Winter Garden in Show, but this was the last performance of the evening, and the one he'd been waiting on all night. He couldn't miss it.

"Is that her?" Marc asked, squinting up at the stage and pointing.

"Nope," Nate whispered, grabbing Marc's finger and repositioning it to the opposite side of the stage. "Second row, last one on the left. There, the one in the sparkly slippers and little crown."

"They're all wearing sparkly slippers," Trey said, knocking their hands down. Holly would be horrified if she saw her uncles singling her out. "And it's called a tiara."

"They do this every time," Gabe complained while using the zoom on his phone's camera to look for his daughter. "It's like some sick joke they play to mess with us. The moms stand backstage doing final touches to the hair or whatever, leaving the dads in charge of recording the performance, but they dress them all the same so that we can't tell whose kid is whose."

The music started and all five rows of girls took three dramatic steps forward and, arms out to their sides and right toes pointed toward the audience, struck a ballerina pose. A hush fell over the room and everyone went silent—well, everyone except Gabe, who was mumbling under his breath, the camera scanning the formation frantically.

"Regan's going to kill me," he hissed.

Trey zeroed in on the front row, just right of center stage and sent a wink. A small smile snuck past Holly's lips before she went back to poised and professional. There might have been twenty-five girls in matching silver tutus, ice-crystal tiaras, and sparkly dance slippers, but Trey knew exactly which one was Holly. "She's front and center."

Gabe set him a disbelieving look, then zoomed in. "How did you know?"

"It's her posture," Trey leaned over and whispered, wondering how they could *not* know. Holly spent the past two weeks twirling around the house with a shower rod taped to her arms, extending her neck like a giraffe. Her goal: master the art of looking bigger than you are.

She'd nailed it.

When all three brothers turned to look at him, he explained, "She's the smallest one in her class, so she's been working hard on elongating her lines to move in sync with the taller girls." Trey had also been helping her clean up her point. No one wanted sloppy feet. "Which is why they all look the same, to blend in. Not to stand out and draw attention. So stop gawking or you'll embarrass her."

Ignoring the crazy-ass stares his brothers were shooting his way, Trey sat back and focused on his niece. Tongue peeking out the side of her mouth, she gave a few quick taps of the foot and they were off, arms waving, feet gliding across the stage, and not a single girl was in sync. It was beautiful.

Then the music swelled and at the precise moment that Holly did a little leap, metallic flakes fell from the ceiling, drifting down over the girls like a light dusting of snow. And Trey knew it was almost time for the big finish.

"It's the twirly part," Gabe said, jabbing Trey in the ribs as though Trey didn't already know about the twirl situation. Hell, he'd been living that nightmare ever since Sara put it in the routine. "She said she was nervous about a bunch of twirls on one leg. Does she look nervous to you?"

"One leg?" Nate asked. "Why would she only let them use one leg when two would be safer? Is that like some kind of handicap for dance?"

"I don't know," Marc said, eyes fixed to the stage. He was leaning so far forward he was practically kissing the seat in front of him. "Don't tell Lexi I know, but we're having a girl, and I swear to God, if this is what it's like, I think I'm going to be sick."

So was Trey. Fists clenched, pulse pounding, it was like the final pass in a game of sudden death. He knew how hard she'd worked, knew how much she wanted this to go perfectly, knew that regardless of what happened, he would be damn proud, but when Holly dug her toe in the floor—no sickled feet there—and pushed off to begin her twirls, Trey's lungs just stopped working.

One . . . Two . . . Three . . . And—

Trey was on his feet clapping, a warm feeling of pride bubbling up and taking him by surprise. At the audition, Holly couldn't even land one of those turns, and she'd just nailed four—with him acting as stand-in dad. And okay, there was a little wobble on the last twirl but she also knocked elbows with Lauren—who needed to work on pointing her toes.

"She was amazing," Gabe said beside him. "She was the best one up there. Did you see?"

Small but mighty, Trey thought, wondering if this was what it felt like to be a proud papa. Not that Holly was his, but for the last two weeks she had been. And in that short amount of time, she'd grown so much.

"You might want to keep your comments to yourself," Nate whispered. "Since everyone around us thinks that their kid was the best."

Gabe shrugged, still clapping. "I can't help it if they're wrong."

Trey felt a warm hand rest on his arm and he turned to find the most beautiful woman he'd ever seen. Tonight, her hair was pulled back into a loose bundle of curls at the base of her neck with little white flowers securing wisps of soft waves that framed her face.

From the front, her dress appeared simple and elegant. A pale-pink fabric draped from her shoulders to her collarbone, hugging her body all the way down to pool at the floor. She looked like a starlet from the forties. But when she turned around, things got interesting. The back was pretty much nonexistent, except for a single strip of pearls that pulled across her shoulder blades, holding the dress together, with another string cascading down to the lowest tip of her back, leaving everything between bare.

"She really did rock the tiara," Sara said, and it took everything Trey had to not bend down and kiss her. Right there. In front of his brothers and Roman, who, he was certain, was lurking around.

He looked at her lips, glossy and lush, and wondered what she'd do if he did kiss her. Then he wondered if she was able to wear panties with that dress. Then he stopped wondering all together because his pants were getting a little too crowded to pull off discreet.

"Is that your professional opinion?" Gabe asked and the man was serious.

Sara tempered her smile, but Trey could see the amusement bubbling up in her eyes. "It is."

After a round of gentlemanly "hellos" and compliments on a job well done, she turned the full force of that smile on him and discreet went out the window.

"ChiChi is starting to show her teeth." She leaned in and lowered her voice. "She has it in her head that since she told you to wait by the arbor and you aren't by the arbor that there was foul play involved. She has Deidra cornered in the ladies' room and I'm afraid that waterboarding may come into play."

"Well then, I guess you'd better take me to her," Trey said, picking up a little white box from beneath his chair and offering her his arm, in the most friendly and non-date-like way imaginable.

He wove them through the sea of candlelit tables, past the arbor, and into the cool night. Once they were out under the stars, he took her by the hand and led her away from the lights of the tent which covered most of the community park.

"Your grandma is over that way," Sara said, jerking her head back toward the tent, but he noticed that she didn't pull away from him.

"Which is why we're going this way."

She glanced down at their intertwined hands, which were swinging idly between them. "I never took you for a hand-holder."

He shrugged and glanced down at her out of the corner of his eye. "Sometimes it's better to hold hands. As for our destination, I want to go anywhere isolated enough so that I can look my fill of you in that dress without worrying about getting caught."

Actually he was heading toward the community rose garden and pond. Located on the back side of the park, it was always decorated with tea lights and floating candles. It was romantic, quiet, and the perfect place to tell her how proud he was of her.

And give her a little gift.

He'd spent all night watching her flit around the ballroom, now he just wanted one selfish moment to have all of her attention before the dancing began.

"I agree. Holding hands is better." She laced her fingers tighter and moved a whole lot closer. *Thank you, Coop.* "Although, I was hoping you were taking me someplace to make out."

"That's for later. After I kiss you good night at the door and then charm my way into your bed. Remember?"

"You might want to bring a coat so you don't get cold waiting outside for an invite." That didn't sound promising. "Since I'll be in your room. In your bed."

"Right. Then you better get started with all the sweet talk and compliments because I can tell you right now I don't just let anyone charm their way into my bed. I'm very particular. And I have lots of rules," Trey said in his best "Sara" tone.

"I like rules." Yes she did. Almost as much as she liked breaking them. "And how about your pants." She stopped on a bed of rose petals that covered the pathway to the pond. "Are those charmable?"

He had a witty response, one that would guarantee him a smoking-hot night with his smoking-hot girl, but she looked up at him and everything inside him went still. His thoughts, his heart, even the earth seemed to stop spinning. The little flowers, which were tucked in her hair, sparkled under the soft glow of the floating candles while the moon spilled across her face, illuminating those eyes that saw right through him and turning her dress a shimmery white.

She looked beautiful. And like the woman he could spend the rest of his life loving.

"I brought you something," he said, looking down at the box in his hand, suddenly unsure. But he'd already opened his mouth, she was staring at the box, and it was too late to turn back. So he handed it to her and felt his ears go hot when she pulled out the corsage.

"It's beautiful," she said, offering him her wrist. He slid the corsage on, bumbling a little like he was back in high school and this was the prom. But she didn't seem to notice; she was too busy fussing over the flowers. "Are you pinning me, Trey?"

"I know we're a little old for corsages," he began. "But it's tradition."

"A woman is never too old for corsages."

Same thing Frankie had said when he'd picked it out. She also told him that he should think about the meaning behind the flower, because women get off on that kind of thing. Her words, not his.

"I know it's Valentine's Day and that you can't be my Valentine." He looked over the top of her head at the soft glow of the tent. "At least not here. But I wanted to get you something that let you know how proud I am of you. You made every girl in there, including my niece, feel like a princess."

She tilted her head and he could see the moisture in her eyes glisten. "I couldn't have done it without your help."

"Yes, you could have. Because you're that strong, Sara. And I admire that. I admire you." He cupped her cheek. "Which is why I was hoping you'd wear my flowers. The yellow ones around the outside are alstroemerias. They stand for friendship."

"Friendship?"

"Yeah." But when Sara's brow furrowed in confusion—and maybe disappointment—he quickly added, "The only thing I can think of that would be better than stripping you out of this dress is spending Valentine's Day dancing and laughing with my friend."

"And the big white one in the middle?" she asked, tracing the edge of a petal, not letting him off that easy.

"That is an aster and it symbolizes patience."

"You've been very patient," she whispered, this time tracing the edge of his lapel and he wondered if she could feel his heart trying to hammer itself right out of his chest. God, he was nervous.

If that right there wasn't terrifying proof about just how far gone he was, his next words sealed his fate. "I have, but that's not why I picked it. According to legend it's an enchanted flower."

"Enchanted?"

"Like its owner." He laced their fingers and kissed the palm of her hand. "I've never been enchanted before, but you, Sara Reed, everything about you has me mesmerized."

She threaded her free arm around his neck and brushed her mouth over his. The simple contact was enough to make everything start spinning again.

"You're the best friend I've made since moving here, Trey." She kissed him again. Only longer and with more heat and when she pulled back, his hands had somehow found their way beneath the fabric at the small of her back. "And when you're ready for that dance, I'll be the one by the punch bowl. Proudly wearing your pin."

"Please welcome to the floor our last finalist of the evening." The MC adjusted the mic and extended a dramatic hand to the entrance beneath the arbor. "The eighteen-time finalist and nine-time winner, Chiara Amalia Giovanna Ryo."

The band struck up a smooth intro and Trey escorted his nonna to the floor, waiting until they passed Deidra and her partner, who had already taken their place, before giving her a showy spin that had her dress catching air.

"You sure know how to sweep a lady off her feet," she breathed, her cheeks flushed, when he pulled her into his arms. "That dance teacher worked wonders."

Sara had worked wonders, in every possible way—even ones he'd never imagined. She'd made what should have been a difficult visit home . . . enchanting.

God, did he really use that word earlier?

Trey found himself smiling. He had used it. And meant it. Just like everything else he'd said in the garden. He'd had a lot of women over the years but he'd never had one he considered a friend. Sara understood him better than even his own family. She accepted him for who he was, faults and all, and that meant more to him than she could ever understand.

"Now, if you'll all turn your attention to the floor for the sixty-ninth annual Winter Garden of the Year Finalists' Waltz." The MC gave the band leader a nod and then stepped away from the mic. The violins struck the first note and a soft melody filled the tent as all seven finalists and their partners began to move around the floor.

Trey had danced with Sara to this song during several of their lessons. In fact, she insisted that they practice to this specific song. She might pretend to be Switzerland with the grannies and Deidra, but she was more Team Trey than she'd let on.

With a practiced step forward, Trey led ChiChi right up the middle of the dance floor, wowing the crowd with a complicated turn combination. When ChiChi looked thoroughly impressed, and Deidra utterly shocked, he stealthily scanned the crowd until he found Sara sitting demurely at a table—with Super-Ro-Man and his rippling biceps. The good news was that her eyes were locked on

Trey, sending him all kinds of secret messages. Roman's eyes—the prick—were on the nonexistent back of her dress.

"You look so much like my Geno, it warms my heart," ChiChi said, patting the handkerchief of his tux. "Thank you for doing this. You don't know how much your being here, sharing this dance with me tonight, means."

Trey broke the rules and looked down at his grandmother. Her smile was shaky, her eyes watery, and *he* felt like the prick—a selfish and cowardly prick.

"Ah, Nonna. Don't cry. I want to be here, I was just . . ." *Just what? Being a chickenshit?* "Sometimes I get so caught up in my own shi . . . stuff it's easier to assume that Gabe or someone else will handle things at home, and I don't stop to think that they might be busy, or that you might need me."

"I always need you, child. You're my favorite," she assured him and he rolled his eyes. "But tonight I needed you to help me say good-bye."

That got Trey's attention. "What are we saying good-bye to?" Please God, she wasn't dying, was she?

"The past," she whispered, and a point went to Sara for the semi-choreographed routine or this dance would have ended badly with those two words.

"You are so much like your grandpa," ChiChi said reverently. "More so than any of your brothers. You have the same fire about you and boyish charm and you love your family with every ounce of your soul. He would have been so proud of the man you've become."

Trey didn't know about that. Geno had been loyal and reliable and would never have considered moving halfway around the world to be free of his family.

No, his nonno had been a family man who would do anything for his loved ones. Trey didn't know how to love someone without disappointing them. If anything, the old man was in heaven wondering when the hell Trey was going to figure out his life.

"I don't know if being loved by me is a good thing." The moment the words left his mouth, Trey's whole chest caved. It was the first time he'd admitted out loud his biggest fear.

"I do," ChiChi said in that tone that dared him to argue. "You love selflessly, Trey. Unconditionally and more fiercely than anyone I've ever met besides my Geno. You make sure that the family business runs smoothly, even picking up the pieces when your siblings overindulge."

"They just want to see it grow, make it the kind of company Dad and Nonno would be proud of." Which was why he kept his head down, didn't bitch when they screwed with his job—well, not too much—and just took care of business.

"They tend to jump in, and you smooth it over, make sure everyone feels taken care of," she said. "Geno had the same uncanny ability to connect with people, only you care about their path until it consumes yours. It's a blessing and a curse. You commit yourself with abandon, which means that just like your nonno, you're selective of who you let in because once they're in, they get all of you."

He wasn't just selective, he was shut off. And until recently, that had worked for him. But lately, ever since Sara and Cooper, shutting off had become more and more difficult.

"No one is more capable of loving than you." Her voice went soft. "Which is why I wanted to dance with you tonight, Trey. To help me let go, say the kind of good-bye to your grandpa that I wanted to, so I can move on."

"I don't understand." She wanted to move on? What did that even mean?

"I was still mourning my Geno when your parents passed." ChiChi managed to make the sign of the cross and not even miss a step. Trey, however, nearly took out two other couples. "And you kids needed me so I had to put all my good-byes on hold."

Trey never knew how to respond when people brought up his parents' death, especially when it was one of his family members. He'd hoped that by now he would have figured out some magical phrase that would make it easier, because "sorry" didn't even begin to make up for their loss.

"I forgot how close together it all happened."

Geno had passed not too long after the Gala. His parents followed a few short months later. ChiChi moved into the family house to help take care of everyone. Trey had never once considered how difficult that time must have been for her, juggling five grandkids and her own loss.

"If I never said it before, thank you for being there for us," he said.

"A busy household gave me something to fixate on. I wasn't ready to let go of Geno or your parents. And you weren't either. But carrying around all that emotion, all that pain, isn't good for either of us. I'm ready."

"To let go?" he had to ask, because he wasn't ready. Letting go of the pain meant letting go of the guilt, and he couldn't do that. Not without the fear that he would also let go of all of the memories, that they would fade with the anger.

"I've been ready for some time now. I've just been waiting for you."

"Nonna," he whispered, slowing his pace. She sounded so tired, so weary that Trey wanted to give her what she needed, but he didn't know if he could.

"I came here tonight to have my final dance and remember my

first love, my son, and my beautiful daughter-in-law. Your siblings are happy and settled for the most part, and I want to get to the next chapter of my life before I'm too old to live it." She looked up at him and he saw something in her eyes that made his chest tighten to the point of pain. "But I promised myself at your parents' funeral that I wouldn't let go until you're ready, Trey."

Sara watched from her table as Trey waltzed his grandmother in circles around Deidra. Best fan kicks in Vegas or not, ChiChi and her partner were the Fred and Ginger of the evening. Hands down.

The tables' crisp, white table linens played off of ChiChi's red dress to perfection, and the crystal vases and flowers seemed somehow to accent her jewelry. Even the elegant chandeliers that hung from the main support of the tent seemed to be the perfect illumination for her complexion.

But watching Trey take his grandmother in his arms, giving in to the showy moves that she'd taught him, just to make ChiChi smile and impress the crowd, was what had Sara going dreamy.

"I see that someone already pinned you," Roman said, fingering the petals of her flowers.

Sara nodded, remembering the way Trey had looked when she opened the box. Shy and vulnerable and like he was hers. "A friend gave it to me."

"I had hoped to give you this." Roman slid a clear box with a cluster of exotic red and orange orchids in it across the table. "But it seems I'm too late. Something that's been happening a lot lately."

"It's beautiful," she said. Beautiful, bold, and so not her.

He reached across the table and took her hand. "Am I too late, Sara?"

They both knew he wasn't talking about the flowers anymore.

"I wanted it to be about time," she said, "because then it could have worked with you. But I think it's more about the right person than the right time."

"Ouch."

"No, I mean," she placed her free hand over their joined ones, "you are a great dad who is nice and reliable and comfortable and . . . safe."

Sara looked out on the dance floor and spotted Trey with his nonna and realized that he made her feel safe too. But in a different way. He wouldn't have waited six months for the "right time" or let her analyze them into the neutral zone. Trey took an interest in her, in what she needed to feel comfortable moving forward, and then gave her that. He also made sure to give her every reason to take the leap.

"I sound like a golden retriever."

She smiled and gave his hand a squeeze. "You sound like me. Don't you get it? We're the same person. Kissing me would be like kissing yourself."

"I'd like the chance to prove you wrong," he said with a little smile.

"We agree on everything, we love our kids first and foremost, we're so busy being polite and careful with each other that nothing would ever happen." She lowered her voice. "I'm your safe bet, Roman, your excuse to stay in that protective bubble and not take a risk."

Roman looked out at the dance floor, silently watching the couples. She was right, and he knew it.

"I tried passion once," he admitted. "She left me for my best friend. Safe sounds nice."

She looked down at the flowers. Roman didn't want a girl-next-door dance teacher who drove a wagon. He needed someone to bring some fire into his world. "Maybe you just tried the wrong kind of passion."

Sara closed the box and slid it back across the table. Roman tapped it once with his hand and then put it into his jacket pocket. "Promise me you'll be careful. Trey is a great guy, and it's obvious he cares for you, but the whole town knows he's leaving. It's what he does."

"Maybe." The music began to fade and the dance floor was coming to a halt. "Or maybe it isn't so much that he leaves, maybe it's that he hasn't found the right reason to stay."

With an understanding smile, that was in complete contradiction to the defeated grunt he released, Roman reached out and cupped her cheek. "Yeah, well, I hope he knows what a lucky son of a bitch he is."

"It's starting," Charles said, hobbling up to the table, a little out of breath and interrupting their moment.

He looked dashing in a vintage, dark-gray tuxedo with a crisp white bowtie and matching kerchief. In one hand he strangled his silver cane, and in the other was a box much like the one Trey gave Sara earlier.

"Artie told me one more song and then it's time. You'd think a hundred bucks would buy the right to pick what time the song played, but he said he's the band leader so it's his call. Artistic license or some baloney."

Sara looked at Roman to apologize and he gave an understanding nod. "It's all right, go."

"Oh no you don't," Charles said, tugging her off by the arm. "That sneak Stan is making his move. I saw him buying petunias. The putz. Who would buy a woman like ChiChi petunias? Hurry up, he's headed right toward her, box in hand. I'm not going to miss pinning her again."

"Hey, Sara," Roman said and she gave a last look over her shoulder. "If you ever want to test the 'just friends' theory, let me know, because I still think I can rock your world."

Sara gave him one last smile before Charles, who was quite spry for a man with a cane, pulled her toward the dance floor. Together they moved through the swelling crowd and under the twinkling ball of roses that hung from the center of the party tent, cutting Stan off.

"Chiara Amalia Giovanna Ryo," Charles said, dropping Sara's hand and touching the top of his flower box.

"Charlie," ChiChi turned around, her hand smoothing down her hair. The woman took one glance at the extended box and looked ready to cry.

Trey, however, looked so shocked to see Charles offering up his heart on a platter that he sputtered. Or maybe it was that ChiChi wasn't battling him off with a broom.

Charles did some sputtering of his own. One glance at ChiChi and it was as though the walls were stripped away and all that was left was a man desperate to claim his true love.

"You look even more beautiful than the last time I stood here with a flower, hoping to pin the prettiest girl at the Gala." He looked at her wrist and let out a breath of relief when he saw it was still bare.

"What took you so long?" ChiChi asked, her hand clutching her chest, her lashes fluttering. Sara could almost feel her heart thump with the music.

"Sixty years of stubborn pride," he admitted and ChiChi's eyes filled with tears. "I used to think that the biggest mistake of my life was not telling you how I felt before Geno did."

"And now?" she whispered.

"Not realizing sooner that it just wasn't our time. We both had lives to live, families to raise, with other people, before our journey could begin." Charles took ChiChi's hand in his. They were both shaking. "You once asked me to let you know when I was done being angry. Well, I'm done, Chiara, and I would be the happiest man here if you'd allow me the honor of pinning you."

"I've been waiting a long time to get pinned by you Charlie," ChiChi said saucily as Charles slid the corsage on her wrist. "You'd better be worth the wait."

Trey cleared his throat. "You're in a crowded ballroom, Nonna, with your grandchildren around you."

But she wasn't listening, she was too busy staring at the corsage. It had a cluster of bright-blue flowers with a few sprigs of lavender.

"Forget-me-nots," she said, then looked up, her face firm. "You buy these from Deidra?"

"No, ma'am, picked them myself."

"From my garden," Lucinda said breathlessly and she scurried over, Pricilla on her heels—both of them moving Charles aside. "Sorry to interrupt, but this is a matter of the cheat's been caught."

"We've got the proof," Pricilla said excitedly, her pudgy hands rubbing together.

"Mary Lambert says Deidra's been buying dye from the same supplier that she uses for the Prune and Clip. Can you imagine, hair dye in flowers?" Lucinda said. "The supplier told Mary that Deidra keeps it behind the water fountain."

"All we have to do is take the mayor down there and show him, and she'll be disqualified."

"But we gotta go now," Lucinda said.

ChiChi looked at Charles, who was slowly backing away and sending Artie the band leader a panicked expression. "I can't right now."

"You've got to," Lucinda demanded, her voice shrill. "The MC will be reading the winner's name in just a few minutes. And once the name's read, she'll win." Lucinda looked between ChiChi and her brother and then to the corsage. "He'll understand. Right, Charles?"

"You go," Charles said and Sara wanted to cry for him. "I've waited sixty years, I can wait another twenty minutes."

ChiChi looked at the red-and-silver Best Winter Garden in Show sash that hung on display across the podium, at the trophy that sat up top, and then back at Charles. "I can't."

Everyone stared wide-eyed as ChiChi walked away from her chance to take down the great Deidra Potter, in the name of bamboozled green thumbs everywhere, for a chance at romance.

Charles smiled and Sara cried—just a little—when he bent at the waist and, hanging his cane over his forearm, extended his hand. "Chiara, may I have this dance?"

She took his hand. "If you play your cards right, you can have my whole dance card."

And as if the night couldn't be any more perfect, the lights dimmed and Artie gave the signal. The first few strings of "At Last" eased over the crowd as Charles took his first and last love to the center of the room. Pulling her into his arms, Sara watched with her heart in her throat as he took his first step toward recapturing old memories and creating happier times.

"You knew about this?" Trey asked, his rich voice sending tingles across her bare back. Or maybe it was the heat of his hands resting just below the dangling string of pearls as he eased her into his arms.

"He's my special private," she finally admitted, her hands taking a little detour of their own, to move over the ridges of his chest before wrapping around his shoulder.

"Old man Charles?" Trey laughed, and what a great laugh it was. It was deep and relaxed and real. In fact, everything about him looked relaxed and lighter, as if a big piece of the world had just been taken off of his shoulders. "Do you know how many nights I stayed up obsessing about who your privates were with?"

"You thought it was Roman, didn't you?"

He leaned down, his lips grazing her ear. "I didn't care who it was with. It wasn't me."

Sara had to force herself to swallow. Trey pulled back enough to lock gazes, his intense eyes drank her in like he wanted to fill up her dance card. And maybe for longer than February.

His hand stayed in the perfect place for the proper dance position, but his thumb traced back and forth across her bare skin. "Is this dress a test?"

"Why, are you afraid you'll fail?"

"I hate to fail." He trailed a single finger along the string of pearls to the lower edge of her dress. "Then again, no one's perfect."

"You're pretty close," she whispered. He expertly led her in a series of sweeping turns that had their bodies brushing and her heart skipping. "What were you and ChiChi talking about during your dance?"

Trey faltered for only a half-beat, but Sara noticed. Just like she noticed the way his shoulders tensed slightly. She ran a hand to the base of his neck and gently rubbed until he took a deep breath and let it out.

"About knowing when to hold on and when to move on."

"Where are you at?" she asked, looking up at him. "Holding on or moving on?"

The minute the words left her mouth, Sara found breathing difficult. She was ready to move on. With Trey. Only he was moving on to Italy. She didn't know how they could make it work but she was willing to put her heart out there and give it a try. Except he had to be willing to meet her halfway.

"I'm ready to move on," he said and Sara felt her stomach bottom out. Did he mean move on, as in pizzas and Ferraris—and without her? Or move on from what he'd been running from?

As if sensing her panic, he leaned down and brushed her lips in a kiss. Not even a kiss really, just a gentle connection that slid all the way to her toes. "But tonight I realized that even though I'm ready to let go, to move on, there are certain things I can't walk away from. Things I don't want to walk away from."

"What kind of things?" She needed to know. Because that just sounded like a declaration of some kind.

When he only smiled, pulling her closer until her cheek was resting against his shoulder, she breathed him in and listened to the steady beat of his heart over the music.

Trey's hands brushed lower, as though testing to see just how far the dress line plunged—one more inch and she might melt into a puddle at his feet.

"Did you know," she said quietly, "aster flowers close their petals when it rains? Supposedly fairies take shelter beneath the petals."

"Fairies, huh?" he murmured and she felt him smile against her hair.

"It's their sanctuary from the storm."

Trey pulled her even closer and whispered, "Kind of like you, Sara."

CHAPTER 16

I think this is where you're supposed to kiss me," Trey said, standing by the door to his suite. He'd been dying to get Sara out of that dress ever since she walked into the Gala. It was the new *numero uno* on his bucket list. Hell, getting her out of that dress obliterated the list. But a deal was a deal, and he wanted pretty words. "And make it good."

With a smile, Sara closed the distance, the skirt of her dress brushing his thighs as she walked him back a few inches until the door was pressed at his back, and she was pressed at his front, causing a whole lot of pressing to go on in his pants.

She rose up on her toes, leaning into him until she was plastered against him, stopping when they were close enough to share the same breath. She didn't look away, didn't go in for the kill, instead met his gaze and held it as she tugged his lower lip between her teeth.

"Make it *good* or make it *fuck-yeah*," she whispered, her mouth brushing his with every word.

Normally he'd go for the *fuck-yeah*, he always went for the *fuck-yeah*. But for some reason, it didn't fit tonight, didn't fit him anymore, which made no sense.

The air around them simmered with growing sexual heat and Trey's body was all but high-fiving its way out of his clothes. The woman had him so primed, he wasn't sure he'd be able to make it to the bedroom, and yet the only words that came to mind were "Real. Make it real."

"Real is my specialty." She pressed her mouth to his, her lashes fluttered closed and—specialty was an understatement. Her kiss officially blew his mind. It was everything that he needed and nothing that he'd ever felt before. All of the crazy emotions from the evening, and the gentle way her lips caressed his, tangled into one complicated lump in his chest.

He wrapped his arms around her and deepened the kiss until he didn't know if he'd be able to let her go.

Which was the only excuse he had for lifting her in his arms and carrying her into his suite. Kicking the door closed, he never let go of her mouth as he moved her into the bedroom with the sole intention of getting her into his bed. Immediately.

Only when he got there, he remembered the back of her dress—and the single strand of pearls holding the entire thing together like a gift begging to be unwrapped, and decided to set her on her feet. Right next to the bed. Then he pulled back to just look at her.

"Why are we stopping?" She stared back for several long seconds, then a teasing smile appeared, flashing that dimple that he adored. "Is it because you like me too much?"

"I can't stop, because I like you too much." Neither could his hands, which were on her hips gliding up her ribcage and sneaking around the back side, inches from her breasts. He smiled when her breath caught, only to release when he didn't make direct contact. "I just wanted to test a theory."

He reached behind her with one hand to flip the clasp of the pearls and watch as—holy hell—he fucking knew it. The dress swept down her body and pooled at her feet—leaving her in nothing but her heels.

"Christ," he groaned, taking in every inch of her.

She was perfect. Compact, curvy, and everything he could ever want. And for tonight, she was his. A little voice inside of him said that it could be for longer, all he needed to do was tell her that he didn't want this to end.

"Well, I want to test out your bed," she said, doing some pretty blatant staring of her own. "But no matter how hard I try, I don't think your clothes will come off with one sweep of the hand."

It didn't mean that she didn't drive him insane in the process. She pushed his jacket to the floor, smoothed her palms down his chest, across his stomach, and right over his hard ridge to take him in her hand. The heat from her touch seeped through the wool of his pants as she caressed and gently squeezed before lowering the zipper and—*hello*—Trey's eyes rolled to the back of his head.

"Christ," he growled again because, how could he not? Her elegant fingers were firmly wrapped around him, stroking him from base to tip, driving him so completely out of his mind.

"I guess I *can* get you off with one sweep of the hand," she whispered, giving another long caress. "But I want to see you first."

Which worked for him, except she was no longer stroking, she was stripping, making quick work of his clothes. Finished, thank God, because her hands were back on him, not where he wanted, but close enough. She walked him back until he was sitting on the end of the bed, completely naked, and the girl of his dreams straddled him.

"God, you feel good." He immediately reached for the globes of her ass—his second-favorite part, right after her smile—and pulled her against him.

She groaned and, pressing his erection between their bodies, rose up and rubbed herself deliciously down his length. The friction of her smooth skin was almost too good to handle, so of course she did it again.

"Much more of that and you will charm us into the grand finale before I even get to appreciate the opening act."

"We have all night," she said and—lucky guy that he was—did another long sweep of her heat all the way up his outer ridge. "You can appreciate later."

"I want to appreciate now *and* later."

Not wanting to risk her moving again, he rolled over, pinning her to the bed and dropped an openmouthed kiss to the valley between her breasts. Since he was in the neighborhood, he moved up and paid a lengthy visit to a particular pair of perfect breasts, making her arch off the bed. Which was brilliant on his part because one more little roll of her hips and he was either a) going to go off like some teenager and embarrass himself, or b) start spouting sonnets that compared her incredible body to a Ferrari and embarrass himself.

Her coming apart in his arms was the better option if he wanted the night to go as planned. And the morning.

God, thinking about waking up with her next to him, soft and sleepy and sliding her leg over his thigh so he could help ease her into the morning by easing himself into her had him right back to almost embarrassing himself. Because Trey didn't do morning-afters and he certainly didn't do morning-after brunch. The idea usually made him want to run. Only with Sara it made him want to stay— for a long time.

Whatever was happening between them felt real and right, like he was on the edge of the biggest moment of his life. But what if it only felt temporary for her?

Like an idiot, he'd told her that she was his sanctuary and she'd told him she was his . . . *for as long as you're here.* His stomach knotted and he found even breathing hurt. Those were her exact words. And—

"Trey," she said, framing his face with her hands. That one simple contact was everything that he needed. "It's okay, I feel it too."

"Thank God," was all he could manage before they were kissing and—*holy hell*—it was a sudden slam-to-the chest, life-altering kiss that went from zero to everything from this day forward in no time flat.

Her skin was hot beneath his palms as they slid over her breasts and lower, until he met hot, wet skin.

Oh yeah, one touch and she was already making those noises he loved so much. Two passes and she bit his lip—hard. The third pass, he slid a finger inside and she gasped, her body tightening round him, almost begging him to go deeper. So he did and her hands fisted in his hair.

"Trey," she panted, her chest rising and falling with every labored breath. "Can you . . . that thing . . . I like it when you—"

Her words caught on a cry, because he knew exactly what she liked. Knew what turned her on, what made her cry out in sheer unadulterated pleasure—and knew that what he was feeling right now was different—that he could never go back to the way things were.

Not with his family, not with his job, and not with her. Sara moved into his heart and made herself at home, giving him things that he'd been too scared to even contemplate having before. More important, she made him believe that he deserved them.

Made him believe that he deserved her.

"Trey," she whispered, gently pushing against his hand.

"I got you," he promised, keeping the pace slow, driving her right to the edge and back, waiting for her eyes to flutter closed, for her to turn her head, because staying still was too hard. Instead she held his gaze, never once looking away, even when he finally took her there and she melted into him.

He wanted to take it slow, worship every inch of her, so when her legs wrapped around his middle and she arched up, he kissed his way down the path she was clearly indicating, devoting special attention to her breasts. But when he realized that she was reaching for the box of condoms he'd put on the nightstand, he got on board immediately.

In two seconds he was wrapped and ready and sliding home in one long thrust. They both moaned and even before he could catch his breath, she lifted her hips, taking him all the way, and giving some little twist at the top that made the room spin.

"Hold up," he whispered, gripping her hips and stilling her, because that's just what she felt like—home. He laced their fingers and pinned them over her head. "Just give me a minute."

A minute to process what he was feeling. To try and understand what she was doing to him.

"Trey, you can have me as long as you want."

He looked down at her and that's when he saw it. That same look ChiChi got when she talked about her husband. That same smile his mom saved for his dad when they thought no one was looking. And he got that same feeling in his chest that Gabe had been talking about.

Everything went into slow motion and Trey realized that he might just take forever.

"Does anyone in this family ever knock?" Trey asked Abby, tugging a T-shirt over his head and closing the door on the gloriously naked woman sleeping in his bed. Okay, so she wasn't sleeping, she was in a post-orgasm coma, and it wasn't *his* bed, since he didn't own one.

Something that, after last night, he was giving serious consideration to changing. But to own a bed meant he needed his own place, and since the reason for his sudden change in priorities lived in St. Helena, he was considering all kinds of things. For example, he thought, glaring at Abby who was making herself right at home on his couch, no spare keys would be given out. Except to Sara.

"It's after ten, which means any reason to knock is already gone," Abby said, waggling her brows. "I guess today's special."

She had no idea.

"You want to talk about it?" she asked, pulling her legs beneath her.

It must be the overexposure to estrogen, because he did. He wanted to tell his sister that he'd met a freaking amazing woman and he didn't know where it was going to lead exactly, only that it was somewhere he wanted to be. And if that wasn't reason enough to kick her out, Sara was just a room away.

"Want to talk about why you weren't at the Gala last night?" he asked, walking over to the coffeemaker and starting a pot.

"You don't want to talk about who's in your room?" Abby shrugged. "Got it. But it makes me think that she must be pretty special to make you smile before you've had your coffee." When Trey said nothing, she went on, "I mean, you're glowing."

"Maybe it's from hanging out with pregnant women for three weeks," he mumbled.

"I can't believe that Peg Stark won Best Winter Garden in Show."

Trey grabbed two mugs, holding them up to indicate he wanted to get back to his guest in case Abby had any ideas of staying. She shook her head, as though he'd just offered her coffee. Defeated, he set them on the counter.

"Nonna said it was the green vote, something about recycled corks and the country going to hell," Trey said.

Not that she'd seemed to mind. ChiChi and Charles danced the entire night. And when they weren't dancing, they were huddled in a corner, whispering and laughing as the whole town stared in shock. After sixty years, ChiChi and Charles had finally managed to let go of their long-standing feud and were moving on. Together, apparently.

Something that sounded good to Trey.

"Regan said that Deidra flipped out. The mayor had to carry her out before things got ugly."

Trey heard the tub in the bathroom turn on and Abby raised a curious brow. Too bad all Trey could picture was a wet and naked Sara lathering herself up with soap. Then he pictured Sara wet and naked, with him lathering her up, and suddenly he needed to get Abby out of his place.

"If you wanted to talk about the Gala, you would have gone to Lexi, not come here. So tell me what's up, then you can leave."

Abby sighed and it was as though her entire body deflated. "I think we're going to lose the property."

Visions of a wet tango disappeared and Trey set the mugs on the counter. He walked over to sit on the couch, pulling Abby in for a side hug. She crumbled into him and rested her head on his shoulder.

On a completely selfish scale, Trey didn't think that losing the property was such a bad thing. He'd meant what he'd said: DeLuca

Wines was being pulled in too many directions, just like Trey was, and at some point they'd both snap. But his family wanted this deal to happen, so Trey wanted it to happen.

"Why do you say that?" he asked.

"The attorney screwed up. He put the wrong date on the escrow papers, so instead of having until the end of the month to get everything signed and in order, we have until Friday."

Everything inside Trey stilled. "Is there any way to get an extension?"

She shook her head against his shoulder. "No, there is another interested buyer who is just waiting for us to fall out of escrow. And if we do, then he will counter and I can't be sure that Mr. Rossi won't consider his offer."

"Abby." Trey pulled back, hating to be yet another guy who let his sister down. "I can't go right now. I need until at least next week here. March would be even better."

"I know. I hate even asking, and if there was any other way," she said, her heart in her eyes. "I know that you're busy finalizing your sales team and getting everything ready to move. But you're the only one who can sign the papers."

"How long would it take?" Trey heard himself asking.

"It's just a week. You'll be back before you know it."

Something in his chest twisted because it wasn't the coming back part Trey was worried about. It was the walking away.

Twenty minutes and a lonely bubble bath later, Sara finally gave up and got dressed. She found Trey, sitting on the couch with his head leaned back and eyes closed. She plopped down next to him.

"It was the bubbles, wasn't it?" she mused. "Too girly."

He rolled his head toward her and gave a tired pout. "Don't tell me that I missed you in the bath."

"Afraid so," she whispered, snagging his mouth in one hell of a good morning kiss. "Although we can try it again, without the bubbles."

"There is nothing I'd love more than to spend the day scrubbing your back." He kissed her long and hard. "But I can't, I have to pack."

With a sigh, she fell back against the couch. "Yeah, us too. Cooper wants to unpack so he can check off the pack list again and then repack everything. Plus, I told Lexi I'd be there by eleven." She looked at her watch. "I'm late."

Kissing her lazy morning, and her sexy man, good-bye, she stood to gather up her things, but he took her hand. She looked back and her breath caught. He wasn't worn out from last night, he was upset. And disappointed. And something else that she couldn't identify, but it sent a wave of panic swelling in her chest.

"No, Sara, I have to get ready. Pack. I'm leaving."

Everything inside Sara stilled. "For Italy?"

"I fly out tonight."

"Tonight?" she repeated, because her heart was pounding so hard in her ears, she must have misunderstood.

"There was a mix-up in the terms, which means I need to get over there and get everything straightened out."

"Can't you straighten things out from here?" she asked. He couldn't do this. He promised her February, and after last night, she'd thought that maybe he could promise her forever.

And there it was again, that look, only this time she recognized it, felt the familiar pressure press in on her chest until it crushed her heart. It was the same look her dad had given her when she was five and he took the job in New York. The same look her mom had given every time Sara's school events conflicted with the dance studio's schedule. And it was the same look Garrett wore when he reenlisted. No matter how much she knew that they loved her, it always felt like they were saying, "I love you, but not enough to stay."

"What happened to leaving in March? What about training your replacements?" *Oh God.* "What about Team Bros? Cooper is so excited about tomorrow. What am I supposed to tell him?"

"I'll tell him," he said, gently tugging her down next to him. Which was good because she was afraid that her legs would give out any minute. "I'll explain everything before I go, and make it up to him when I get back, I promise."

"He's five, Trey. How are you going to explain heartache to a five-year-old?" she asked, her voice shaking. "Because I've tried. And believe me, no matter how sorry you are, how gentle you think you're being, it will crush his little world."

"You don't think I know that?" his voice was shaking now too. "God, Sara, the last thing I want to do is hurt him. Or you."

"Then don't," she pleaded. She would recover, it would be hard and heartbreaking, but eventually she would move on. She'd done it so many times, she could do it again. But Cooper? He didn't ask for this. He just wanted to go race his car and camp in a tent with a man he admired. "Don't go."

"I have to." Trey let out a heavy breath. "Someone screwed up, and if it doesn't get fixed by Friday, there is a good chance we'll lose the land."

Not we *will* lose the land, but a good chance. He was willing to disappoint Cooper, walk away from something real because of a possibility. "You don't have to go, you're choosing to."

He shook his head. "I can't let my family down."

"And I can't let Cooper down."

She understood what he was saying, but she also knew there had to be a compromise. A solution where no one lost out. She knew what it felt like to be disposable. She didn't want that for Cooper, and she didn't want that for herself—not anymore.

"You can't let Cooper down. He's counting on you, Trey. I'm counting on you to be the man I know you are. The kind of person who understands that showing up is more important than pretty promises."

"I already told my family I would go."

"You also said you wanted to make this work." She patted her chest, whether it was to see if her heart was still beating or to hold the pieces together while it quietly shattered, she wasn't sure. "With me. You said you wanted to make this work with me."

He took her hands in his, and she could feel his body vibrating with desperation. "I do. God, Sara I do, more than anything. I meant what I said last night, about you being my shelter. And when I get back, I want to get a place here, make St. Helena my home base." He pressed his lips to her open palm. "Make you my home base. But I have to do this first."

And there it was. Maybe it had been there all along, but she had been too caught up in seeing what she wanted to see, that she missed what was real. What was right in front of her.

"Then I have to say good-bye." Sara leaned over and brushed her lips across his. One last time. Then stood. Thankful that her legs didn't collapse. "I can't spend the rest of my life coming in second."

"Good-bye? What?" He stood too, and for such a big, strong man, he looked ready to break. "I'll be back in a week, tops, and then we can figure this out. I called Gabe when you were in the bath, told him I want to split time between here and Europe."

"That's just it, Trey," she said. "I don't want to be a complication, someone else you have to prioritize, a place to escape to when your real life gets complicated, especially when I always seem to come in last. I'm tired of being a stopover, I want to be the destination. I want to be the person you rush home to every night because there is nowhere else you'd rather be."

"I feel that, when I'm with you." He cupped her face. "With you I feel alive and whole and like I'm home. You feel like home to me."

"Oh, Trey." She wrapped her arms around his neck, and he clung to her so tightly, she could feel his body tremble. Sorrow burned her lungs and tightened around her throat, because he didn't even know what he'd just said. And there was nowhere for them to go. "You told me yourself, you'd never be able to stay home forever."

When Trey looked at her, saying nothing, she wondered how she was even breathing, because she knew he agreed. The truth hit her hard and broke her heart. "I just want you to be happy, Trey. To be the man you want to be."

CHAPTER 17

B ut you promised you wouldn't leave," Holly said, her thick lashes fluttering in a practiced pout. "At least not until after dessert."

And because Trey couldn't stomach the idea of letting down another person in his world, he shoved the giant stuffed llama under his shirt and plopped his pregnant ass back down. His knees hit the tot-size table and the seat of the chair cut a little too narrow for comfort. "Just trying to get comfortable, kiddo. Want to pass me the sugar?"

Holly gave a squeal of delight and clasped her gloved hands together. "Daddy, can you pass Uncle Trey the sugar?"

"One lump or two?" Gabe mused, shifting the frozen soda can to his other hand so that a teething Baby Sofie could keep gumming her way to a tear-free hour. He passed a piece of ChiChi's finest china around the table—his pinkie stuck way up in the air for added flair.

Trey had a finger of his own to stick in the air, only there were kids present.

"So the soda can works?" Marc asked as though taking mental notes.

"Better than any of that hippy shi—" Gabe paused as Holly waited for him to say the dirty word. "Holistic stuff Regan bought."

"We weren't even gone two weeks. I can't believe she got her first tooth," Nate said.

Neither could Trey. In the time they'd been gone, Baby Sofie had grown a tooth and her vocabulary by nine sounds, Holly had learned that babies came from Amazon, and Trey had discovered that being home wasn't so bad. Even when he was forced to sip tea from dainty cups and birth a llama.

Yeah, Trey decided while looking at his brothers, all of them wearing tiaras and pearls and baby bumps like his own—it wasn't so bad. Plus it took his mind off of Sara and how he'd blown it. And how the look on her face, the one that ripped his heart out of his chest, broke something inside of him that he knew would never be the same.

He looked around the room and laughed. Nothing was the same. Not a damn thing. And it never would be.

Gabe's media room looked more like the inside of a dollhouse than a man cave. The bar, normally stocked with DeLuca wines and microbrews, was serving punch and lemonade on tap. The sixty-four-inch plasma screen was permanently dialed to *Hello Kitty*. His brothers were in the middle of playing maternity tea party and smiling like they were sitting on the fifty yard line at the Super Bowl. Hell, they were always smiling—because they were in love.

The only thing that hadn't changed was Trey's uncanny ability to screw everything up. Even when he tried to do the right thing, tried to earn his place, to be a better man, everything fell to shit. Then, like the coward he was, he ran.

Only this time, he really thought he'd figured it out. He was doing what was best for his family, doing what his grandfather would have wanted him to do. And he still managed to disappoint Sara and Cooper, the two most important people now in his life.

Fuck. He hated himself right now.

Holly gasped her outrage at the dirty word, which he had apparently said aloud, although her excited giggle ruined the effect. Gabe had his hands on Baby Sofie's head in the earmuff position, and Marc and Nate were sharing concerned looks.

"Sorry." Trey forked over a quarter for the offensive language.

Holly waved off the dirty-word fine and patted his hand. "That's okay. I get sad too when I have to go away from home."

Then she leaned in and gave him a hug—and damn if his heart didn't split right open. Even this was different. As always his niece smelled like apple juice and little girl, and her inquisitiveness about birth still gave him the cold sweats, but instead of wanting to pry her sticky little fingers off of his pressed shirt, all he could think about was never letting go. Or that if he did, he'd never get this moment back.

"I don't want you to go," she whispered. "Team Terrific will be one Lady Bug down. And lonely."

He pulled back and tugged her hair. "You've got your dad."

"But you don't have anyone," she said, her expression one of lip-trembling concern. "And that makes my heart sad."

Yeah, it made his heart sad too.

"Hey, honey," Marc said, patting Holly on the shoulder. "Why don't you go ask Auntie Lexi about dessert?"

Holly was about to object when Gabe gave her a stern look, that lost all power when he added, "When you get back, we can all play kitties. Again."

Still not sure, Holly gave Trey one last look and then, since watching her grown-ass dad hobble around on all fours meowing was too much fun to pass up, she hurried out of the room. But not before kissing Trey on the cheek.

When he'd shown up for the impromptu family dinner, he was surprised no one had grilled him about Sara. Especially after the dance they'd shared last night at the Gala. He figured that either his sisters-in-law hadn't spilled the beans yet—highly unlikely—or they decided not to bring it up. Even more unlikely. The women in his family couldn't help but try to fix him, and the men couldn't resist telling him what to do—or more specifically, what he did wrong. So when Holly left the room, and his brothers leveled him with a look, he knew they'd just been waiting.

"Want to tell us what's going on with the dance teacher?"

"Nothing's going on. She's great and we had fun." He shrugged, but even that hurt. "I'm leaving, she's not. End of story."

Gabe studied him, seeing way too much. "I don't think you want it to be the end. And from what Regan told me, neither does Sara."

Sara had talked to Regan? "You don't know what I want."

"Maybe not, but I know that look," Gabe said.

"Yeah, and what look is that?" Trey asked, because the masochistic part of him wanted to know if it looked as awful as he felt.

"The 'holy shit I screwed it up beyond repair and lost her forever' look," Marc said, setting his cup down and confirming Trey's worst fear.

"Don't take it so hard," Nate said rationally and calmly, making Trey feel anything but.

"We've all worn it, bro." Marc clapped him on the shoulder. "Being a DeLuca, we are genetically predisposed to screwing it up when it comes to the right girl. Good news though, when it's the right one, you can't screw it up beyond repair. All you have to do is admit she gets to you, then tell her how much she gets to you, and do whatever it takes to win her back."

"You can borrow Sofie," Gabe offered.

"It's not that easy," Trey said, hating how his brothers were all nodding in unison, as though making forever work was as simple as renting a baby for the day or buying a picket fence. "Plus, I have to be on a plane in about four hours."

Marc shrugged. "Then don't go."

"What about the land?" Trey asked. "I'm the only one who can sign on the dotted line."

"So, we work it out," Nate said. "I can call Mr. Rossi. There's always a way, but I think Marc was talking about you not moving, as in living here."

Trey looked around, confused. "I thought you all agreed we wanted someone in the family looking over the construction?"

"What I want is my family to be happy," Gabe said.

"What the hell do you think I'm trying to do?" Jesus, it was as though men were from Mars and women were from Venus, and he was from Uranus, because every time he tried to explain this situation, everyone looked at him like he was the dumb-ass who wasn't listening. "I'm trying to make this work, trying to make it so that everyone gets what they want and no one has to miss out."

"What about you?" Gabe asked. "Where do you fall on that list? Because I'm betting that when you said you wanted to move to Italy, babysitting a house wasn't one of the benefits of moving."

No it wasn't. Neither was managing Abby's pet project or overseeing Nate's new grapes. What he wanted was to find a place where he fit—a place where he could feel like he paid his dues, earned his spot—and find peace. Only, that would have to wait until . . .

"I don't know." And that, right there, was the problem. If he couldn't even find time for himself in his own life, how could he make room for Sara?

Easily, he thought. Everything with Sara was easy and natural. She made him feel like everything was all right, that he was all right. That with her, he could be himself and that was enough.

"Well, maybe it's time you figured it out because you're my family too," Gabe said. "So tell me, what makes you happy, Trey?"

Gabe looked over at him and Trey felt everything he'd been holding back pull free and threaten to take him under. His parents, his job, his family. He was so tired of carrying around the guilt, the disappointment, the sorrow.

Then there was Sara and Cooper. They were his fresh start, not Italy. They were what he wanted.

"Sara," he forced her name out. "I'm so fucking happy when I'm with her and Cooper that I don't know if I could handle losing them."

"So let me get this straight," Marc said. "You're willing to walk away from a woman who likes you enough to put up with your shit, a kid who thinks you're some kind of hero, because you're scared that you might lose them? Well, easy solution. Man. The. Fuck. Up. And give them a reason to pick you."

"I'm not scared." He was terrified. After his parents, Trey kept it simple, fun, his emotions dialed to low to avoid the whole love and caring part of life, because loving someone like that again only to lose them—he didn't know if he'd survive it.

But nothing about the way he felt about Sara was simple or emotionless. Just thinking about not being a part of Sara and Cooper's life made his chest burn and his throat raw. He had a genuine shot at being the luckiest bastard on the face of the planet.

If he got on that plane, it was game over. No second chance. He'd forfeit his place in her life because of fear.

Only an idiot would walk away from a chance at a life with Sara over something as stupid as fear. Because she loved him. He didn't know how or why, but she did. He saw it in her eyes. And he still couldn't believe it.

"I can't go to Italy," Trey said, standing. "I have to pack for my camping trip. I still have to buy a sleeping bag. And tell Sara I love her. Holy shit, I love her."

"Figured as much," Nate said.

"That wasn't so hard, was it?" Gabe clapped him on the shoulder.

"Say it again, just to get used to it," Marc encouraged. "The more you say it, the better it feels."

"I love her," Trey said again and—nope, it still scared the shit out of him. But it felt insanely right.

"Another few hundred more times and you won't break out in a sweat every time you say it," Marc laughed and pulled him in for side hug. "Welcome home, bro."

"Yeah," Trey said, clinging tight—wussy or not, nothing could make him let go, because this time he meant it. He was ready to move on and come home.

"She thinks I left and so does Cooper." He ran a hand down his face. "She must hate me."

"She'll get over it." Gabe stood and slapped him on the back. "We all do."

"Even so, you might want to consider picking yourself up a pair of steel nuts while you're out," Nate said with a smile. "Last I heard, Frankie was the one who went over to help Sara roll up the tent and pack up the car."

Sunday morning Sara lugged Cooper's backpack out of the truck, her body rebelling from what felt like an endless night. She'd spent the first half of it helping a very confused and sad Cooper pack for his first campout, and the rest of it sobbing her way through a batch of cupcakes. Which was probably why her dance pants were tight and her head pounded. That she was holding back the tears and trying to be brave only made it worse.

"Got your toothbrush and toothpaste?" she asked, kneeling in front of Cooper.

"Yup," he said, clutching the shoe-box garage Trey had built to his chest. "Do you think he'll come?"

Sara took a deep breath and cupped her son's cheek. They'd been over this a dozen times already that morning. "I don't know, honey, but either way you're going to have a great time."

"He promised I could use his flashlight. At night. When it got dark." Cooper's lip started to quiver.

The mother in Sara wanted to call the whole thing off, but the woman who knew that her son was about to start his own adventure, zipped up his windbreaker.

"You have a flashlight in your pack. A Batman one. Side pocket, remember?"

Cooper exhaled a shaky breath and slumped back against the wall. "Trey's is brighter."

Cooper had never actually seen Trey's super-secret flashlight to know if it was brighter, but Sara didn't bother to argue. She understood what Cooper meant. Everything with Trey seemed brighter.

"I put extra batteries for it on the counter. Did you remember to pack them?"

He gave a shaky nod. "It was on the list. Under hairbrush."

Cooper didn't have a brush, which meant that Sara would need to stop by the drug store to buy a replacement later. Right now though, it was all about seeing Cooper off. And watching him stare longingly out the window, in a pair of jeans, his dad's old Semper

Fi hat, and a too-big tee, which had a picture of a car burning rubber on the back that read TEAM BLAZE: EXTINGUISHING THE COMPETITION, she wondered if she had made the right decision.

Closing down the studio for three days hadn't been an option, but neither was Cooper missing out on his first big campout. She didn't want him to spend his school vacation wondering what he did to make Trey go away. Sara would be thinking that enough for the both of them.

Which was why yesterday, after a good cry in the car, followed by a pep talk where she assured herself that she would be fine, that she could survive two nights in that house alone and not fall to pieces, she'd given Roman a call. He'd been wonderful, assuring her that Cooper was going to have a great time and would handle himself like a champ, not asking the obvious questions about why Trey wasn't going or why she sounded like she'd been bawling her eyes out.

She refused to bawl again since Roman was due to arrive any minute to take Cooper on his first mommy-free camping trip as the honorary member of Team Blaze—yesterday's conversation with him had been embarrassing enough.

"He's here," Cooper said, smashing his face against the glass. "He's here."

Oh God, not yet. Sara looked at the clock and felt panic kick in. She was supposed to have ten more minutes to run through phone numbers, emergency instructions, a dozen or so last hugs before Roman walked in, since Cooper informed her last night that hugs were for babies and not allowed in mixed company.

"Remember, Roman has a phone. If you need me, call. If you get scared, call. If you just want to say hi, call."

Only Cooper wasn't listening, he was actually vibrating with excitement and waving out the window. Okay, she'd made the right decision.

"Don't touch any red plants, or anything that slithers or has a stinger, and remember, I'm coming Monday to see the race and then I'm staying the night."

"On the other side of the lake," Cooper clarified. "With the girls."

"Right, with the girls," Sara assured him.

A knock sounded. Sara opened door and screen to say hi and felt her heart drop to her toes. Instead of Roman with his friendly, you-can-count-on-me smile, Trey stood at the door looking as handsome as ever.

Dressed in his Team Bros T-shirt, a new rucksack, and a cap that said MANNY UP, he looked like a Hubby-for-Hire. Only she wanted permanent employment, she reminded herself painfully, and he still considered himself a contractor by nature.

"Trey!" Cooper yelled, getting airborne before wrapping his arms around Trey's body. "You came. I knew that you'd come. He came, Mom, see?"

"I do see," Sara said carefully. "It was nice of him to come and say good-bye."

She was too afraid to allow herself to believe this visit was anything more than just that—a promised good-bye. And she didn't want Cooper to get his hopes up only to be let down again.

"I couldn't miss seeing you all geared up for your first big bro-bash, now could I?" Trey said, hugging him back. His gaze met Sara's, tired and unsure. "You look like you're all packed and ready to go."

Cooper unraveled himself from Trey's legs and smiled up at him. "Yup, I made a list, like you told me to so I didn't forget anything. 'Cept the tent, I don't have a tent." And there went the hands in the pocket and the nervous swaying. "Or your flashlight."

"I brought the flashlight." Trey reached in his pack and pulled it out. It was silver, metal, and completely normal, but somehow it did look brighter.

"Wow." Cooper's eyes went wide with awe. "I have one too. Batman. With extra batteries. But it isn't shiny like yours."

"That's the magic working."

"I can tell." Cooper said with a reverence to his voice that made Sara's chest pinch.

One didn't have to be a kid whisperer to figure out that Cooper took Trey's unexpected appearance as a sign that he'd changed his mind and Team Bros was back in business. Sara went to defuse the situation before things got bad—strike that, worse—when Trey ruffled Cooper's hair and squatted before him.

"I know that you are sleeping in Roman and Matt's tent, but if your mom's okay with it, I'd like to tag along." He was talking to Cooper, but his attention was solely on Sara.

"Really?" Cooper looked up at Sara with so much hope in his eyes, breathing became impossible. "We can be Team Bros just like you said?"

"If it's all right with your mom."

"Why don't you go grab a juice box from the kitchen for the trip and let me and Trey talk about this?" Sara said quietly.

Cooper studied the two adults, then with a jerky breath looked utterly crestfallen. He gave a small nod and turned to leave. Sadly, he already knew how this worked, because he stopped at the hallway and turned back. "If Mommy says no, will you go away before I get back?"

Sara watched Trey struggle to swallow. "No, buddy. I'll be right here waiting for you."

After Cooper's sneakers disappeared down the hall, Sara pushed through the pain and managed to speak without breaking down.

"You didn't have to come all the way over here, but thank you. You made Cooper's day."

"I made him a promise and I want to show him that I'm not the kind of man that bails on promises."

"Oh." She forced herself to smile through the tears. Now she and Cooper were two other people he was afraid to disappoint. She didn't want him here because he felt morally obligated, she wanted him here because there was nowhere else he'd rather be.

Trey set his pack next to Cooper's smaller one and reached out to take her hand as though what he'd just said hadn't hurt. Or that yesterday, a part of her world hadn't ended.

"I also came because we never finished our dance." He pulled her into the perfect proper dance position and Sara felt all of the tears she'd been holding inside fight for release.

"So you came here to dance?" She loved him with everything that she was, but this was just too hard. She took a step back, out of his arms. "Shouldn't you be on a plane or in Italy?"

"It doesn't matter, because where I need to be is here, with you. And Cooper."

"Trey, Cooper and I will be just fine. He's going to camp, I have it arranged so I can see the race, everything worked out," she said, hoping he'd just leave. It had taken everything she had not to lose it in front of Cooper, and she was holding on by a thread, but if he kept talking about her as another item on his list to be checked off, she'd crumble—and wouldn't that be humiliating. "So see, you don't have to do this."

"Yes, I do."

"No. You don't. I get that you made a promise, but life happens and Cooper will understand. This time he will understand, next time it will crush him."

"I don't want to hurt him, or you ever again."

"Then go," she pleaded. "Our life is here and yours is waiting for you, just a plane ride away until you get to start breathing again, following your dreams, living the kind of life that you want. Believe me, I understand." At least the logical part of her did, her heart unfortunately wasn't listening. "You were honest about what you could offer. I was the one who changed mid-adventure."

"You are my life," he whispered, closing the distance. "You make me happy. And around you, I can be the kind of man my nonno would have been proud of. My whole life has been a series of adventures and stopovers, Sara. The only place I have felt connected to since my parents died is right here." He pulled her into his arms, his palms sliding down her back to cradle her against him. Slowly, he started swaying. "You and me, just like this. This is my home, Sara."

"For how long?" she whispered, because she wanted to be his home. She wanted to be his family.

"When you asked me to be your February," he leaned over and brushed his lips against hers, "I think I was half in love with you then, but I was still too busy running to realize it. I'm tired of running, and I want to come home to you and Cooper. Every night."

She stumbled slightly and sucked in a breath. "You love me?"

"Every piece of you," he breathed, his hand tightening around her. "I love the way you smell, the way you feel in my arms. I love the way you love your son and that you don't take my crap. And I love the way you look in those skirts." With a low sound of male appreciation, he pulled her flush, waltzing them slowly around the family room. "God, I love dance skirts. I even love station wagons, because I read online that they have one of the highest safety ratings, and what's not to love about safety ratings?"

She gave a little laugh, but it came out more of a half sob.

"And I love you. I don't need Italy or a new job. I need you, Sara." Trey gently draped her over his arm in an elegant dip. Their gazes locked, their bodies pressed tight, his mouth hovered over hers, and Sara felt her heart swell. "But you know what I love the most?"

Unable to speak through the tears, she shook her head.

"I love how you look when you're happy. And if you'll let me, I want to spend the rest of my life making you and Cooper happy. Building a life here in St. Helena or wherever you want to live. As long as it's with you."

"I love you too," she whispered.

He smiled and everything inside her stilled. Garrett was her first love and would always be her first love, but she knew in her heart that Trey would be her last.

"Sara, will you be my forever?"

"Only if you'll be mine," Sara whispered.

Trey captured her lips in a kiss that shook her to the core. It was gentle and possessive and so right, she knew that this was what she'd been waiting for. He was who she'd been waiting for. Everything in her life had merged to prepare her for this one moment—this one man.

The kiss ended and Sara buried her face against his chest, breathing him in, listening to his heartbeat while they gently swayed. And Sara knew, at last, what forever felt like.

FROM THE MOMENT WE MET

Available Summer 2014 on Amazon.com

Most women spend an average of 150 hours fantasizing and dreaming about the perfect wedding. Not Abigail DeLuca. Nope, she'd spent the past seven years planning the perfect divorce, which as of—she glanced at her watch—eight hours ago had finally been granted. And nobody was going to ruin her first day as a happy divorcée.

Nobody, she thought grimly, looking at the bear of a man in grease-stained coveralls standing on her front porch, except her pencil-dick of a two-timing ex.

The man pulled his Rodney's Recovery, Repossession & Party Rentals trucker hat low on his forehead and flashed a copy of Abby's marriage certificate. "Are you Abigail Moretti, wife of Richard Moretti?"

"Ex-wife. As of today," she clarified, pulling her robe tighter. Her new, silky blue robe that did amazing things to her skin—and her cleavage. She'd bought it specifically to wear today, wanting a perky start to her new life. A bold and confident start. None of which included coming face-to-face with Rodney. "And my name is DeLuca. Abigail DeLuca."

She stopped going by Moretti the day she discovered that Richard's favorite pastime during intern season was playing hide the salami.

"Abby?" A weathered voice called out from over the picket fence that separated her property from the busiest busybody and gossip in St. Helena, save her Nonna ChiChi. "Is everything all right?"

"Yes, Mrs. Kinkaid. Just getting the morning paper."

"Well, you might want to invite your gentleman friend inside before tongues start wagging," Nora chided, peering over the fence. "This is a respectable neighborhood."

Nora was the self-appointed Neighborhood Watch Commissioner of the cul-de-sac and took her job seriously. She meticulously chronicled her neighbors' comings and goings, being sure to report any odd findings on her Facebook wall. Even issuing citations for infringement of the Good Neighbor Code.

Nora had been looking for a reason to cite Abby ever since her cat, Cujo, allegedly sharpened her claws on Mrs. Kincaid's magnolia tree.

"He's not my gentleman friend," Abby said, and because she was raised in a house where being rude to one's elders was considered a sacrilege, she refrained from pointing out that spying on thy neighbor was not a respectable hobby.

"If you say so," Nora said, unconvinced. "It would be a shame if the neighborhood became a drive-thru for the town's bachelors."

Nora would be ecstatic if that happened, because she'd capture each and every transgression on film and post it on Facebook. Not that there would be any transgressions of the male variety. Abby was finally single and she meant to keep it that way.

So with a polite smile she said, "And he was just leaving."

Only Rodney didn't budge.

Raising a brow, Abby reached for the door handle and, as though anticipating her next move, which was to disappear back inside her house, pull the curtains, and toast her first D-Day with a mimosa, he took a step forward. And wasn't that just like a man: self-centered, domineering, and, even though he was the one who was crapping all over her good morning, determined to be heard.

Abby took in the receding hairline, frown marks, and tow truck parked at her curb—her gaze landing on the REPOSSESS part of his title—and rolled her eyes. "If you're here to repossess Richard's car, you wasted your time, because like I explained only seconds ago, that's my car in the drive and Richard is not here."

Nor was he her problem.

"So if you'll excuse me, I have to get ready for an appointment." Which was not until tonight. But standing on the front porch in her sexy robe, talking to a strange man, while her neighbors idly placed bets on whether he was the first post-D-Day walk-of-shamer, was not her idea of easing into a respectable singlehood.

"I'll make it quick then. The name's Rodney, of Rodney's Recovery, Repossession & Party Rentals." He pointed to the logo on the front of his hat as though that was all the identification required and extended a newspaper clipping. "I need to confirm if you are the Abby Moretti, uh, the Abby who placed this ad in the local paper."

Abby's face heated as she looked at the front page of the *St. Helena Sentinel*. It was a copy dating from last summer, boasting a missing person's announcement with a photo of Richard that had been taken on their wedding day. He was dressed in a tux, looking handsome and faithful, and like a man in love. Abby nearly snorted.

"Yes, I was trying to locate my estranged husband so that I could"—she paused, her face heating—but this time with anger.

"Wait. Don't tell me that the son of a bitch is trying to sue me for defamation of character? It was an ad. That I had to place because he refused to show his cheating face so I could serve him with divorce papers."

Richard had successfully managed to elude her, her family, and the law for the past seven years.

Rodney raised a brow. "The headline reads, HAVE YOU SEEN MY DICK?"

"It was the question of the hour for women everywhere, I assure you."

"I'll take that as a yes, you are Abigail Moretti, who married Richard Moretti in St. Helena, California, eight years ago."

When Abby only crossed her arms, Rodney gave a decisive nod. Turning around, he waved his hand, signaling—who, Abby had no idea, but her stomach sank all the same when he hollered, "Bring it on in. This is the right house."

Before Abby could process what was happening, a loud beeping echoed throughout the cul-de-sac announcing the ginormous truck backing up—right over her lawn, the garden bunny one of her piano students had painted for her, and straight through the center of her dahlia garden. Her beautiful dahlias that she'd planted and nurtured into a masterpiece of horticulture supremeness.

It was the centerpiece of her yard. Hell, it was the centerpiece of the whole damn neighborhood.

"What are you doing?" Abby yelled, racing down the steps and waving a signal of her own. "Stop!"

"Sorry, but we only get paid if we make the delivery as per the instructions." Rodney hollered after her. "And we had some pretty specific instructions on this here delivery."

"But my dahlias!"

Rodney at least had the decency to look apologetic, but the

truck didn't stop, not until it had torn up a good half of her lawn and smashed every last bloom in her garden. Then the beeping became more alarming and the open flatbed of the truck lifted and that was when Abby knew that Richard was a complete bastard.

Before she could say a word or throw herself in front of the oncoming disaster that was quickly becoming her life, an Adonis-inspired statue slid down the ramp of the truck, landing gracefully on her lawn with a small thud.

"Oh my," Nora sighed with an expression of sheer appreciation. "Isn't that an eyeful?"

Eyeful indeed. Standing well over six feet tall and, except for the embellished bulge and generous amount of hair, the marble statue was a spot-on replica of her ex. Even down to the smarmy smile and trademarked wink.

"Impressive, isn't it?" Rodney said, making Abby realize that she was staring.

"I'll say." Nora started fanning herself and a series of impressed grunts came from the two men who exited the delivery truck to take in the sight.

"He wasn't that big," Abby felt the need to point out, then realized how *that* sounded and clarified. "Tall. I meant that he wasn't that tall. The man was only five ten. With lifts."

Looking extremely satisfied with himself, Rodney extended a pen and a clipboard. "I need you to sign here, here, and here."

"And I need you to remove that"—Abby waved a hand at the statue—"monstrosity, before I call the cops."

"No can do." Rodney rocked back on his heels. "I got paid for a delivery. It's been delivered."

"Then I'll pay you to deliver it somewhere else."

Mulling over her request, Rodney sized up Abby, then took his time sizing up the statue, finally shaking his head in pure-male awe.

"You sure? It's a statement maker. Really brings out the character of your yard."

"My yard has plenty of character and *that* is not the kind of statement I want to be making."

"Plus it's in violation of GN Code 27C," Nora explained. "Garden art can't be more than three feet tall with a base not exceeding half the height, unless it has a water element to it, and then you must get board approval of the fixture."

"Oh, it's got a water feature all right," Rodney explained ever so seriously, resting his hand on Richard's shoulder. "All Mrs. Moretti's got to do is run a water line to the base and then water shoots out his—"

"There will be no shooting," Abby insisted, her right eye beginning to twitch. "And it's not staying. In fact, I will pay you to deliver it back to where it came from."

She was tired of being manipulated by men. There was no way she'd let Richard weasel his way into her life—not again. She wasn't that lost, heartbroken college student anymore. She was a successful, independent, man-free woman who was in charge of her own destiny and—

Oh. My. God. Abby froze at the sight of a real-life Adonis pounding the pavement—pavement that happened to be covered in her Neighborhood Watch territory. Moving with a confidence and masculine grace that was far too natural to be manufactured, Abby had no doubt that Jack "Hard Hammer" Tanner was 100 percent unadulterated male perfection—no embellishment needed.

At six feet five and two hundred and fifty pounds of solid muscle, Jack Tanner was a mountain of testosterone and sculpted male perfection. He was sporting a pair of black jogging shorts slung low on his hips, a San Francisco 49ers ball cap, and matching T-shirt, which—*sweet baby Jesus*—dangled from his waistband instead of covering his chest, leaving miles of tan torso that made her mouth dry and her palms wet.

Which was why she sagged with relief at the sight of him jogging down the cul-de-sac and past her house.

Her premature celebration ended when, as though her morning wasn't complicated enough, Tanner's footsteps slowed as he passed her lawn and, without warning, abruptly retraced his steps, coming to a stop at the curb of her driveway. He took in Shrine de Richard, then his gaze drifted to Abby, pinning her with an amused look before releasing a lethal smile that left more than just her hands wet.

Another in a long list of reasons to stay away from him.

"Before we can talk terms," Rodney said, and Abby had to strain to understand him over the blood pounding in her ears, "we have to close out this transaction."

"Fine." Abby grabbed the clipboard and scribbled her name. A here, here, and here later, she was one step closer to eliminating Richard from her life, and it gave her something to do besides gawk at the way Tanner's muscles played as he jogged up the driveway—straight toward her.

Rodney took the clipboard. "I can get your package—"

"It's not my package," she clarified as Tanner strode up. He didn't talk, just silently situated himself way too close for her to ignore. But she did her damnedest.

"That signature there says it is," Rodney reminded her, his meaty finger stabbing at her signature scrawled on the delivery slip. Then he flipped the page and wrote up a new delivery form and handed it to her. "Now, if you want to hire me to ship it back, then that's going to cost you nineteen-oh-four, with tax."

"Fine. I'll go get my purse."

"We don't take checks."

"I have cash," she said.

"I don't know if I feel comfortable carrying that much money around on my person," Rodney said, running a greasy hand down the front of his coveralls.

At his comment, Abby looked at the total he'd scribbled on the paper and felt her heart plummet straight to her toes. "You're going to charge me two grand to return a statue that isn't even mine?"

"You signed for it so it's—"

"Mine. Yeah, yeah," Abby mumbled. "But two grand?"

"You see the size of him," Rodney said, his eyes straying back to Richard's package.

"He wasn't that big!"

"Need any help?" Tanner offered sweetly from beside her. She could feel him staring, feel his amusement pressing down on her.

"Nope, I've got it." Abby squared her shoulders and signed the form.

Last year, she'd set out to get herself a divorce and living arrangements that didn't include her childhood bed or her nonna as a roommate. Check. And check. This year, she was determined to prove to this town—and herself—that she could stand on her own two feet. Starting today.

And that didn't include a man.

"Do you take credit cards?" Abby asked, the twitching behind her eye now encompassing the entire front lobe of her head.

"Yup. Let me call the station and make arrangements." Rodney disappeared into the cab of his truck, leaving Abby alone with Tanner.

"I got to hand it to you, if that's your solution to ward off would-be suitors, it's working, darling." The way he said darling, low and husky, felt like an intimate caress. Too bad he was staring at Richard's over-embellished ego. "It's enough to give most guys a complex."

"You intimidated, Jack?" she asked, pulling her robe even tighter.

"Nope."

Of course he wasn't. The man was far too capable and accomplished to give into anything as silly as intimidation. Most people admired that about Tanner. Abby just found it annoying.

Almost as annoying as the way her heart picked up as Tanner's gaze took a lazy journey down her body. She resisted the urge to smooth down her hair, just like she resisted the urge to kick him in the shin, when his gaze reached her feet and he chuckled. She didn't need to look down to realize that she was wearing her Godzilla slippers—they were big, green, badass, and growled every time she walked.

"And I'm not just any guy," he said, leaning in until she could smell the clean sweat and male perfection wafting off of him. "I'm a Hall of Famer."

Abby rolled her eyes. "For most pass receptions in the NFL."

"Yup, that too." His lips twitched and so did her thighs.

"What are you doing here?" Because this could not be happening. Today was supposed to be the start of her new life. And she didn't want to begin it with an eerily lifelike replica of the man who had broken her heart, her confidence, and the bank when he absconded with twelve million of the town people's dollars. Not to mention staring down the man who'd taken her virginity and something so much more valuable—her ability to trust.

"Darling, half the town is here." He pointed to the curb, and sure enough every neighbor was on their lawn—or hers. She waved. "When Richard came up Main Street it was as though he was Jesus, walking on water and people just started following him. I saw your grandma making the sign of the cross as she hobbled out of the Sweet and Savory to watch the procession. She'll be here any minute."

Great.

"So you came to watch the show?"

"Nope," he tucked a piece of hair behind her ear and heat curled low in her stomach. "I came to see if you wanted to go grab a bite to eat. The show's just a bonus."

"You already asked me out on a date. I said no." Although she'd wanted to say yes. Not to the date part, she'd always hated dating. But to the good-night kiss part that usually followed said date. And maybe even to what naturally followed the kiss.

"You said you were still a married woman, so I backed off." He smiled. "You're single now, so the question is still on the table."

"She's not divorced," Rodney hollered over the hood of the car, informing everyone in a three-block radius.

Nora pulled out her phone and began filming.

Abby felt everything inside of her still. "Excuse me?"

"That there isn't just a piece of masterful art carved from a rare marble found only in remote parts of Italy. It's a vessel," Rodney said, pointing to the vase in the statue's hand and taking in a moment of silence. "I'm sorry to inform you, Mrs. Moretti, but your husband, Richard Moretti, passed away three months ago, long before that there divorce decree was signed. And as his wife, you are the sole heir to all of his assets."

ACKNOWLEDGMENTS

Thanks to my editors Maria Gomez and Lindsay Guzzardo, and the rest of the author team at Montlake, for all of the amazing work and support throughout this series.

As always, a special thanks to my fabulous agent, Jill Marsal, for agreeing to take this awesome journey with me. To my constant cheerleaders and plot buddies: Hannah Jayne, Jacee James, Diana Orgain, and Marni Bates. You girls keep me going! And to Jessica Beane and Brittney for sharing your awesomely funny and incredibly sweet mommy stories, and helping me understand the world of little boys.

Finally, and most important, thanks to my daughter, Thuy, and my amazing husband, Rocco. You guys are my rock.

ABOUT THE AUTHOR

Marina Adair is a #1 national best-selling author of romance novels. Along with the St. Helena Vineyard series, she is also the author of *Sugar's Twice as Sweet*, part of the Sugar, Georgia, series. She lives with her husband, daughter, and three neurotic cats in Northern California.